What people are say

The Womanp.....

T0032246

Dr. Stafford Betty weaves mystery and intrigue into this powerful story, set in the second half of the century. Macrina McGrath, an American Southerner, challenges the limits set by the Catholic Church and after many roadblocks gains the priesthood for women. But this is only the beginning of her ascent. Betty builds into the story, with its many twists and turns, deep insights about the human condition. I could hardly put the book down. It would make a great series on Netflix.
Tina Antonell, Life Counseling and Coach, Mindfulness and Meditation Teacher

Although I am a long-lapsed Catholic, I still feel a certain affinity with the Church and very much appreciate the spiritual foundation and moral compass it provided me. Professor Betty's engaging book prompted much musing and pondering over the history of the Church, its faltering prominence, and its possible future. It offers many feasible twists that I had not considered and that much of the world in the years ahead will probably see unfold—some with delight, others with dismay. A standout novel for thoughtful Catholics, ex-Catholics, and anyone interested in the story of a single woman who shakes the world.
Michael Tymn, author of *The Afterlife Revealed* and *No One Really Dies*

Dr. Stafford Betty's writing is captivating. He has found a style in which he can address theological, political, cultural, and gender issues in an assertive, yet thoughtful and scholarly way. His latest novel, *The Womanpriest*, offers an inclusive view of world faiths, while maintaining a solid grounding in Christianity. In a time of doubt and darkness in the world, Dr. Betty offers the possibility of hope.

David Atkins, Marriage and Family Therapist

In this daring and unusual story, Stafford Betty puts us not in the twentieth-century shoes of a fisherman, but in the twenty-first-century shoes of a fisherwoman named Macrina, destined to become the first female pope. He takes us on a bittersweet, breathtaking journey of self-discovery and unflinching service to the church, the world, and the One who called both into being. Along the way, Betty wrestles with more pressing personal and social issues, more spiritual and secular conflicts, than would seem possible in a single book. Yet they hold together, work together, in the life of a captivating character large enough, strong enough, brave enough, to embrace them all. Here's a roller-coaster ride with ups and downs, twists and turns, that matter even more than they amuse. Take a seat, I urge you, and hold on.

Newton E. Finn, retired public interest attorney and community organizer, ordained American Baptist minister, award-winning author (Kogan certificate)

The Womanpriest

The Womanpriest

Stafford Betty

ROUNDFIRE
BOOKS

Winchester, UK
Washington, USA

JOHN HUNT PUBLISHING

First published by Roundfire Books, 2023
Roundfire Books is an imprint of John Hunt Publishing Ltd., No. 3 East St., Alresford,
Hampshire SO24 9EE, UK
office@jhpbooks.com
www.johnhuntpublishing.com
www.roundfire-books.com

For distributor details and how to order please visit the 'Ordering' section on our website.

ISBN: 978 1 80341 124 8
978 1 80341 125 5 (ebook)
Library of Congress Control Number: 2021922903

A CIP catalogue record for this book is available from the British Library.

Design: Stuart Davies

UK: Printed and bound by CPI Group (UK) Ltd, Croydon, CR0 4YY
Printed in North America by CPI GPS partners

We operate a distinctive and ethical publishing philosophy in
all areas of our business, from our global network of authors to
production and worldwide distribution.

Previous Titles by Stafford Betty

Non-fiction

Vadiraja's Refutation of Sankara's Non-Dualism: Clearing
the Way for Theism
The Afterlife Unveiled: What "the Dead" Tell Us About Their
World, 9781846944963 (O-Books)
Heaven and Hell Unveiled: Updates from the world of Spirit,
9781910121306
When Did You Ever Become Less by Dying? Afterlife:
The Evidence, 9781786770042
What Does It Mean to Be a Christian? A Debate
(co-authored with John F Crosby) 9781587319365

Fiction

The Rich Man, 0312681054
Sing Like the Whippoorwill, 0896223248
Sunlit Waters, 0896224147
Thomas, 9780140278545
The Imprisoned Splendor, 9781907661983
The Severed Breast, 9781910121849
Ghost Boy, B075YRCTQQ (Our Street)
The War for Islam, 9781789040425 (Fireside)
The Afterlife Therapist, 9781786771353

The Womanpriest

Greg McGrath: I am looking at a video on my computer that my father, Clifford McGrath, made in October 2020 by an old technology known then as Facetime. Twin babies, boy and girl six months old, lie on their backs next to each other on a blue flannel blanket wiggling their legs. My name is Gregory, and I am that baby boy. My sister's name is Macrina.

Three months ago, in January 2084, I retired from my job as a health care lobbyist to tell the remarkable story of my sister's life. Other biographers will undoubtedly beat me to the finish line but don't have access to her online "Journal" or her paper diary in seven notebooks of varying quality that I keep locked in my safe. And, of course, they don't know and can never know her as I do. I should mention that I have been offered millions of dollars for this trove of information.

Mom (Jan McGrath) and Dad, now in their late 80s, live in a retirement community in Mobile. They have kept their wits, have sharp memories, and have been a tremendous resource to me.

I have never written a book and don't think of myself as a particularly creative individual. But lobbyists typically have many contacts, and I am no exception. I know where to go for information. Throughout this book my contacts will speak for themselves, either in writing or vocally. Sometimes I have asked them to dramatize the events they describe, even to the extent of creating a dialogue for more interesting reading. Sometimes I've done so myself. I have edited expressions that lacked clarity, but I have retained as much as possible the exact words as they came to me.

Luckily, Macrina was such a public figure that many of her interviews, her debates, her peculiar turns of phrase, her trenchantly logical mind, her wit, her prayers, her tears, her love life, her faults, her muted fury, the whole indomitable woman that she was have been electronically preserved. I have made good use of them, so she will often speak for herself. Her memory for detail is exceptional.

I will introduce the speakers by listing their names, their connection with Macrina, and the context of their comments where necessary.

Jan McGrath, voice recording: I was sure I was pregnant two weeks after I missed my period. When the first wave of nausea swept over me, I made an appointment with the gynecologist, a friend of mine. I'll never forget her face when she held up the scan and looked at it with a grin and slowly nodded her head. "Oh my God!" I thought. I could see us going to the poor house. As it happened, they were born April 13, 2020, when the world was in full lockdown. One of our friends called them the "COVID twins."

Clifford McGrath, voice recording: We were selfish Generation Z-ers. We wondered if we even wanted a child. Then came two. We thought we were being punished for our selfishness. But then you and Macrina were born. We felt so blessed. You were the big one, a whiner, a boisterous baby. Macrina was calm. She put up with your scrambling all over her. She didn't seem to mind. You didn't look like each other. She was dark-haired and blue-eyed. You had light brown hair and hazel eyes. From the start you favored me in appearance. She favored your mother. Your mother was working as an English teacher downtown at the Alabama School of Math and Science. She didn't make any more money than me. She took six months of maternity leave. I continued to work. We struggled but survived.

As you know, we named the two of you after your mother's favorite saints: Gregory of Nyssa and his sister Macrina. Who would have guessed that our baby girl would grow up to be a woman of such worldwide distinction?

Jan McGrath, in-person interview with Greg: Both of you were happy children. But Macrina said things that puzzled, even troubled me. When playing with her dolls, she would sometimes take them to see her "other mommy" — those were her words. When I asked her about this, she spoke as if her "other mommy" was real. Very strange. Once she began pre-school, I never heard of this again.

Then there was little DeeDee, Melissa Johnson's child. You might remember Melissa — she's dead now. Did you know DeeDee had what psychiatrists call "an imaginary friend"? DeeDee was an only child and lonely, and Melissa asked if Macrina could come over and be a *real* friend. "Sure," I said. Well, wouldn't you know it? I pick Macrina up and she tells me the friend *is* real.

Our conversation went something like this:

"You saw a ghost?"

"A ghost?"

"DeeDee had an invisible friend who played with her, right? You saw her?"

Macrina looked at me as if I were crazy. "Her name is Squatsy, Mom. She didn't like me and told me to go home."

"She didn't like you? Why on earth didn't she like you?"

"She wanted DeeDee for herself. She was afraid I would take her away."

I was amazed. "What did she look like?"

"Just a little girl, like me. She wore a pink sweater with yellow polka-dots."

That's how it went.

Clifford McGrath, in-person interview with Greg: When Macrina was just short of five, we were walking in the neighborhood, the four of us. We came upon a dead bird. It was a cardinal if I remember. It was lying on the sidewalk, dead. She asked what was wrong with it. "It's dead," I said. She reached down and picked it up. Then she shook it. She kept on shaking

3

it to make it wake up. "It's dead, darling," I said, "it won't wake up."

I've told this story many times but can't vouch for its exact accuracy. But this is fairly close to the way in unfolded.

"Will you die, Dad?"

I stopped and thought, Do I tell her? Maybe she was too young, but I decided there was never a better time than now. "Yes, I will die—someday."

"Will Mommy die?"

"Yes, someday Mommy will die too."

"Will Greggy die?"

"Yes, a long, long time from now."

She looked up at me with tears in her eyes and asked, "Will I die?"

"Yes, everybody dies, darling. But that is a long time away. But why are you crying? Are you crying because you'll miss me?"

She thought for a moment. "No."

"Are you sad because you'll miss Mommy?"

"No."

By now she was sobbing. "Are you sad because you'll miss Greg?"

"No."

"Then why are you so sad?"

What she said next floored me: "I'll miss myself."

How could a child say this? It was as if she understood the whole tragedy of existence. She sounded like a French existentialist! That evening we sat down in the old rocker. She was in my lap. I told her the dead bird was flying around somewhere in its new body. I told her she'd have one too. She knew she wouldn't miss herself.

Mindy Carlisle, Macrina's childhood friend, text message: She was a very determined child. We must have been six or seven, and we decided to have a contest to see who could hold their breath the longest. We stood up and took a deep breath. Maybe a minute passed, and suddenly she fell over in a dead faint. Just fell over. That's how determined she was not to lose.

Jan McGrath, in-person interview with Greg: She was a plucky little thing. I think she was seven, and we drove into the garage. There, climbing up the back wall of the garage was a snake, a long black snake. I was shocked. She jumped out of the car and rushed over to where a hoe was hanging on its rack. She grabbed it before I could stop her and attacked the snake as if it were the devil itself. She slapped at it with the hoe until it dropped at her feet. It tried to wriggle away and she kept chopping. She was the wrath of God, I tell you. When Cliff got home, he gave her a little lecture about a snake's right to live, then helped her bury it. She said a prayer for "Mr. Black Snake" and asked him to forgive her.

Jan McGrath, email to Greg: We limited the time you were allowed to play video games to one hour a day, and television another hour. There was no limit to what the two of you could read. And of course Macrina had her clarinet and you had your golf. Still, there was plenty of time to kill on the weekends or in the summer. And the cemetery across the street, not much bigger than a couple of acres, was your playground. Huge live oaks shaded the area, and the gates were never locked. About the only activity there besides the games you invented was people being dead.

I watched the two of you sitting on gravestones and imagining what life must have been like for a Mr. and Mrs. Flew, who died within two weeks of each other in October 1948, or a dog named Klondike buried next to his master with only a small headstone to remember him by. She asked if Klondike was in heaven with his master. I had the impression that Macrina's imagination kept you endlessly busy. Then there were the times you went out trekking, walking all over Spring Hill College, down the beautiful Avenue of Oaks, out across the golf course, and then perhaps back up to the Church, where light shone through the gold-tinted windows and an air conditioner kept the place cool in the stifling heat of summer. At these times you were in charge, and Macrina would come home happy and exhausted. Sometimes I went with you. The happiness you found in each other's company was something to see.

Jan McGrath, email to Greg: After the Catholic Church formally decreed that women could be ordained as permanent deacons, Macrina was curious to know what that meant. I told her they could do everything a priest could do except consecrate the bread and wine, hear confession, and perform the sacrament of confirmation. "Why can't they go on to be priests?" she asked. I told her it was because all Jesus' apostles were male. She didn't like that answer.

You and Macrina had been playing the game of saying Mass. You would always be the priest, and she would be your acolyte, no questions asked. If any of your friends were over, they would attend as parishioners. But after the Church's decree, she tried to push you aside. It led to arguments, but you would usually yield. It was hard not to yield to Macrina. And truth to tell, she preached a better sermon than you!

Clifford McGrath, in-person interview with Greg. She was curious for a 10- or 11-year-old. Especially about astronomy. She wanted basic information about what made summer and winter. She wanted to know why the moon would rise later each night. That sort of thing. I told her how big our galaxy was. I told her how many galaxies there were in the universe. "Probably billions of inhabited worlds like ours," I said, or something like that. She sulked. Which amazed me. Most kids like big things. She wanted them little. "I'm too little for God to hear my prayers," I think she said. I said that God was infinite and could hear all our prayers at the same time. She was unconvinced. That night she didn't say her prayers.

Carrie Franklin, Jan's friend, text message to Greg. I'm an old lady now with a bad memory. The thing I most remember about Macrina was her serving Mass with you. The two of you were precious, but I couldn't help noting that you didn't resemble each other in the least.

Jan McGrath, in-person interview with Greg: How in the world did you find Carrie Franklin? I thought she was dead. One of Macrina's favorite activities was serving Mass. She liked dressing in her cassock at St. Ignatius and mastering all the little things that servers had to do. But she envied Greg because he always got to swing the censor because he was bigger.

Greg: The fifth through eighth grades at St. Ignatius came and went. Macrina was always the standout girl, and Richard Davis the boy I couldn't quite catch. Dad drove Macrina hard to master her clarinet and gave me the freedom to do whatever I wanted, which was usually to play golf with my friends. It was as if he didn't think I was gifted enough to bother turning me into a wunderkind, and he was right. Macrina also kept up with her reading, especially on the subject of astronomy. Dad gave me a child's science book on our twelfth birthday. I didn't read it for more than fifteen minutes, but Macrina took to it. She became fascinated by earthlike planets and told me there were millions in our own galaxy. She also got into writing poetry and entered a poetry contest for kids, once winning a second place, which sent her into a day-long sulk.

When high school at McGill-Toolen downtown came along, Macrina did two things that impressed me as remarkable. In sophomore religion class we were studying the Psalms, and the teacher asked us to write a personal reflection on Psalm 139, one we had to read aloud in class. What she wrote I saved in my computer, the first time I ever did that. It inspired me to create a "Macrina folder," to which I have added countless entries over the years. The thoughts expressed in her poem would serve as an early indication of—well, here it is:

My God Is Too Big
People say your God is too small,
But my God is too big.
"He counts the number of the stars
And calls them all by their names," says the Psalm.
But my God counts the galaxies,
And the number of stars is greater than
The number of grains of sand on the beaches of earth.
In all this bigness I feel lost.
Do you really know me by name, God?
Are you "acquainted with all my ways"?
Did you "form my inward parts and knit them
Together in my mother's womb"?

How many light years does it take
For my prayer to reach you?
Will you excuse me if I reach up to lesser heights—
To your lofty creatures, your angels, your saints?
The Chinese pray to their ancestors—
I laughed when I first heard this,
Pitied them, but now I understand.
But I crave to be heard by you anyway.
But where do I go to find you?

Ah, so that's it.
Not in a grotto on one of Saturn's rings,
Not at the controls of the Virgo Supercluster,
Not on a throne at the edge of the universe,
But right here, inside me, sharing space
With the tininess that I am,
Our Father who art in heaven.

She recited it aloud without notes. She had memorized it. For
about three seconds after she finished, there was total silence.

What she said seemed to come from her depths, her very soul, it wasn't just a class exercise. There was an uncanny solemnity about it. It was awe-inspiring. I remember being tremendously proud of her. I also remember what the teacher said when she finished: "Macrina, did you write that without help?" "Yes, m'am." As she went back to her seat, there was a smattering of applause.

Then there was that other event. Once or twice a semester the whole school would gather in the gym, usually for a pep rally before a big football or basketball game. This time wasn't any different, except that there was a preamble to the main event. A chair had been placed at the half court line of the basketball court. Without any introduction, Macrina walked out holding her clarinet and took her seat. As the crowd seated in the bleachers on all sides of her quieted, she lifted her instrument to her mouth. I remember what a deep breath she took. Then she let fly a barrage of notes like no one there had ever heard, not even the band director who put her up to it. The piece, written for piano, was called "Dizzy Fingers." Played on the clarinet by a sixteen-year-old girl, it was a *tour de force*. Three minutes later the whole place erupted. My friends were slapping me on the back congratulating me. Not even Benny Goodman, who made the piece famous, I later heard, played it any faster. Incredible.

It's odd. She must have practiced the piece at home over and over, but I don't remember it.

Macrina, Journal kept on her computer, first entry: I've decided to keep a journal to record my secret most intimate thoughts. I'm only 17, and it might well be that later in life I will have no interest in what I had to say. Maybe I'm just too wrapped up in myself, caught up in my own precious thoughts. Surely, they will have no value to anyone but myself.

About Lorenzo. He is a year ahead of me. Since I was 12, and he 13, we were sometimes partnered on the altar at St. Ignatius.

From the beginning I was struck by his dignity, by his kind instructions to more junior acolytes, and by the way he towered above the silly boys who were his friends but without making them feel inferior. They loved him. Everybody did. But no one loved him more than I. When he spoke to me, I tingled all over. But I would never let myself think I meant anything special to him. I knew he was dating Connie, another acolyte. But once he gave me a special smile and said, after he had served his last Mass, that he would check to see how I was doing when he got back from Notre Dame, where he was starting college. Check on me? I was amazed. Why would he check on me?

Oh, Lorenzo! You did check on me! You say you thought of me a lot, missed me. It's Christmas time, and you say you've not met anyone like me at Notre Dame. We've seen each other every night over the break. Dad is a little worried, but he shouldn't be. You know where to stop when we hold each other. Besides, we have such interesting things to talk about. You are opening to me a world of philosophy, and you listen when I tell you about the stars and galaxies.

You are so different from Greg. Greg is my other half, my bodily other half, but you are my soul's other half. Between us there is a greater bond, a spiritual bond, one that is eternal, just as you said last night.

Three weeks have passed, and you head back to Indiana tomorrow. How incredibly fast things have developed. Last night you said you wonder if we have a future together. Oh, how I hope we do! "Have you thought of going to Notre Dame?" you said. I tell you I plan on going to Georgetown on a scholarship, or rather a collection of grants I've applied for. "That's not too far away," you say. "I have a car, self-driving, of course."

Life is so astonishingly wonderful!

Greg: Macrina graduated second out of 245 seniors, and I graduated eighth. Out golf team lost by two strokes to Randolph in the state championship, but second isn't bad. Lorenzo is home, and Macrina is blissful. He goes off next week to Oregon to be a camp counselor.

Greg: Macrina suffered a terrible loss July 4, 2038. She had never known anything like it before, and I hadn't either, nothing even close to it. Lorenzo drowned trying to save a child who ventured too far into the current of a river that the campers were picnicking next to. Lorenzo's parents conferred at length with Dad. From what I remember, Lorenzo jumped into the river without hesitation and swam frantically after the child, until he too got swept away. The river was strewn with boulders and rapids. A bump on the head was all it took, even for a strong swimmer like Lorenzo. They found his body the next day hung up against a tree branch. To my knowledge they never found the body of the child. I remember Dad saying that trying to save the child was almost suicidal. That's how dangerous the river was. But how could Lorenzo do less? I might have done the same.

Macrina spent most of her time in her room with the door closed. I remember trying to cheer her up but without success. Mom did a little better, but nothing we could do would have made much difference. What she was hatching in her traumatized mind flew in the face of all the counsel she received. It was utterly bizarre. In a sense it launched her entire career. It was as if destiny could not be thwarted. Georgetown was not part of it, at least not right away.

Macrina, Journal: Oh my darling, where are you now? Do you see into my grieving heart? Will you pity me as I babble on? Do you find me tiresome as I lash out at you for leaving me so utterly desolate? Lorenzo, Lorenzo, Lorenzo—the mockingbird outside has a hundred different songs, but all I hear it sing is Lorenzo. I must pull myself together, you would want that, I know.

What were your last thoughts as the waters closed round you? Did you think of me? How can I be so selfish? Forgive me. But I want to know anyway. Did you realize what you were losing? I hope not. But no, I hope so! For then you would understand what I feel.

I've decided not to go to Georgetown. I would only think of you, think of you driving down from Notre Dame. Do you know how much I anticipated that? Do you know?

I happened to read an article about the U.S. Marine Band, and I've decided to enlist. I need a complete break from all that is familiar. It hurts too much with you not a part of it. Everything reminds me of you. Dad was horrified when I told him I had my sights on Okinawa. I remember you said you wanted to honeymoon in Japan when we married. Oh my God, even there I won't be able to forget!

Macrina, Journal: I dreamed of you last night, but it wasn't a dream. Nothing like those dim, shadowy, ghostly things I see every night. It was a visit. You were there. Your face shone as if in sunlight. And you were smiling, smiling radiantly, so happy to see me. And happy to be where you are. And urging me to be happy where I am. That was the message you gave me. And when I woke up this morning, I *was* happy. Thank you. Thank you so much for coming.

I've begun to wonder what it's like up there. Are you in heaven? Or maybe purgatory? This I know. You are in a good place.

I'm going to get out of the house and go for a walk under the Oaks with you alongside me. You will be there, I know you will if you can. If you're not busy doing something better.

I'm healing, I'm finally healing.

Cousin Brian Kent, email to Greg: One of my fondest memories of Macrina as a teenager was a discussion we had in your home on Thanksgiving—it might have been in 2037. I was a senior at Spring Hill and had finished the required philosophy and theology courses. She asked me about them. I don't remember what I said or even what the specific topic was. All I remember is her curiosity, her persistent questioning, and the pleasure she took in the conversation. She became dear to me on that day. We must have talked for over an hour. It was a warm day; I remember we went outside to get away from the hubbub inside.

Macrina, email to Greg: You'll be amused to learn that I came in first in marksmanship in my company. Could it be that those god-awful duck-hunting trips Dad took us on in the bayous is paying off? But I never hit a duck with Dad! Life is full of mysteries.

Basic training is no fun. Imagine crawling on your belly through mud with tracer bullets whizzing by over your head. The worst part is the way they intentionally dehumanize you, yelling in your face if you laugh or smile. Was I crazy getting myself into this? But it will end soon. The good thing about it is that I'm not obsessing over Lorenzo. I'm more back to missing you.

Then it's on to the School of Music in Virginia. They were impressed by my audition and practically promised me I'd finish in half the time—that means three months. Then on to Okinawa. I'm counting the days. I'll be Lance Corporal, pay-grade E-3. How about that, big boy?

Macrina, email video recording: Don't worry, Dad. The men in the band are not the type to assault a woman.... The band practices three hours a day. Then after lunch I practice with the other members of the woodwind quintet, two men and two women, all college graduates except me. And thanks, Mom, for the happy nineteenth birthday greeting and the shawl....

They really keep us busy. We give concerts on Japan's main islands and Korea. And with the thaw in our relations with China there is talk of our traveling to Beijing. This is all so interesting... I love it.

I'm taking three courses at the local junior college, one in the Japanese language, another in Buddhism and Shinto, the third in Hinduism, my favorite, all taught in English. I guess it's becoming obvious where my interests lie. I'm staying busy. I hope to be halfway through college by the time I'm done....

No, Mom, I couldn't miss Mass even if I wanted to. I'm the Catholic chaplain's server....

Congratulations, Greg, on making South Alabama's golf team. Third man as a freshman is not too shabby....

I love you all so much.

[Dad salutes her as they sign off.] That's funny, Dad!

Greg: Macrina wrote me frequently, going into all the details about Marine life in Okinawa. She did Facetime with Mom, Dad, and me gathered around. She was in great spirits and had been promoted to sergeant. She especially liked the band director, who played the French horn when he wasn't directing. She said he excelled on the piano as well. I remember her telling us that he asked her to play a piece by Schubert, a sonata written for piano and a different instrument but adaptable to the clarinet. I think they actually performed it at one of the band concerts on the island. It was this, I think, that made them close.

Jan McGrath, in-person interview: I thought my little girl was destined to become a loser after what happened, not in her inner character—no one who knew her could ever say that!— but in what life would give her. I was shocked. Your father wanted her to rotate out and come home for good. The decision she eventually made both saddened and relieved us. It was probably the most momentous decision she ever made.

Macrina, email to her parents: Dear Mom and Dad, I was sorry, more than you can imagine, to spring this news on you over the phone. I promised to give a full account in writing. Here it is.

David is 28, his rank captain. He is a gifted musician both on horn and piano. He could have selected anyone to join him on the piano in off-time. He chose me, and I felt deeply honored. I felt even more honored when he asked me out on a date, at great risk to his career. It wasn't hard falling in love with him. What he saw in me, a mere 21-year-old whelp, I don't exactly know. He could have had anyone.

The Marines never stop warning us women to avoid pregnancy, to take precautions, and so on. But they also make it clear that pregnancy doesn't get you sent home. You continue doing your job and living with the same girls in the same billet. You get 12 weeks of maternity leave, and they provide free child care when the baby arrives and the best medical care. With this in mind, and above all with the presumption we would marry — he made it clear that I was the girl he had always wanted — well, I just let it happen. From that point on I was on birth control, but it was too late.

What a fool I was! Dad, I am so sorry. Mom, how can you forgive me? You had warned me so many times what could happen if — well, I didn't listen. I just didn't believe it could happen to me. Or if I did, that David would turn out to be — I can't even find the words. Here is what happened. Be sure to destroy this message once you've read it. I am too ashamed.

David's forceful, sometimes even fierce personality makes him a great leader. No one wants to disappoint him. He inspires excellence in all of us. He is pure Marine. He's also quite good looking.

Naturally I was attracted to him. We all were. But the very force which makes him a great director undid our relationship. He was aware that I was a practicing Catholic and that I was assisting the chaplain, but I had no idea what he really thought of it. He is Catholic by background, and I assumed he would go along with whatever happened.

When I told him I was pregnant, in my innocence I expected him to be pleased, even excited. We had talked about children, and I knew he wanted them. Still, I was a little apprehensive when I brought it up. We certainly hadn't planned on having them so soon.

A look of distress spread over his face. I can't remember exactly what we said, but this is pretty close:

"You're pregnant? I thought you were protected."

"Really? Why would I be? I wasn't sexually active. You must have known that."

We were in his jeep, driving along by the seashore. It was not self-driving. He was at the wheel. Seagulls circled offshore.

"Well, you need to take care of it. I'll help you in every way."

"What do you mean?"

"I mean you'll need an abortion. I can arrange it."

"An abortion?" That word was a like a dagger through my heart. "David, I would never even consider an abortion."

"Why not?"

"I would never kill my baby. And it's against my religion."

"Baby?" He spoke that word with contempt. "It's not a baby, it's a fetus."

By now I was near tears—not just over that word, spoken with such contempt, but over the man I was discovering him to be.

"Macrina, your religion is riddled with superstition. You need to grow out of it." He almost snarled when he said the word *religion*.

"Slow down. Slow down, please!" He had gunned the jeep to a dangerous speed without realizing it.

"Look, this is not the time to bring a kid into the world. Doesn't your religion put marriage first?"

"Of course. So didn't we talk about marriage? David, didn't we?"

He shook his head and started screaming at me, just driving along screaming at me. I was weeping by now, totally distraught. I couldn't believe the horror that was happening in front of me.

At some point I asked him to stop and let me out. I was ready to hitchhike back to the base. This calmed him a little, and he began attacking the Church, especially Mary.

"Do you really believe that Mary was a virgin and that she was immaculately conceived and was assumed into heaven without even dying? All of that is ridiculous. I once believed it myself because I was a child and didn't know better. But once I began to think for myself—for God's sake, Macrina, grow up. Your Church has made big mistakes. And what it says about abortion is one more."

"David, it's *my* baby. I'll take care of it. We'll marry, and I'll take care of it. They're plenty of single moms who are Marines. If they can do it, it'll be easy for us. Just trust me to do it."

"Macrina, you're assuming we're going to get married. Look, I do love you. But marriage is—it's not something I am ready to do."

I was shocked to hear this, almost too shocked to continue speaking. But I calmed myself and said something like, "I wasn't either, but now things are different. We have to be flexible. We love each other, and we have to be flexible, David." You can see how determined I was to marry him, how determined to bring him around. I really thought I could.

We argued on and on. He said he would refuse to raise a child in the Catholic religion or any other one. He said that religion was the cause of most of the wars the world had ever known. At some point he turned the jeep around and headed back to the base. I couldn't change his mind. I argued with all the force I had—you know how persistent I can be—but to no avail. We got home and parted.

As I lay in my bed, I wondered what kind of husband he would make if we did marry. I had never seen such fury in a human being. It occurred to me that the forcefulness that made him such a great director in the recital hall might make him a terrible husband at home.

The next day after practice he called me into his office. Photos of the band playing at various sites hung on the wall behind his desk, and ribbons and plaques decorated the office even further. He called my attention to them and, this time using a different tactic, said he could be demoted, or transferred, or even court-martialed if I remained stubborn. He told me his fate was in my hands and that if I really did love him I would make the sacrifice. By now I was quivering, I could barely think as I studied the face of the man I would have died for only yesterday. Such threats were like a giant tidal wave sweeping over me. I think he said something like being open to a child in the distant future—"when we would both be in a position to get married."

As I sat there listening to him talk, all I felt was the devastating loss of his love. I felt worthless, forever unlovable. In my desperation I even offered to live with him if he would help me raise the child and be a father to it. He wouldn't consider it. I left his office wishing I could wake up from this nightmare. I went back to my billet and wept and wept.

I woke up the next morning dreading the day. I mechanically went through the motions of greeting the girls as if nothing had happened, washing up, putting on my uniform, braiding my hair, applying lipstick, and getting ready for the concert we were giving.

As I was leaving the barracks, a daring thought occurred to me. I decided to protest my treatment by not showing up. I didn't care what happened to me. I would show him. I caught the bus into town and bought a ticket to Sefa Utaki, a sacred Shinto site I had always wanted to see.

It was while standing in front of a huge overhanging rock with water dribbling down its face and a cool wind blowing through the canopy of trees surrounding it that my decision was formed. I faced the fact that David and I were finished and that I would be bringing my baby into the world without a father to help me raise it. I hated the thought of this, especially if the baby were a boy. On an impulse I decided to give the baby up. I would give it to a mom and dad who would raise it together without interference from me. The thought horrified me, it was like swallowing acid, but I knew it was in the baby's best interest. I decided to put my baby up for adoption. The Shinto gods dwelling in the shrine seemed to bless the decision.

On the way back on the bus, I realized there was more to it. I wanted the freedom to follow whatever my dream might be. I've always loved my religion and been drawn to the lives of the saints. I remember promising Lorenzo that I would enter the convent if I were ever to lose him. Am I cut out for a normal life? Maybe what this affair with David is telling me is that I'm not.

One thing is clear. There is something more important for me to do than play clarinet in an orchestra for the rest of my life.

I've consulted an adoption agency and will let you know once the process is underway.

Try to forgive me for the mess I've made of my life. There was a time when I thought that some special destiny awaited me, such as writing a famous novel, but I see now that it was nothing more than the fantasy of a swollen ego.

Humbly and contritely, and with all my love,

Macrina

Greg: This is the earliest long letter in my Macrina file. I made a copy of it without my parents knowing. Why did I do this? I don't remember, but probably it was—I don't know, maybe I had an inkling it would be useful for something.

I remember how distressed Mom was as we stood together in the kitchen and listened to Dad read the letter on his laptop. I had never seen Mom cry so uncontrollably. Dad sat her on the sofa in the den and held her. "That's my grandchild she's giving away!" she moaned. I remember that distinctly because it surprised me so much. I thought she would be more concerned with Macrina. Dad told her there would be more grandchildren and that Macrina was doing the right thing. He never lost his cool. My reaction was that I wanted to kill the bastard who did this to my twin sister.

Macrina, email to her parents: the priest I serve Mass for is a friend with a childless couple who are thinking about adopting. Both have law degrees, but she gave up the practice, went to seminary, and is now the rector of the local Episcopal church—yes, a woman—right next to our base. They hadn't even contacted an adoption agency yet when I heard about them. It sounded so ideal that I wasted no time looking into them. I went to her church two Sundays ago, watched her preach in Japanese, and had the most amazing conversation after the service. This beautiful lady—her name is Rev. Grace Onishi—was extremely interested in my proposal. She invited me over to meet her husband, and within two hours we came to an agreement. They would take the child at birth, and I would forfeit all rights until the child turned 21, at which time she (my hunch is she's a girl) would be told she was adopted. Then she could contact me if she wanted. Grace and I will stay in contact. The child will be raised bilingually.

Mom, you might hate me for this, but the idea of a closed adoption (no contact) was mine. I studied the question for a long time before deciding it was better for the child not to be confused by two sets of parents.

David is still not happy with my decision, but he's relieved he won't be paying child support. He won't be here much longer anyway. He and the director of the Marine band in Hawaii will be trading places—a clean swap. I asked our commander not to punish him and took much of the blame. My desire for revenge is gone. He is, after all, the father of my baby. Dad, I have not forgotten the advice you once gave me: *Never hold a grudge against anyone.* Thank you for that....

Jan McGrath, voice recording: My poor child was alone without family in Okinawa. We did a lot of Facetime with her to keep her spirits up. Her pregnancy wasn't difficult, not like mine with the twins, thank God! But she kept second-guessing herself. I had to remind her that the pact with Grace was final, even though it was breaking my heart. I told her she was doing the bravest, most selfless thing she would ever do and that her depression was normal and would pass. "But someone else will be raising my baby," she would say. We let her cry, and she would feel better. Clifford told her she couldn't allow it to interfere with her job. Mention of duty always seemed to revive her. I don't need to tell you how it all turned out.

Macrina, email to her parents: The baby's name is Anna Onishi Cowan. I chose Anna because it's a common name in both English and Japanese....

Macrina, Journal: I had so well prepared myself for the handover that I let her go as soon as she was born. The nurse held her up for me to see, then washed her and took her away. She asked if I wanted to see her again. A flash of profound regret shot through me. I was like a suicide changing her mind halfway down, giving anything to be still standing on the bridge from which she jumped. I said no and started blubbering as I lay alone in my bed. Mom had offered to come over and help me through the ordeal, but I forbade it. Exhausted but resting, I wished I hadn't. Once my head cleared, I called her. Again she told me I was doing the right thing even though it cost us both. I had made up my mind, and I wasn't about to let Grace down....

I watched the baptism at All Saints. Grace, being the rector, performed it. I lived through a kind of double reality: "There's a baby up there that a woman is holding in her arms and baptizing, and that baby is mine." I imagined myself holding the baby, feeling a kind of horror that I wasn't, but then I looked at Grace's loving face and was happy for her. "I baptize you, Anna Onishi, in the name of the Father... the Son... and the Holy Spirit." Three little splashes on the forehead. Who was that other lady? My God, I'm not even the godmother! The link is severed for all time. Deep sadness. But also a deep sense that I've done the right thing. Happiness for Grace. Happiness, yes, happiness for Anna too.

Greg: Macrina put in her four years as a Marine and came home. She no longer dreamed of going to Georgetown; she thought Spring Hill, a Jesuit college, could teach her the same thing she'd get at an elite university. Personally I think she stayed home to recover from the trauma of what happened to her in Okinawa. She needed to be around the people she knew would always love her, never betray her. It wasn't like she was shattered, but I could tell by the way she clung to us that she had gone through hell.

Surprisingly, she recovered rather quickly. It wasn't long before she began to take interest in how to heal others. The sprightliness and nervous energy so typical of her began to awaken. It manifested in a way that would become her trademark.

I transferred from South Alabama to Spring Hill for my senior year after my golf scholarship ran out, and Macrina arrived as a sophomore after her units transferred from Okinawa. We found ourselves in the same theology class during that first semester together. It was strange being reunited with her in the classroom—the first time since high school. There it was again: the extraordinary quickness of her mind. She would carry on a conversation with our professor, a young Jesuit in training for the priesthood, as his equal. The rest of the class just gaped.

They became friends, she and the professor—Tom, as he invited us to call him. He was ministering to a small Black community of Catholics in Crichton, a rundown neighborhood, actually a slum, two miles into town, as distant from the lovely ambience of the college as a curly-tailed stray dog from a pure-bred lab. On one occasion he invited me to accompany him on a mission to give basic instruction in the faith and baptize babies.

He told me he needed someone to stand in as godfather in homes where the father was unknown and no males available. Perhaps he mainly wanted to show me how the rest of the world lived—I don't know. Anyway, I couldn't turn him down. As a result I have a few godchildren of unusual vintage.

When Macrina got wind of what I was doing, she wanted to come along. She became a regular at our weekly visits. She would hold and love the baby as if it were her own, and she helped clean the house and fix little things. The women in these small, drafty, tumble-down houses loved her.

When the semester ended, Tom was transferred, and I assumed that would be the end of the mission. Not so. Not so at all. Macrina stepped right in and took over. The first time we went together without Tom, I told her it was a waste of my time, but she insisted it wasn't. She asked me to stand in as godfather as usual, asked for a volunteer to serve as godmother, and... I remember asking, "What are you doing, Macrina? What do you think you are doing?" "Hush," she scolded in a hiss. "We've got business here." She picked up the baby—it was a boy about six months old, I'll never forget—said the prayers, poured the water over the baby's forehead, and baptized him—as if she were a self-made priest reporting to God alone.

Macrina, Journal: When Tom left town, I wasn't content to let the mission end. I loved those humble women, and they loved me. The trick was to get Greg to continue helping. I pushed him hard and, God bless him, he finally consented, not knowing what I had in mind.

According to Canon Law anyone, cleric or layperson, can administer a valid baptism as long as they use the right formula and intend what the formula says. But for the baptism to be licit—that's the word the Church uses—the parish priest or deacon has to do it. But there are exceptions. In an emergency a layperson can do it. As far as I am concerned, this was an emergency. That baby was not going to get baptized unless I did it. And the mother was finding it impossible to get to church—no car, no real desire. A flimsy Catholic at best, though she did say, at my urging, that she intended to bring the child up as a Catholic.

What gave me the grit to take this on? Before me stood the example of Grace holding my own baby: "I baptize you, Anna Onishi, in the name of the Father... the Son... and the Holy Spirit."

Greg: Something happened in that Hinduism class she took in Japan that ignited an interest that didn't fade with time. What was it? Was it mere curiosity? It had to be more than that. Maybe she wanted to put her own religion to the test, to see how it held up against a contender. Or maybe she just found it attractive. Or maybe—but who knows? Anyway, Macrina graduated from Spring Hill in December of 2044 and left a week later for India. Her journal shows her jumping from one corner of the country to another, sometimes nothing more than a brief scribble, sometimes much more. What happened in India was pivotal to her spiritual development and, I believe, her future.

Macrina, Journal: Okay, girl, force yourself to sit down and write it out. Wow, where to start! It goes back to that course in Hinduism I took in Okinawa.

Dad hated the idea of my traveling alone in India for two months. One of his reasons, strange to say, was the high incidence of snakebite deaths—over 70,000 annually. Another was the threat of rabies from the packs of wild dogs that roamed India's city streets. He was also concerned over threats from our own species: men eyeing a young unprotected white woman of average height and size, or the notoriously poor drivers in a country that had not completely converted over to self-driving or even electric cars. He tried to dissuade me from going up to the day I left.

The crowds in all the cities—Kolkata, Delhi, Mumbai, even in cities of 10 million I'd never heard of—shocked me. The traffic creeping along, horns blowing, swarms of humanity getting from one place to another, 1.7 billion souls thrown together in a space one-third the size of the States. The smell of gas fumes, the litter everywhere, the bazaars spilling out onto the city's roads, pedestrians dodging in traffic as they j-walked across streets, and, yes, those dogs lying all over the sidewalks as people stepped around them—at first I was appalled. But as the days passed, I found my ability to navigate through all this congested space exhilarating. You were on your own, girl, and you could do it!

I landed in Kolkata just before Christmas and threw myself and my pack into the back of a rickshaw, or tuk tuk as they call it. "Mother Teresa's Home for the Dying." The driver knew exactly where to drop me off. I tipped generously from my Marine Corps savings. And there they were in their world-famous blue-striped cotton saris. Nuns from Mother Teresa's Missionaries of Charity, the most famous missionary order in the world. They bustled with their smiles from one emaciated patient to another, washing them down, feeding them, medicating them, loving them. One of the sisters told me to wait until they went back to the Mother House. "Place your pack there, and if you don't mind, would you feed him?" No wasted motion. Thus began my on-the-job training. After Crichton, I was in my element.

I'll never forget the first morning—awakened at dawn by a call to prayer from a nearby minaret. I had almost forgotten that 24% of Indians were Muslim.

Three days later they spirited me north to a leprosarium at Titagarh, where Brothers from the order nursed 600 lepers of all ages. Three of the Sisters and three volunteers, including me, were needed to help celebrate Diwali, India's Festival of Lights. My job was to dish out servings of rice. Have I ever seen so much rice? After the meal the lepers came up to me, women first, and gave me hugs. Then followed the men as they saw I wasn't afraid of being infected.

I paid a visit to the community cobbler, a man about 40. He had to fit every shoe to the unique foot of the client—one with no toes, another with three or four, another with not much more than a stub. I was intrigued by his talent—he had only two fingers and a thumb on one of his hands and half a thumb on the other, yet he had mastered the art of cutting and gluing leather. One of the sisters was with me, and she spoke English. I asked him, through her, if he took pleasure in his work. "Yes," he said, "but I still want to die. I look forward to a normal life next time." This was an opening I couldn't resist.

"Do you envy or resent healthy people?"

"No. They have their karma, and I have mine."

"Does your family visit you?"

"No. I don't want my mother to see me. It would be too painful. My condition worsens. I write her every six months."

I couldn't resist asking further, "What do you look forward to?"

He didn't hesitate. "My 13-year-old nephew is a leper too. He hangs out at a railway station begging and visits me once a year. I send him some of the money I make." He hesitated, then said, "Someday I want to go home to die." I took his stubby hand and thanked him.

I bloodied my forehead on the thorns of a lantana bush while picking flowers the next morning and looked up to see five lepers passing by, staring at and pitying me. It was an odd irony.

I was eager to get out on my own and bought a ticket for Chennai, far to the south and a thousand miles away—a 21-hour overnighter by train if all went well. I indulged and bought a first class ticket so I could sleep. My destination was the alleged tomb of St. Thomas the Apostle, who, according to legend, carried the faith to India, where he was martyred.

Macrina, Journal: I had the great fortune of being seated in a compartment with a saintly man in his 70s who spoke good English. Mahesa Sastri, a retired university librarian and a Brahmin, gave me a short course on "Lord Shiva," the Creator and Master of the Universe. "My only remaining goal," he said, "the only thing worth doing for an old man like me, is to realize unity with the Lord and liberate myself from rebirth." He was headed south to Mount Arunachala, where his guru, a saint named Ramana Maharshi, had lived and died. Meeting Sastri has changed my life.

Of darkened teeth, silvery hair plastered to his forehead, and serene expression, Sastri viewed Mount Arunachala as the "heart of Shiva," a place whose abundance of grace was unmatched by any other place on earth. He showed it to me on his laptop. To me it was just a rocky, treeless mountain rising out of a vast, flat, somewhat parched plain, not even a low hill to keep it company. According to Ramana, whom he referred to as "Bhagavan," it was more than a symbol. It was literally the all-knowing, all-powerful, all-loving supreme Lord of the universe. Some said that to be in its presence, even to gaze upon it, guaranteed liberation from rebirth. Sastri was heading south to more than gaze. He intended to climb it with thousands of others during a festival.

All Arunachala's devotees recite a mantra, "Arunachala Shiva," repeated three times. Sastri demonstrated it to me as we bumped and lurched our way toward Chennai in the train. It has a definite rhythm and melody that I will never forget. For twenty minutes he whispered it with eyes closed and concentrated on the picture of the mountain in his mind. Twice during our trip he went into this meditation. He claimed it removed all barriers between himself and God. His religion teaches that God is identical to one's true self. In other words, God is not only inside the mountain in a special way, but inside each of us. Meditating on the mantra put him in contact with this great fact, the fact of our own divinity. That is Sastri's religion, as I understand it.

I am always curious when it comes to somebody else's religion, and I didn't hold back with my questions. At some point, long after we had shared pictures of our family on our phones, he asked for permission to ask me about *my* religion. I was only too happy. Thus began one of the great teaching moments of my life.

It began by his asking me if I found any significance in my being a twin. No, I said. It was just the accident of two eggs being fertilized instead of one. It had no religious significance. "You've never wondered about it?" I admitted I had, but not seriously. "Maybe God really had planned it that way," I added, "but even if he had, I can't see how it matters." Sastri's face lit up in that wonderful way of his, that almost childlike way, as he said, with eyes sparkling, "We Hindus think you had some karmic connection with your brother in a past life. You two were very close, so close that you chose not to be separated, so you arranged to come back as brother and sister, as twins. That connection guided the science." Then he smiled in that lovely way of his.

This quaint speculation was fun to consider, but I didn't see what it had to do with religion, at least as it's practiced. But this led to something that did—in a big way it did. It struck as the very heart of religion—of *my* religion. This is the way it unfolded, as close to word for word as I can remember.

"If you don't mind," he began, "tell me how you pray. What's going on in your mind as you pray? I see my precious mountain when I pray. What do you see?"

This really caught me off guard. I thought of the Lord's Prayer we recite at Mass. "Frankly, most of the time it's rote. I'm not putting much effort into thinking about what I'm saying. I'm just absentmindedly reeling off words I've memorized."

"I understand. At your age I didn't make room for religion.

Football, my studies, and my friends took up all my time."

I was a little miffed at this. Did he think I wasn't serious about my religion? "But there are times when I do concentrate, especially when I thank God for his blessings, or ask for healing or protection, or pray for guidance. Or when I seek closeness with God, seek to feel his love for me, and my love for him."

"Wonderful! Those are the moments I am asking about. What is going on in your mind when you feel close to God, when you are truly concentrating?"

I had to think carefully. "On the words of the prayer, I guess. On the meaning of the words I use, the words I use to place myself in his presence."

"Do you visualize the words, see them spelled out in your mind?"

"No."

"Would you like to go deeper?"

Startled, and somewhat reluctant to take instruction from a Hindu, I said, "I'd always like to go deeper."

"You must anchor your mind in something. God is formless, but the mind cannot grasp that formlessness. It needs a form. And the form must be steady. It cannot wobble. It cannot shift. It must make the mind still. Only then can it tunnel into your unconscious mind and change you at the deepest level. Deep inside we all have our psychic scars, the resentments that we carry around, our disappointments, our hungry egos that never get enough to eat. My form is Arunachala, the mountain. You must find a form. Then you will find God."

I haven't found my form, but I'll be looking for it. It made total sense when Sastri explained it, and it still does. It keeps him focused, keeps his mind from wandering away, keeps him on track as he goes deeper and deeper into the God within his own depths, the God he calls Shiva. Concentrating on that mountain appears to have formed his beautiful character. He is the holiest man I ever met, and he's not even a Christian.

As we approached Chennai, I asked what would happen to him when he freed himself from rebirth.

"We merge with God. Like a raindrop falling from the sky into the mighty ocean, we merge."

I had a problem with this analogy. "But the drop is you, and it disappears? So how can you experience anything?"

"The drop disappears, but not the atoms in the drop. They disperse and spread throughout the ocean. Only God is left. That's all we were in the first place. We have come home. All that's left is bliss."

"No more forms?"

"No more forms."

We parted in Chennai, promising to keep in touch. I mean to keep that promise....

The Basilica San Thome, a beautiful bright-white neo-Gothic church on the seacoast. Said to be the place where Thomas, Doubting Thomas, my favorite apostle because he dared to doubt, was buried after being martyred in AD 72. Visited the crypt under the church, saw the head of the spear that killed him. St. Thomas known as the patron saint of India. Nice meditation in the church. Still no Pope Thomas after 20 centuries! That's what he gets for doubting. If I were a pope, I would be the first Pope Thomas. If you don't doubt, you don't grow.

Greg: One of the most precious letters I got from Macrina goes back to her India days. Bear in mind that she was an attractive woman in her youth. She could turn heads of discriminating young men who saw her beauty — as much inner as outer. What happened to her in a city named Thanjavur tickled me no end.

Macrina, email to Greg: Well, brother, you'd have been proud of me if you'd seen this. Everywhere in South India there are temples, and as I was walking back from one of the remoter ones on the outskirts of a city named Thanjavur at the end of a hot day, I felt a violent tug. A man was trying to wrench my backpack off my shoulders. He had it halfway off when I turned around and without thinking hit him in the sternum with my knuckles. He was shocked, let loose, fell back, then rushed at me. I timed it perfectly. I kicked him in the balls, and he fell to the ground sprawling and cursing. I didn't become a marine for nothing, and I was, if you remember, a good marksman!

Macrina, Journal: Fifteen miles east of Thanjavur is a village named Venni, the site of one of the greatest battles in India's history. Is it my military background that drew me to this place? A Tamil poet who was on the scene described the battle in gory detail. I just had to see the place for myself, see if I could recognize the topography he described 1700 years ago.

The old relic of a bus to Venni was filled with goats and people. It lumbered across potholes and made stops along the way. When I stepped off it in the mid-afternoon heat, a small crowd, including a dozen or so children, gathered. The children just gazed at me, an American oddity clothed in jeans and a straw visor to keep off the relentless sun. When I explained that I had come to see where the Battle of Venni was fought, universal puzzlement was registered on their faces. Why would anyone do that? Yes, they had heard of the battle, but that was many centuries ago. Venni wasn't in anyone's tourist guidebook, that's for sure. Anyway, everyone was concerned for my comfort and wanted to show me around. Someone produced a bicycle, and off I went with a few other bikers and excited barefoot kids running behind. Many of the houses had mud walls and thatched roofs—little changed from the time of the battle.

Two features of the village especially stood out. As I was being shown around, we came to a tiny shrine at one edge of the village dedicated to the virgin goddess Kammiamma, protector of snakes. The village's snakes lived around her; you could see their holes, from which they came out at night. The villagers respected her and prayed to her for protection, but her first concern was the snakes themselves.

We turned back and rode down a different path, when suddenly my friendly guide explained in broken English that he could go no farther. "Harijans live here," he said with alarm. *Harijans* is the local word for untouchables. I was amazed. But I kept going, but now with no one following. This part of Venni was rundown, its darker-skin inhabitants looking at me with incomprehension bordering on suspicion. Did they too disapprove of my entry into their sector?

Back to the battle. As it turned out, there was nothing in the landscape surrounding the village that fit the description I had read about. Forgotten by the villagers, I walked out by myself to an uncultivated area and took a stand on baked yellow earth. Since I couldn't find signs of the battle, I decided to relive it through my imagination. I imagined cavalry, elephants, and chariots charging each other, guttural screams of men splayed out on the ground in their death agony, men with spears standing on piles of bodies to gain the advantage of high ground, wounded men limping or crawling through yellow dust as they fled the slaughter, trunkless elephants bellowing in agony and charging blindly in any direction, riderless horses bleeding from deep dripping gashes or from arrows stuck in their sides, the terrifying zings of notched arrows, the clicking and clanking of swords and spears, the soil turned into a shallow black-red mud cluttered with corpses and smashed standards. Finally I imagined the snakes cowering in their holes beneath the pounding footfall of men gone mad. This was the way that an ancient Tamil poet described it. To this peculiar ex-Marine, it was thrilling.

As the sun was setting, I left Venni without fanfare and caught the bus back to Thanjavur.

Macrina, email to Cousin Brian Kent: Dear Brian, how is my cousin? Well, as you know, I'm trekking through India, this chaotic, overpopulated, fascinating country, the land of peppers, coconuts, and curries, with still two weeks to go. I miss home terribly, miss the hamburger, the milk shake, and the gym, but wouldn't trade this experience for a million rupees.

I would bore you with stories of all the temples I've visited, but two stand out.

In the South Indian city Mysore, as I was about to enter still another temple, a priest with a V inscribed on his forehead in sandal paste blocked me. He said I couldn't enter—I wouldn't have the proper attitude. Now most Hindus make room for all kinds of people, but not this guy. I was surprised, even shocked. Had he lumped me in with untouchables, who presumably would desecrate the temple? I decided not to let this pass, if not for my sake, then for the sake of the people he repressed. "Sir," I said, "I love God and will not profane your temple. I want to get out of the heat and pray a little." He said it was reserved for devotees of Krishna, the major incarnation of Vishnu. I told him I knew a lot about Krishna and took a course on Hinduism. I wasn't a gawking tourist. He was adamant. "Look," I said as I grew a little heated, "Hinduism is famous for its tolerance. Krishna would be happy to have me in your temple." He was more adamant than ever. "You're giving your religion a bad name," I barked, and tried to push past him, but he kept stepping in front of me. I had no option but to withdraw.

As my anger abated, I thanked God for the lesson it taught me. I could feel this man's contempt for me, and I hated him for it. It occurred to me that for a billion Indians born to the wrong parents this was an everyday experience. It was a strange, disquieting moment of truth that I won't forget.

But this was the exception. All the others temples were open, and especially the great Krishna temple in Udupi, a city on the Arabian Sea below Mumbai. This vast temple complex attracts pilgrims from all over South India who come with one central purpose: to see the Lord Krishna and, much more importantly, be *seen by him*. I marveled at the sight of hundreds standing for an hour or more in a long winding line to glimpse him through a small window with nine holes. What exactly did they see? An image at the back of a dark enclosure lit by ghee lamps. You looked at Krishna for ten seconds when it came to your turn; then the assistant moved you along to keep the line going. What struck me was the awe on the faces of the pilgrims. We Catholics are supposed to believe that Jesus is present in the Eucharistic bread and wine—"body and blood, soul and divinity"—the Real Presence. I can tell you, Brian, that I've never seen such conviction in any Catholic Church as I saw on the faces of these Hindus. For them Krishna was present, *really* present, looking back at them, blessing them. It made you tingle just to see such faith—humble people, of all castes, who had come from long distances for these precious few seconds. A few cows and a huge elephant roamed freely inside the open-air temple, mingling with the pilgrims. If an animal peed on the floor in a spreading puddle, no problem. You stepped around it. "A pilgrim never goes away disappointed," one of the priests told me. Even the animals feel blessed!

The devotees manifested their faith in another way. The same priest, who seemed to take a shine to me, led me to a room with a huge marble basin shaped like a birdbath at its center. The basin, about eight to ten feet in diameter and three or four feet deep, was filled with thousands of manuscripts written in long hand. Each manuscript contained the entire Bhagavad Gita. Some individuals had written a dozen or more Gitas, a few by memory. Try to imagine a Christian copying the entire Gospel of Mark, and you have something comparable. Why did they do it? What was their motive? The same need to be seen by the Lord, to get his attention, to be blessed by him. The nature of the hoped-for blessing? That would be known only to the pilgrim and to Krishna. I have never seen such faith in action....

I assumed all Hindu priests were male because that was all

I saw. Just like us Catholics. Four days before my flight home from Mumbai, my priest friend happened to mention he knew a female priest. Wow, that was a surprise! I asked if I could meet her. "If you're willing to go to Pune. A school there trains female priests. She is one of the teachers." Immediately I changed my plans when I saw that Pune wasn't far from Mumbai. Another train ride took me there, and I met the students and their teacher. Classes were conducted in both Marathi and English. The youngest student was 30. Most were older Brahmins who had raised their kids and wanted something meaningful to do in old age. To me, as I visited one of their classes, they were an inspiration. Not dressed in the traditional white that most priests wore, they were decked out in colorful saris. They claimed that Hinduism did not forbid women from practicing as priests. Only tradition stood in the way, and that meant males, who had dominated the profession for thousands of years. My mind was buzzing as I took a bus from Pune to Mumbai. Why was Catholicism so backward? If Hindus could break through the glass ceiling, why not Catholics?

Greg: I'll never forget what Macrina told me when she got home: "I feel like a lone passenger on a big bus traveling toward an unknown destination."

India changed her forever. The experience in Pune awoke in her a fierce determination to do something about women's second-rate status in the Church. And the experience in Venni, with its invisible barrier separating one half of the village — those with status and wealth — from the other half — Harijans condemned by birth to lives of poverty and hopelessness — awakened in her a sense of responsibility that the rich should feel for the poor. Her Crichton experience years before back in Mobile had had an impact, but nothing like India. From that point on politics began to occupy her thoughts. In her Journal she looks back to the first Pope Francis' vision of "land, housing, and work for all." She cites a passage in which he extols a "healthy restlessness" in young people "to build a better world." She was beginning to respond to that challenge.

Clifford McGrath, Word of Mouth: She had saved some money in the Marines and asked me to invest it, which I did. She was amazed how much it had grown. She considered it a fortune. She asked me the best way to send $10,000 to a friend of hers in India. She said she would ask him to give $1000 each to ten destitute people. Any less, she said, and she wouldn't feel the loss of it. I strongly opposed this. Eventually I persuaded her to send $1000 total on the grounds that so much money to a poor person might get them killed. Which she did. She put ten $100 bills in an envelope and sent it to God knows where. She was a strong-willed girl, to put it mildly. And I adored her.

Jan McGrath, Word of Mouth: I consider myself an open-minded, liberal Catholic, but her glowing admiration of the Hindu religion was worrisome to me. She showed me photos and videos that her new-found friends sent her on the phone. Most appeared to be lovely people.

Greg: Macrina had a number of addresses in her Journal. She doesn't say which she sent the money to, but my hunch is it was Sastri....

She returned to Spring Hill, now as a graduate student in their Theology program. She zipped through the program in three semesters.

She began researching Ph.D. programs in theology and religious studies and chose Georgetown, the university she almost attended before joining the Marines. I remember how impressed she was by its diverse faculty, which included specialists in both Asian religions and Christian theology. I remember her doing interviews on her computer through Zoom and spending long hours online learning Hindi and Spanish after they told her she had to get an M.A. first and learn two languages. She also published her first article—in *America,* the first of many in that Jesuit weekly. I have it in my collection of her writings. In it she describes the growing Hindu movement toward female priests and makes the first of her many pleas for the Catholic Church to open its seminaries to women: "If one of the most patriarchal countries in the world can make room for a female clergy, then why can't we? The Catholic Church is a top-of-the-line Tesla stuck in the mud."

Macrina, Journal: Wow, what a grilling I took in that Zoom interview with Georgetown! I could tell they were suspicious of my credentials from the start. No wonder. Most of their graduate students got their B.A.s and M.A.s from more exciting places than little Spring Hill—places like Harvard, Cambridge, Boston, Vanderbilt, and international universities all over the world, especially the Middle East. And their interests tended to focus on Islam and Buddhism, not Hinduism. A few even had a major publication, one even a book. Why did they accept me? I could tell they were intrigued by my trip to India and knowledge of Hindi. Another liked my publication in *America* and my interest in women's issues. But what really swung it, I think, was a woman I would come to know as Professor Dasgupta. She was from New Delhi, and I could tell by her accent and headdress that she was Hindu. She would be my advisor and primary instructor if I were accepted. I had the impression that she was competing for someone to mentor—an apprentice, someone she could teach Sanskrit to, someone she could make over in her own image. I knew she would pull for me. I was tremendously relieved when they accepted me. It could easily have gone the other way.

    Greg: Macrina was 26 when she arrived at Georgetown in August 2046. Her Journal entries about the university— its location on a rise above the stately Potomac, its classic architecture, the new dorm for on-campus graduate students where she lives, the park-like atmosphere of the grounds, the many trails that lead into the city, her professors and fellow students, and the graduate program as a whole—tend to be rhapsodic. She is clearly thrilled to be part of a great university in the nation's capital. She has a full ride: room, board, and a monthly stipend. Her mentor, Professor Dasgupta, is at first intimidating, but Macrina's rapid progress in Sanskrit, partly due to her knowledge of Hindi, impresses Dasgupta. All this one could expect, but there were surprises.

Macrina, Journal: Jordyn, my dorm mate down the hall, has become a problem. She is lesbian and says she is in love with me. Last night she challenged me to see if I might be too. Until now it never seriously occurred to me. "You'll never know until you give it a try," she said. She suggested lying together on my bed. When I said the thought of it did not appeal to me, she argued that my religion had biased me. When I said I was sure it hadn't, she asked if we could just test it. I finally gave in, and she pulled my head toward her and kissed me on the lips. When she opened her mouth, I pulled back.

Jordyn is a pretty brown-eyed woman, the same age, and a talented linguist in Latin and Greek. She's fun to talk to and knows the District backwards and forwards. She showed me around, walked through the Capitol Rotunda with me and explained the paintings. Her personal habits, her hygiene, and her thoughtfulness make her a great friend. Except that she is in love with me.

Our experiment got me to thinking. When her lips touched mine, why didn't I feel a sexual stirring, as I would have if she had been a man? Did I block it because of my upbringing, as she claimed? It doesn't seem so. It seems natural for me to feel sexual arousal only when with a man. Why is Jordyn so different? She claims that, as far back as she can remember, she never felt attracted to boys, but always to girls. No traumatic event can explain it, she says. I remind her that the whole reason for the sexual urge in the first place is to bring children into the world and propagate the species. That's what any basic course in biology would say, and it's what the Church teaches. She felt boxed in when I made this point and said there are other reasons for the sexual urge—for example, the need for intimacy regardless of one's gender. So why not with another woman instead of with a man?

Jordyn is a beautiful, sincere, vulnerable person, and I refuse to press the point. But I also refuse to experiment further.

One thing is certain. I could never say she was "wrong." Or that her nature is twisted. Or that what she wants to do with me is abominable, as some traditionalists in the Church claim. To enjoy sex with someone you adore and adores you back is a precious experience, especially in a marriage where you pledge yourself to the other for life, even more when a child comes from that union. For me that is the ideal. How boringly conventional I am!

The question remains, why am I and Jordyn so different? Jordyn tells me that according to neurophysiology it has nothing to do with brain function, at least nothing discovered so far. So does God just make us different? Does God look down at the world and see how overpopulated it is and make more and more of us gay so we won't add to the crowd?

Who knows? It's a blustery day outside, and I'm going to put on my old navy-blue parka and take a long walk before getting back to parsing Sanskrit verbs.

Jordyn Graf, recorded phone message: Macrina, of course I remember her—who could forget? When we were at Georgetown she was an enigma, devout Catholic but dedicated pluralist. She had a great love for India, for Hinduism.... She was my first love, vivacious, pixie-ish, and to me adorable.... I wanted to believe she was lesbian like me but couldn't convince her... as if that were possible! How did you find me? Yes, I remember now. She had a twin brother she loved... and that must be you....

It's horrible what happened to her.... What an achievement, she changed the Church all by herself.... I left the Church and never finished my dissertation.... I have followed her all my life.... I'm so glad you contacted me. My heart goes out to you....

Macrina, excerpt from a paper written for a theology course in her fourth semester at Georgetown: Sometimes the students I meet in the Student Center—almost always young men, not too far removed from boyhood—tell me they are atheists. I ask them to describe the God they don't believe in, then tell them I don't believe in that God either. Then I launch into the God I do believe in. Their puzzled frowns amuse me....

My experience with these freshmen and sophomores, so full of themselves, has taught me that the roots of atheism are often found in primitive, narrow views of God picked up in preteen years. Waking up to the absurdity of God condemning non-Christians to hell is enough to blow into smithereens the childhood faith of many a thoughtful adolescent. A God who created the universe a few thousand years ago by merely wishing it into existence out of nothing is just as fatal. For others—and this goes for older people too—it's the belief that God will bless us with what we pray for if we pray hard enough, or that everything that happens to us is supposed to happen. Or that God inspired everything found in the Bible, or the Qur'an, or the Vedas, or the Book of Mormon. To believe in such a God is to fly in the face of reason and evidence. It's almost asking for trouble, for such theologies don't square with the human experience. It's daring the universe to throw you a curve ball designed to wake you up. Too often all that's left is atheism.

But there are alternatives. The best is a God whose nature doesn't contradict reality as we know it—a God that doesn't trip up when placed alongside the physics of the universe or the suffering of little children or the scoffing of brilliant minds in high places.

What does such a God look like? First—and this will surprise many—this God would be personal—not an It—but not personal in the fallible, limited way we are, not categorizable by a Myers-Briggs personality test, but having a unique intellectual and emotional structure infinitely beyond ours. Not an impersonal mystical power like the "Force" served by Jedi warriors, but a matchless Being who knows us, values us, even loves us— loves us because we are that Being's creations. More than that, because this Being ensouls us. We are not related to the Divine as pottery to the potter, but as child to parent. We are made of the very stuff of the Divine. Therefore it's natural for the Divine to watch us, follow us, expect great things of us, forgive us when we fall short, preserve us beyond death, keep the soul-making adventure going. Why? Because the Divine's love for us is as infinite as the Divine Him/Herself.

Wouldn't it be wonderful if there really was such a Being? But doesn't the evidence point in another direction? Surprisingly, on balance it doesn't. True, it doesn't point with compelling force to the conclusion we might hope for. But the door is open....

While in the Marines at Okinawa following a personal tragedy, I lost my faith. I was miserable at the prospect of a world without meaning followed by a death I'd never wake up from. "A flash of light between two eternities of darkness," as the philosopher Unamuno put it—that's all we amounted to. By then I had escaped the cramping theology I grew up with, but what I stepped into was even worse. After much soul-searching and the help of an Episcopal priest—a woman—I found something far superior to both: a joyous, compassionate, loving, powerful, boundless, light-filled Reality at the hub of the universe with an outreach that extended to the epicenter of my soul, a Being that would resonate with a Hindu as well as a Christian. A God roomy enough even for an atheist.

Greg: Macrina came home for the summer following her second year at Georgetown, and I can't resist letting the world see this undiscovered part of her nature. She was 28 at the time. She was more than a theologian.

Macrina, Journal: Just back from Georgetown for the summer, and Greg rents a canoe, straps it to the top of his car, and tells me we're going to see the Bottle Creek Indian Mounds up in the delta, north of Mobile. The day before, Alabama is deluged with five inches of rain, and the Mobile River is at flood stage. We hadn't reckoned on that.

The weather has cleared and it's already hot. We paddle along, Greg in the front, me in the back. Cypress and oak, pine and gum trees enclose us—it's like the Amazon on a small scale. No one around within a thousand miles. Quiet except for the plop of our oars in the black waters of the creek. Not a breath of air.

A whole litter of dark slimy creatures slide down the low bank of the creek. "Look! Otters!" Greg whispers. Wonderful!

We move west toward the river. Slow going. Limbs and snags block our advance. On toward the mounds, built by Indians in the thirteenth century. But first we have to cross the river. It's broad and flowing fast. We paddle hard to the other side.

A smudged sign points ahead to Mound A, the highest of the mounds. The path is drowning in rainwater. Can't find a way through the deep puddles, like small lakes. Greg checks his compass, and we navigate west through dense underbrush, a palmetto jungle. Come upon a pile of sticks with snakes coiled and warming themselves. "Water moccasins," Greg says. Had enough. We decide to turn back.

Halfway across the river we realize we're being carried south by the current. "We might not make it back to the car," he warns. "We might get swept down into the Bay. We've got to row *hard*."

We row upriver at the water's edge where the current is a little slower. Creep forward anxiously looking for the creek. Row almost frantically, never talking. Finally see the creek.

Turn down it toward the car and home. Pass a large alligator eyeing us as we paddle by. Utterly exhausted, not in battlefield shape. Our expedition has failed.

I found the whole experience exhilarating. There is a wildness in my nature, a love of forests, swamps, dangerous creatures out in the wild, prehistoric civilizations, and adventure.

Thank you, Greg!

Greg: While in Mobile that summer, Macrina volunteered for L'Arche. She worked with mentally handicapped kids and adults, took them on excursions, enjoyed their personality quirks, corrected them, loved them. She took me along one time to McDonald's, and one of the kids turned his strawberry ice cream cone upside down and squashed it against the forehead of his best friend. When the victim laughed, so did we.

Her third year at Georgetown was supposed to be dedicated to study for her Ph.D. qualifying exams, but she was already thinking about her dissertation. And about Fr. Anthony La Coste.

Macrina, Journal: A month ago a priest joined us as a volunteer at L'Arche. He pastors Pure Heart of Mary, Mobile's main church for Black Catholics. He's Black himself, or, more technically, mulatto as we say down here. In personality he's the exact opposite of David. Anthony LaCoste is the sweetest, most loving man I've ever met. He showed me around Mobile's downtown Black neighborhoods—boarded up houses, trash dumped in vacant lots, but also homes freshly painted and lawns mowed. "That's the difference between the addict and the churchgoer," he summed up. "For so many of them, short lives, no jobs, crime," he continued as his old Chevy Bolt drove us along. "Turn left," he said, and there it was, his church.

"Are you lonely?" I asked at one point.

"Yes. Terribly at times. I miss a good woman."

Then what he said shocked me. "If I could marry someone

like you, I'd leave the priesthood."

Was it a purely hypothetical statement or a veiled proposal? I wasn't sure. I treated it as hypothetical.

He hasn't come back to L'Arche. How many Catholic priests there must be who feel just like him. They are the good ones who live by the rules. If he had been raised by African Methodist Episcopal parents, he would be a married priest with kids. He would not be lonely or tempted to leave the priesthood. I feel his hurt tremendously.

My heart goes out to Anthony. I will never forget him.

Macrina, Journal: My friend Sophie, who is specializing in Christian women's studies, placed a most disturbing book in my hands. Thora Wheeler's *The Early History of Women in Christianity* describes a view of women, beginning with St. Paul, I hadn't fully appreciated. In 1 Corinthians Paul says, "Women should keep silence in the churches. For they are not permitted to speak, but should be subordinate, as even the Law says. If there is anything they desire to know, let them ask their husbands at home. For it is shameful for a woman to speak in church." St. Clement of Alexandria writes, "For women, the very consciousness of their own nature must evoke feelings of shame." I assume he has in mind menstruation. Tertullian is even worse: "You [women] are the devil's gateway. You first violated the forbidden tree and broke the law of God. It was you who coaxed your way around him [Adam] whom the devil had not the force to attack." Even the great Doctor of the Church, Aquinas, joined in: "[W]oman is defective and misbegotten, for the active force in the male seed tends to the production of a perfect likeness in the masculine sex, while the production of woman comes from a defect in the active force..." It gets no better with Protestants. Luther says, "Girls begin to talk and to stand on their feet sooner than boys because weeds always grow more quickly than good crops." And when they grow up, "they should remain at home, sit still, keep house, and bear and bring up children." Feminists throw around the word *misogyny* much too freely these days. But that word should be reserved for views like these.

We've obviously come a long way since then, but this attitude insidiously influences Catholic policy, especially regarding women priests.

Macrina, Journal: Dr. Dasgupta is determined to make a Sanskrit scholar of me and an expert in Hindu theology. She's always guiding me toward textual Hinduism, but I'm interested in Hinduism *on the ground* — the religion of ordinary people, their gods and goddesses, the vows they make, how they worship, their village shrines, the images they treasure, their festivals, their pilgrimages, their funeral rites, their belief in karma and rebirth. I must be careful not to offend her — she can get pretty snippy when challenged — but I do enjoy assisting her, especially meeting with her students in the breakout groups. I can imagine myself happy as a professor.

She doesn't see how I can devote so much time to my other interests, especially Christian theology. She keeps saying I need to make a choice. I almost have to meet in secret with Fr. Amicus, my theology advisor. I study Duns Scotus and William of Ockham, those wonderful old Franciscans, on the sly!

She wants me to do a translation of Madhusudana Sarasvati's *Bhagavata-bhakti-rasayana,* written 400 years ago and never translated. She's been carrying around the manuscript forever, just waiting to spring it on some defenseless Ph.D. candidate like me. She showed it to me and said, "This will put you on the map. You can go anywhere in the world if you do it right, and I know you can." She's right about one thing: I could do it right.

But I don't want to. It isn't me. Maybe ten people would read it after it was published, and they would all be scholars. What difference in the world would that make? What I really want to do is go to India, starting in Pune, and interview all those female Brahmin women priests, showing what they do better than men. Then I would be armed to follow my passion: open the leadership of the Catholic Church to women starting with priests, then bishops, then cardinals, and who knows, maybe someday in a distant century, a woman pope. That would be something worth doing. No ivory tower for me, please. I'll need Hindi, but not Sanskrit. A translation and commentary? For me it would be a prolonged hazing, a drawn out torture, to join a fraternity of scholars, nothing more.

But why should I put all this work into reshaping the Church? What are the chances of my success anyway? I could be an old woman and still be chasing a dream that never came true. Why be a Catholic at all? Why should my birth dictate who I am? Is Catholic Christianity the best religion? Have I ever met a holier man than Sastri?

Greg: Macrina had an unrecorded face-to-face phone meeting using Facetime with the president of the Association of Roman Catholic Women Priests. By now Macrina is in her early fourth year at Georgetown. Of course, we have no record of that conversation, but fortunately we have an email reply, which Macrina retained and possibly treasured. The president was a nun who signed off as Sr. Carol, SSS. Here is the communication, uncut.

Sr. Carol, SSS, email: Dear Macrina, It was a delight getting to know you. Your enthusiasm for our organization and our mission was an inspiration. I thought of replying by phone but want to choose my words carefully as I dare to offer you advice (I am 58, twice your age!) about your future.

I understand your frustration regarding the dissertation, but there is nothing that would help our cause more than your seeing it through and landing a good job at a prestigious university or college. Mastering Sanskrit enough to do a major translation is just what will make that happen. Once there, you can do what you want. You can write that book about all those wonderful Hindu women and compare them to what we Catholics aspire to. Even better if you were to do a long, well-researched article on the topic for the *Atlantic* or a series of short ones for the country's major newspapers. You are exactly the person we need, Macrina: young, charismatic, and properly pedigreed. Not a middle-aged nun, like most of us. And, if I may say so, easy on the eyes.

But if this is to work, you must recommit to the Church, not just superficially, but because you genuinely love her. Of course, there is no logical reason you should. You called it a "rubbish heap of outdated doctrine and arrogant old men," and in many ways it is. But it's so much more. Call to mind its art and architecture and music, its saints of the past and present, its current theologians who share our concerns and support us, sometimes at the cost of their careers—dear Macrina, you are not alone! Will you turn your back on your family when it becomes dysfunctional, when it runs aground? Where will you go? Why not pry it loose and lift it? Nothing would help the Church so much as placing women in high places, and that means priests. You could lead that charge. Instead of retreating from the challenge, you could embrace it. Does that sound exciting?

There is another reason to complete the dissertation. No matter how much good you could do for our organization if you were to drop out of academic work and join us full-time, there would be no guarantee we could pay you. Almost all of us have a main job or are on a pension or live on an inheritance. So plan on living on your professor's salary—unless, of course, you started a lucrative breakaway ministry where you work, including saying Mass and consecrating the Eucharist. One of our women has actually achieved that. You might too!

Over four or possibly, in your case, three summer vacations

we would train you to take up the responsibilities of a priest. Such a crash course would require total dedication—no distractions. Needless to say, you would be courting excommunication. The Church's official stance at this time is that we are all guilty of a "grave crime." If this prospect cowers you, the priesthood is not for you. Think this over prayerfully.

Macrina, we are looking for a young leader like you—a Moses to lead us across the Red Sea to the Promised Land. But you should feel perfectly free to decline such a responsibility. Leader or not, you would always be one of us: a woman priest, a pioneer conducting a great work, unloved by men but loved by heaven.

Macrina, Journal: Anna Onishi is now nine. Grace sends photos of her birthday party. My little girl, growing up. Will I ever see her again?

The translation is moving along well as I get more comfortable with Madhusudana's singular style and do more background reading on him. I've even reached a point where Dasgupta isn't of much help. I think I can get it done this year and defend in the fall. I could enter the job market with Ph.D. in hand, then devote the rest of the year to my passion: the book I want to write.

But will I even find a job? They are scarce in religious studies. I have dark moments.

Greg: I flew up to D.C. to visit Macrina. She was missing family. We went to a Nationals baseball game, visited the monuments, did all the things that tourists do and that she had never found time for. Her friend Sophie Higgins tagged along with us.

Macrina, Journal: I came across a biography of Robert Oppenheimer, the "father of the atomic bomb." Like me he was fascinated by Hinduism and learned Sanskrit so he could read the Gita and Upanishads in their native language. What most struck me was his work ethic. He was so intensely focused on theoretical physics that the "real world" around him passed him by. That's the way I feel now as I work on my translation. Twelve to fourteen hours a day—I'm consumed by it. It has become a strange addiction; I've begun to enjoy it, to look forward to the next day instead of dreading it. I've cracked Madhusudana's code and am really flying through, bogging down less and less, almost never now. I get high on my work. But then I sit back and wonder all over again: what's the value of it? How does it feed the hungry and change the world? Am I not in training to be a mere bystander?

Macrina, Journal: Dasgupta pressured me to broaden my introduction. She wanted me to show how M's thinking evolved beyond his masterpiece *Advaitasiddhi.* Good God! That would be a huge undertaking. With fear and trembling, I put my foot down. I found her in her office, with its paintings of events from the Ramayana and brass sculptures of the gods, and told her as discreetly as possible that I wouldn't do it. She looked stunned, and I wondered for a moment if my Ph.D. was in doubt. I held my breath. Then that Brahmin manner of hers, so formal and intimidating, wilted. She said that if I agreed to do an annotated bibliography and an index, that would be enough. Perhaps she's not the bully I thought she was.

Macrina, Journal: Greg and Sophie are engaged! My best friend will become a member of my family. It was that baseball game that started it. Greg sat between us, and the two of them never stopped talking while I watched. The Nationals beat the Orioles 4-3; I remember the double play that ended the game. I wonder if they even remember who played.

It started so inauspiciously. Greg's girlfriend had just dumped him after three years of serious dating, so he was gun-shy. And Sophie dreaded sitting next to him because of the acne scars on her cheeks. No one would argue she wasn't a beautiful woman front-on with her gorgeous blue eyes, broad forehead under thick blonde waves, and fine nose and lips, but those little pits on the side were like little individual monsters sent to torture her. I warned Greg of her complex before they met.

It was as if he never noticed. They began speaking on the phone, then graduated to Facetime. Greg is a great listener, and Sophie, usually so shy, opened up to him as if he were her confessor. "But you'll be living in Mobile," I warned after they announced their engagement. "It's a very hot place for a Minnesotan." I hope she'll finish her dissertation, but I have my doubts. Unlike me, she doesn't feel a call to change the world.

I'm 32, unmarried, and not moving in that direction. Is my ambition getting in the way of future happiness? Pondering the joy Greg and Sophie found in each other's presence cut into my sleep last night. Sometimes I wither under those lonely moments.

Macrina, Journal: The defense went well. Most of the senior students and half the theology faculty attended. Far from defending, I quickly became the teacher. They "sat at my feet," happy to learn what I could tell them. I have never seen Dasgupta so happy. I could tell she was bursting with pride over what "we" had achieved. I shared her happiness. A small champagne party followed, and that evening she took me out to dinner. How different her manner, how lovely she was. She encouraged, no, she *insisted* that I hurry the "book" to publication. But where? She was pushing the Harvard Oriental Series and Motilal Banarsidass in India. She wants to write the foreword. I am feeling very honored. I didn't tell her I never wanted to see another word of Sanskrit if I lived to be a hundred....

Three openings in my field interest me—one at Boston College, one at Amherst, the third, of all places, at South Alabama, three miles from home. To live in beloved old Mobile with old friends and family surrounding me is so inviting. "View it as a temptation to be resisted at all costs," Sr. Carol tells me. "Keep your sights on the goal, which is to reform the Church's view of women. You need credibility. Think credibility." I apply to all three, hoping for Amherst, where I would have to teach only two courses per semester. Plenty of time for other things, like the next book I hope to write. Boston College is attractive, but they are Jesuit. Would I get myself into trouble with my radical views? Amherst is ideal. I've studied their course offerings and see a way to make myself appealing. We'll see.

Macrina, Journal: I got the job! Amherst will be my new home. I traveled up there and fell in love with the place, its quaint towns set among the rolling, snow-covered, rural Massachusetts landscape, and interviewed. They were impressed by the translation and were delighted to know I had contacted Harvard about publishing it. And I didn't discourage them from thinking I'd do more of that kind of work. (Shame on me.) But what pleased them most at the interview was my proposal for their Intro course. It's team-taught and requires comparing one religion to another around a theme chosen by the professors. I told them about my contacts in India and suggested comparing Hindu and Christian attitudes toward women and said I was prepared to take either side. They liked that, especially their Christianity specialist, Douglas Stillwater, who said he would be happy to teach the course with me. I think we'll hit it off. My main job would be to cover their courses on Hinduism and Buddhism. But they left open the possibility of teaching anything I wanted once I got established. I can't wait to get started. I am so grateful, so incredibly grateful. Thank you, God, whoever you are.

Macrina, Journal: With no classes to attend, no dissertation to write, my future at Amherst set for the moment, no regular network of friends now that Sophie has departed, no boyfriend, Christmas behind me, winter in full swing, and moments of loneliness tiptoeing into my life, I've decided to join the Catholic Music Ministry and sing in the choir at beautiful Dahlgren Chapel. We just met for the first time this semester, and the choir director, a music professor, had us practicing a hymn titled "Be Still, My Soul." When I got back to my apartment, I found it on YouTube and listened to it sung by an acapella boys' choir. I melted in tears. I've never heard a more beautiful hymn. I don't want ever to forget the first stanza:

Be still, my soul: The Lord is on thy side;
With patience bear the cross of grief or pain.
Leave to thy God to order and provide;
In every change he faithful will remain.
Be still, my soul: Thy Best, thy heavenly Friend
Through thorny ways leads to a joyful end.

Why was I so moved? I think I know. It's not that I'm bereaved or depressed. It's that I'm a human being living in a world that is not our true home but gives hints of one that is. Is it wrong to hunger for the joys of that better world? Some would say I must be living a life that is unfulfilled, that I'm to be pitied, and that I turn to that fiction called religion as a coping mechanism to drown my sorrows. How wrong this is. What I feel is what we all should feel. Religion provides a comforting solace, the only legitimate solace when we meditate on death. To consider our lives on earth fulfilling in any final sense is to indulge a fantasy, an illusion.

Greg: Macrina wrote an article on purgatory and hell sometime during her last semester, her fifth and final year, at Georgetown. In all her later work, Macrina dedicates herself to retaining traditional Catholic teaching while reinterpreting it for a modern audience. This essay, I believe, is an early example of her future methodology. It also shows her trademark transparency. How different are her engaging metaphors and parables from the formal language coming out of the Vatican!

I looked for the essay in an old computer where she kept her writings from that era but couldn't find a trace of it. I searched through a box where some of her odds and ends were collected and found an old thumb drive. There it was, under the heading "Rethinking Purgatory and Hell." I felt like the widow in the Bible who loses a drachma coin, sweeps her house until she finds it, and rejoices. I've clipped out quite a bit.

Macrina, Thumb Drive:
Purgatory is a wise and good teaching and should be prized by every Catholic, every Christian, but it should be renamed.

Have you ever found yourself in a dark room when suddenly someone knocks at the door and you open it and you can't see who it is because your eyes haven't adjusted to the glare of the sun behind her? All you see is a dark silhouette.

For the newly dead, God's Heaven is like the glare when our eyes aren't ready. If we were lifted straight into Heaven the instant we died, we'd be uncomfortable. We'd feel out of place. We'd feel like we crashed a black-tie party when all we wanted was a place to hang out with our friends in their T-shirts. For the worst of us it would be torture. Purgatory gives us time to adjust. It's not a place of punishment. It's not a place where we get purged, in spite of what the word suggests. It's a place where we get schooled. Schools can be, and should be, very pleasant places.

You might wonder what it looks like. What will be your first impression when you get there? As a child I was told it was fiery and sulphureous, a hideous place. I prefer to think of it in this way: The sky overhead shines a vivid cloudless blue. We fly rapidly toward a vast city laid out below in checkerboard fashion. Parks of forest, meadow, and garden alternate with houses. Brooks twist around the houses and through the parks. Roads or paths separate each of the squares of the checkerboard. People walk along the roads, undisturbed by cars and trucks. They walk on a grassy boulevard as wide as a football field. People come and go, appear, disappear, fly, walk, or stand and talk. The atmosphere is unhurried and mostly serious. At the far end of the boulevard, about a mile away, and leading into the heart of the city, stand three immense, astonishingly tall buildings. The one on the left looms gray and windowless. The one on the right sparkles with a million colors, each distinct. The one in the middle, tallest and thinnest, stands spire-like as it transforms the color of the sky it reaches into: the blue is deeper, purer. Everywhere trees stretch up high and flowery. Birds flit, their plumage as diverse as the colors of a patchwork quilt, their songs more beautiful than earth's.

For basically good people Purgatory is a welcoming place that points upward to a better world, what we call Heaven. But the prize will not come cheap. There is work to be done: mental work, soul work. Purgatory is the place where we correct our flawed character, the place where good but imperfect men and women go when they die.

But what happens to selfish people who are *not* so good, people who made a habit of getting the most out of others and giving the least possible in return? Where do they go when they die? Picture a dull, decaying city in America's rust belt with its abandoned steel mills, stretches of barren fields, and run-down houses. Picture its residents—spiritually dim, morally sloppy, mentally undeveloped. They have a long way to go before they reach the heights they were created for. They are in Purgatory's basement.

Picture halls and schools where study is encouraged and where teachers tell of more beautiful regions above. Over time these spirits gradually wake up and acknowledge the evil they did on earth. Hard as it is, they repent. They learn new habits.

They learn that selfless service brings self-respect and earns them love. Maybe they begin by helping others build their spirit homes, or greet newcomers like themselves when they come over, or tend their new world's many flower gardens. There are a million ways to serve, to practice love. They'll be guided toward the work that's good for them.

I want to stress that Purgatory is not a place of punishment, but rehabilitation. Without rehabilitation we would turn away from Heaven's light, just as thugs and criminals avoid earth's churches. With it we can begin the climb toward God's luminous presence. Purgatory is a school, easy and pleasant for some, difficult and painful for others, but necessary for almost all of us.

As the great apostle James said, faith without works is dead. Purgatory is the place where our works are judged, not by a God sitting on a throne, but by ourselves. We'll be both judge and jury. There will be no escaping the truth about ourselves. We can't hide from it, as we did on earth. The process will be humbling, sometimes painful. But it will also be thrilling because it will rehabilitate us and set us free. We'll be on our way.

This brings me to Hell, a subject that has brought derision down upon us for centuries. It is a mistake to imagine it as a separate world where damned souls live for eternity in a state of perpetual regret and suffering. Better to think of it as the dungeons of Purgatory. Picture it as a casino with its endless jingling noise, its glitzy lights, its cigarette smoke, its seductive games appealing to human greed. No natural beauty, no fresh air, no sunlight, no silence, no churches or chapels, no God. Think of the kind of person who would choose to live there and call it home. That is Hell. That is the place where God is absent.

No one is forced to live there. As C.S. Lewis said, "The gates of hell are barred from the inside." Nothing would please God more than for the place to be emptied. But Hell dwellers are just as free as everyone else. God respects their freedom. He doesn't force himself on them.

Can souls in Hell leave their dungeon? That is God's will for them; after all, they are his loved creatures. But if they choose not to leave, can they work their evil on others of their own kind? Yes, and they do. They are like gangsters looking for a fight. Anger, hatred, and cruelty are their currency. They thrive on it. Can they work their evil on us? The Catholic Church says yes. That's why each diocese has an exorcist. His job is to protect innocent people from these dark spirits.

God sends no one to Hell. When Jesus warned the Pharisees that they would be going to everlasting Hell, where there would be "weeping and the gnashing of teeth," he was speaking hyperbolically, as he often did—as when telling his disciples to gouge out their eye if it leads to sin. No Christian takes this literally. To believe in a Hell where sinners are damned for eternity against their will is a hideous teaching. It turns God into a monster—what Lewis memorably called a Cosmic Sadist. It brings derision to our faith from outsiders, and rightly so. It must be discarded.

But plenty of people don't even believe in an afterlife. All around us we see atheists, many of them basically good people. Are they at a disadvantage for not believing in an afterlife where they are accountable for their deeds? I believe they are. Catholic beliefs about the afterlife are a potent motivator toward virtuous living, especially when linked to Christ's teachings about forgiveness and love of neighbor. Without this motivation, it's too easy to stare death in the face momentarily, then lapse back into one's old self unchanged. Catholics have more incentive to change for the better, even to practice heroic virtue, as their martyrs have done down through the centuries.

To put it another way, if you believe everyone suffers the same extinction at death, from Jeffrey Dahmer to Padre Pio, you lack the motivation that Catholics have when serious temptation sidles up to you. Purgatory and Hell, rightly understood, are a 300-pound lineman pushing you across the goal line. There's a lot to push against. We call it life.

Macrina, Journal: Mobile is the rainiest city in the U.S. (69 inches per year), a fact I've been oddly proud of. But it's a pussy cat compared to Mumbai (93 inches) during the monsoon. On my second trip to India I spent a lot of my time just being wet, but I did get the job done. I interviewed 29 Hindu women priests and many others whom they ministered to. But the crowds are frightening. People fall to death off Mumbai's jam-packed trains on a daily basis. India's population is almost 1.8 billion. The planet is groaning under the weight of foot traffic. Will it protest? Will it send us another plague, but this time more deadly than in 2020, just to make this over-crowded planet more bearable?

Greg: Macrina arrived in Amherst, found a backyard apartment, and settled in. Her relationship with Douglas Stillwater, the co-instructor of their Introduction to Religion course, became interesting from the start.

Macrina, Journal: Doug is Mr. Cool. He's almost 40, but sometimes he tosses off comments like a teenager.

A week ago he dismissed the idea of Original Sin and demonic possession as Christian superstitions. At the time I was afraid to speak up and let it slide. Today I spoke up. We were standing next to a bench looking out over the distant hills covered with forest, turned orange, yellow, and red in their beautiful fall foliage.

The conversation went something like this.

"So you believe we're born with Original Sin because Adam and Even ate the forbidden fruit?"

"Of course not. That story is an ancient Israelite parable. But it makes a legitimate point, like any good parable."

"And the point is that we are born corrupt?" He looked at me as if he thought I was a bit daft. And that's why I'm recording our conversation so carefully — for my own protection in this era of cancel culture.

"No," I went on. "Sin and corruption are not the same thing. As I see it, the doctrine of Original Sin is a reminder that we have free will and are therefore capable of making bad choices. It's in our original nature to sin from time to time, not be corrupt. We all need to be reminded of this. It keeps us humble. It helps us see the sin in our own conduct rather than in our neighbor's. Does that make sense, Doug?"

"Put like that, it does. I'm just relieved to know —"

"It's just that — pardon me for interrupting — I see so much delusion in progressive liberal thought, and I consider myself progressive. Most of us are so sure of our own faultlessness that we can't imagine anything wrong with the way we think but see all kinds of failings in others. I hate this. I see it everywhere. If we took Original Sin more seriously, we'd see it in ourselves. But progressives, even progressive Catholics, seldom go to church. Where are they going to hear about Original Sin?"

He looked at me with something like amusement. I could tell he was thinking of me as a specimen from a prehistoric era. I didn't dare ask him if he went to church.

Then I called him on demonic possession.

He was amazed to learn I believed in it and was intrigued to know why. "So you believe in the devil?" he began.

"No, if by *the devil* you mean an entity named Lucifer who fell from heaven and has been cursed by God to an eternal life in some cosmic ghetto, no, that's all mythology. But I do believe spiritual beings we can't see can bother or oppress us — and in rare cases possess our bodies outright. I do think Jesus knew what he was doing when he cast out demons. Today we call them earthbound spirits, and there is plenty of evidence they exist. The Catholic Church has exorcists who are overwhelmed with work these days. You don't have to look beyond the internet to see what they are up against. It can be quite scary."

He looked at me with a quizzical smile and quipped, "I'll have to be on the lookout for such bad fellows. Do they have pitchforks?" I'm sure I colored with anger. Obviously he didn't take me seriously. This man has a lot of power over me. Maybe I should be more guarded in what I say.

Greg: In one of the boxes in our parents' attic I found class notes and student evaluations from her Amherst days. Students in one of her Women in Religion classes had this to say:

"I will always see you as an inspiration. Many of your students, myself included, find you intimidating but in the best way. You are someone I aspire to be; someone who is confident, intelligent, and skilled in teaching. I thank you for being a remarkable female figure in my life."

"She's an amazing professor who pushes her students to step outside of their everyday thinking. You might feel overwhelmed looking at the syllabus but if you stay on track the class flows."

Greg: Macrina's elevation as a public intellectual began in her third year at Amherst with an article she wrote for the *Boston Globe*. Not only were there too few priests to guide the faithful, she claimed, but too many of the ones they had were morally unfit. Her solution was not better screening of candidates to the priesthood, or frequent counseling along the way, or outright termination, but the ordination of women. "Women do not do these things," she wrote, and went on to contrast the psychologies of men to women. She pointed out the obvious: that men had much higher levels of testosterone and expressed themselves more outwardly and violently, that women by contrast felt just as much outrage at injustice but suffered it better inwardly, and that men were anatomically "sprayers" — she was alluding to sexual expression—while women were "receptacles." She went on to say that young idealists often underestimated their capacity for celibacy over the course of a lifetime and that this was compounded with feelings of guilt over homosexual tendencies: "While in seminary there is no way they can anticipate the difficulty of a life of celibacy or conquering their so-called 'deviant' tendencies.... They can have no idea of the loneliness that total loss of sexual intimacy often brings with it, a loneliness made all the more painful by the heavy load of responsibility that commonly falls upon the overworked priest."

She then asked why bad priests prey on children rather than adults. "Because they are so adorable in their innocence and purity, not so much because they are defenseless." She showed a compassion for the fallen priest not often seen in the writings of outraged women—one angry mother commented she'd rather see her little boy "die" than be molested by "such scum." Macrina went on to praise the virtues of women, noting their capacity to suffer a life devoid of sex—"not because they desire it less, or suffer less the loss of it, but because the urge is less overwhelming. In a word," she continued, "women experience more pain throughout life beginning with childbirth and are better able to deal with it, especially with anti-depressants to help them cope." She cited Gandhi's claim that women were morally superior to men because they suffered more, not because God made them that way. She mentioned the menstrual cycle: "In small ways it curtails the freedom we would like to have and that men enjoy." She spoke of a woman's maternal instinct, often bred into them from childhood. She didn't fail to point out the many instances of female tyranny over children, but the tyranny almost never expressed itself sexually.

She ended the essay by citing the country's total commitment, ever since the Biden administration, to female equality "at every level and in all arenas." She cited our two most recent presidents, then added, "whether it be astronauts, CEOs of General Motors or Amazon, or referees at the Super Bowl, women have found their equal footing—except in the Catholic Church."

Commentary poured into the *Globe,* not all of it positive. It led to invitations from the editorial staff to speak out on other issues: the Church's social teachings, abortion rights, homosexuality, the timetable for a married clergy, and so forth. Boston's Archbishop Driscoll asked to meet her. Television interviews followed.

I'm getting the hang of writing this book. The words are coming easier, and I'm seeing more clearly how the events in Macrina's life should be sequenced.

Greg: The University of California Press published Macrina's book on Hindu women priests during her fourth year at Amherst. She documented the warm reception these women usually got from the people they served and the retaliation they encountered from the priests they replaced. In the last chapter, the longest of the book, she argues that women priests are needed far more urgently in the Catholic Church than in Hinduism. She calls for the Church to repeal its edict of excommunication against women priests and "open its heart to humanity's other half." The book got enthusiastic reviews from the secular press but met resistance from the Vatican—though without threats of excommunication. It earned her television and podcast interviews and an early promotion to associate professor with tenure. She quietly gave her raise, month following month, to Boston's Oxfam America. She cared very little for money, probably because Dad made so much for her.

Clifford McGrath, word of mouth: Macrina's Marine savings had multiplied almost six times. She never asked about it. She showed no interest in money, except as something to give away. She always said she had to give until it hurt. I didn't let her do this. That has led to a very substantial bequest to Spring Hill College.

Greg: In spite of her increasing fame, most of the entries in

Macrina's Journal have less to say about her many interviews, publications, and public acclamation than you might expect. Just as often she writes about the men in her life. Fellow faculty were clearly attracted to her, and she to them. She wonders if one of them might be the "right guy," perhaps right enough to lure her away from a vocation to the priesthood—she had recently been ordained by her organization as a woman priest in an Easter ceremony a few days short of her thirty-ninth birthday. She admits feeling guilty over not telling Sr. Carol about her temptations. Several times she laments, "Why shouldn't priests, male or female, be married?" and mentions Grace Onishi.

Two of her male friends will be of special interest. The first was an English professor two years her senior. In addition to literature, Arlo Tipton loved hiking, camping, and fishing. I met him on one of my trips to visit Macrina. With curly blonde locks flapping back and forth over his long, beardless, blue-eyed face like windshield wipers out of alignment, he didn't look the outdoor type. Gay and unmarried, he fit nicely into Macrina's need for an untempting male buddy. Neither met the soul-deep needs of the other: he wasn't religious, and she wasn't a male. But they gave each other precious company.

Macrina spent the last semester of her sixth year at Amherst on sabbatical finishing a third book on the worldwide travails and challenges of the Catholic Church. She had kept away from the campus as much as possible to avoid seeing students, who distracted her from her writing, but she missed them at the same time. When Arlo proposed a camping trip to the Catskills across the Hudson, she accepted without hesitation. Thus began an adventure that very few humans ever have.

Arlo grew up near New Paltz, New York, and loved its forests, lakes, and rivers. In early May he and Macrina drove east to his favorite place, a campsite along Rondout Creek, which was actually a narrow river flowing into the Hudson. She mentions flat ground under hickories, maples, and birches, "their young leaves dancing in the sunshine," as the place where they pitched their tent.

Macrina, Journal: We caught five smallmouth bass, boned them, and fried them over the fire as the night closed in. Satisfied, our conversation rambled back and forth between the woods we grew up in, as far away from each other as equatorial from polar, and shop talk. A chilly breeze came up, an owl hooted, and the river flowed soundlessly by. The fire was little more than embers.

"Look, Macrina, look at that!" Arlo said in a hoarse but urgent whisper. He pointed to the river.

I turned and saw something with a bright light shining down on the water. It moved slowly to the east toward Kingston. It didn't make a sound, not a purr, not the slightest hum. It hovered about three feet over the water as it glided by. It was certainly not floating. "Christ! What's that?"

The light reflecting off the water lit it up. It was saucer-shaped, about twenty feet in diameter, maybe four feet high. It appeared to be dark gray in color. It glided past us about thirty feet out over the water. I grabbed my phone and tried to photograph it as it receded east into the distance. I was too late to get a good picture.

What I felt would be hard to describe. I was pretty sure we had seen a UFO and vaguely remembered that Harvard had a couple of scientists who took them seriously and wrote about them. I remembered that under the Biden administration military men presented pictures of them. I had always been open to the possibility they existed but never dreamed I would see one. Thus I never quite took them seriously. But now, as we watched the craft slowly glide down the river, my entire body broke out in gooseflesh. A holy dread overtook me. I wondered if they had seen us, if we had been close to being abducted, perhaps even close to death. The craft had passed. We were safe.

There was no reason to think we had ever been otherwise. Still, I found myself shivering.

"Did we really see that?" I said.

Arlo didn't answer.

"Arlo, have you ever seen anything like that before?"

"I've heard stories since I was a boy." He spoke very slowly, in a low tone, almost a whisper. "A lot of old-timers around here say they've seen them. Back in the '80s the Valley was supposedly a UFO hotspot. New Paltz even has an annual UFO fair. I never really took it seriously. But... we'll just keep it to ourselves."

"A UFO. We really saw it."

"Yeah, we did. We just won't tell anybody. It'll be our secret. Our eternal secret."

"It was so close we could have cast for it. We could have hooked it with a fishing line!"

That broke the tension, and we both began laughing, laughing hard.

"We've seen the holy grail," he finally gasped.

"You say there have been other sightings. Somebody must have written about them. I'm going to research it when we get home."

"You're going to share our little secret?"

"Sure. A professor's word should count. Worldviews should shift. Even religions."

Maybe he didn't know what to make of that last comment. Sometimes we argued over religion. He said only, "This won't help your reputation."

I shot back, "It won't hurt it either."

In any case I feel incredibly blessed to have had this experience.

Arlo Tipton, phone conversation: When I read that Cardinal so-and-so challenged her integrity, even her sanity, I was very angry. But I didn't try to set the record straight, and I should have. Yes, what she wrote is just the way I remember it. And I remember it as if it happened yesterday.

Greg: In her next op-ed at the *Globe*—she had become a paid monthly columnist by now—she described her experience and the speculation it aroused in her. Comments came in by the hundreds, some approving, some critical. One said she had "flipped out," another that she was a conscious fraud, a third that she had fallen into heresy and should no longer speak for the Catholic Church. Others praised her for her courage, including her friend Archbishop Driscoll. This, in part, is what she wrote:

Macrina, Boston Globe archives: As a child I was fascinated by astronomy and ever since kept up with it as a rank amateur. Naturally I have been curious about all the sightings claimed by responsible witnesses. I wanted to believe they were real because that would make the universe—and God—more interesting, but I remained unconvinced. The reason was the time it would take for any craft to reach earth from so far away.

But seeing is believing. Now I know that UFOs are real, however long it takes them to reach us. That certainty gave rise to the following thoughts....

Is the Catholic Church destined to be an anachronism? Is that its very nature? Here we are in the middle of the twenty-first century, and we still excommunicate priests who are female or married as they volunteer without pay to serve the needs of a Church whose paid staff cannot come close to meeting those needs. And here we are reciting a creed formulated at a time when earth was thought to be the center of a tiny universe circled by sun, moon, and stars a stone's throw out in space. We say, "I believe in God, the Father almighty, the creator of heaven and earth, and in Jesus Christ, his only son, our Lord," when we could be saying, "I believe in God, the Father and Mother almighty, the creator of all the heavenly worlds and the universe with all its planets, and in Jesus Christ, earth's inspiration and guide," or something along that line, something that educated people really have a chance of believing. Is there some reason we should not update the creed to make it resonate with what we know? Is there some reason we are better served by affirming a worldview that scientifically literate people cannot accept?

I do not know the answer to these questions. It might well be that the creed should be understood today as a banner or pennant around which the faithful gather, not as a statement of facts to be grasped and affirmed, a statement with cognitive content. Our Church fathers, however, thought they were accurately describing God, humans, and the world as they really were. That was the whole point of the creed. So where does that leave us?

Macrina, Journal: Ezra Vilner and I had another good talk yesterday. As I've gotten to know him, all six-foot-four of his rangy body, home to such a brilliant mind, I feel myself being penetrated in the same way I felt with David so long ago. The way he looks at me when I speak, so probingly yet gently, as if he knows me more intimately than I know myself, frightens me. We had turned in our final grades the week before (he's a physicist and mathematician), and the weather was fine. We decided to go tramping, just ambling along with no destination. He had thought to carry water and a snack in a backpack, and he wore a full-brimmed hat.

As we passed through the village and then out into the countryside, he draped his arm over my shoulder but not in a way to pull me to him. It was the kind of thing you might do to to — to a buddy? Or was it something more? It made me uneasy but at the same time pleased me. We walked along the edge of a forest and praised the rural beauty of the fields with their cattle and their tractors turning over the earth, whose rich scent has always pleased me. Following no path, we walked into the woods with its maple and birch, their bright green leaves trading secrets in the breeze overhead. We traded secrets too. He told me of his people, his father a Hasidic rabbi, his younger brothers' obedient sons choosing to live in Brooklyn for the rest of their days, his sisters all married. Finally he told me about the girl his father had chosen for him and how he could not disappoint his father, as he already had in so many other ways. Yes, I was his buddy, and it hurt me to know it. I liked him. He was the kind of man I might have been happy living a long life with: gentle, thoughtful, respectful, nothing like David.

When we reached home, my heart sank. I was pretty sure that marriage and family were not in my future. I took a deep breath, picked up my Journal, and am writing these words.

Macrina, Journal: The most amazing thing has happened to me. Two weeks ago out of the blue, a wealthy lawyer from Boston called me and wanted to know if I would be willing to start a church and serve as its pastor. Good God! What!? He had been following me through my columns in the *Globe* for years, seen me speak on television, and thought I could get a following. Stewart Sheffield, that's his name, suggested taking a leave of absence from the college. "There is an old Presbyterian church downtown that's for sale or rent, and I'd rent it if you're willing. I'd match your salary at the college if the congregation didn't cover it. And I'd put ads in all the right places. I think people would pour into the church out of curiosity at first, then come back once they saw you were serious." He intended to promote it as a "true," not a "Roman" Catholic Church. "There's nothing particularly Roman about it," he said. "But we'll claim allegiance to the Pope and its present leadership. They can disown us, but we won't disown them. The liturgy will remain the same. The only difference will be that a woman is its priest and pastor. What do you say?" That's the gist of what he said.

Wow! How can I pass this up? The Vatican has already excommunicated me, so how can they harm me more? Isn't this what I trained for all those summers? It never occurred to me I might actually use the priesthood anytime soon. For me it was just a powerful symbol of protest, of possible use only in a distant future. I am thrilled at the prospect. The more I think about it, the more thrilled I get. But am I up to it? Can I really do it? Do I really want to be a full-time functioning priest?

I called Sister Carol, and she said, "Hell, yes, you do! You better!"

Stewart traveled to the college and met me in my office. He was amused at my digs. "So this humble tuck-away is where all those big ideas are hatched? I expected to see built-in mahogany bookshelves, a veritable printing press, chandeliers hanging from the ceiling. Christ, this is a cell in a monastery. Wait till you see your office at the church!"

He struck me as a down-to-earth, practical man with a good sense of humor given to exaggeration. He had made his fortune and wanted to do something meaningful with it. His wife, Shannon, is totally with him.

We had lunch at the Black Sheep Deli, then toured the Emily Dickinson Museum just down the street. He asked if I chose the deli because I was a black sheep. I confessed it hadn't occurred to me. We had a good laugh. He struck me as the kind of person who never missed a thing.

Macrina, Journal: Everything's changed. Stewart realized the Presbyterian church is too big. "You wouldn't fill more than a fourth of it. We need to start with something you can fill, then later think bigger." He came up with the most amazing deal. Apparently he knows the Archbishop and offered to buy a little church at the heart of old Boston I'd never heard of, St. Augustine's, actually a chapel. I checked it out on YouTube. Turns out it's Boston's first Catholic church, built in 1819, surrounded by a cemetery with gravestones. Stewart was worried about all that death, but I love it. Catholics welcome death, or at least should. It's like Ash Wednesday nonstop. Or like the Buddhists with the little bird on their shoulder reminding them this could be their last day. And it's beautiful inside—and small. You could shoehorn 100 people into it if you included the choir loft.

I asked if the Archbishop, who was just elevated to a cardinal, knew about our scheme. After all, he doesn't want to get himself defrocked! Stewart had a look of utter delight on his face. "I took a risk and told him about our plan," he said. "And the Archbishop showed me his poker face. It meant he didn't want to say one way or the other. I was actually surprised. I thought our scheme might fail. But I know how he admires you and that you and he have actually met."

In a word, he agreed to let Stewart have the property, chapel and cemetery, for 2.7 million dollars. My first parishioners will be 1000 souls whose bodies rest in St. Augustine's grass-covered soil—some who died when Presidents Jefferson and Adams were producing their famous correspondence. How can this be happening to a 5'6" 130-pound shrimp like me?

I've taken a one-year leave of absence, with hopes of making it permanent if all goes well.

Boston Globe archives: "Archbishop Driscoll said he had long wanted to sell St. Augustine's. The upkeep was costly, he explained, and it functioned more as a mecca for genealogists studying its tombstones than a church. When Sheffield, a Catholic, made an offer, Driscoll saw it as a way to keep the property in the family. "I knew that a few Catholics treasured the site as a kind of monument...." When asked if Macrina McGrath could be considered a legitimate part of the family since she was officially excommunicated, Driscoll replied, "In the eyes of men, perhaps no. In the eyes of God, yes." When asked if he were forced to choose between God and Pope Augustine, he didn't hesitate: "I have long believed that women should be ordained, and the Pope knew that when he made me a cardinal. I don't feel forced to choose."

Jan McGrath, email: Darling, what are you doing? You aren't a Catholic anymore. You've been excommunicated. And now you are taking over a Catholic church as its pastor? I really must say something, love you as I do.

I set up a meeting with Bishop Pooley downtown just so I could get some clarity on the issue. He is not a die-hard conservative, as you know. He admitted being sympathetic to the Womanpriest movement, even hoping that sooner or later women would be ordained. But he was shocked when he heard what you were up to. "It's dangerous enough to lead a movement that ends in excommunication; you might even admire her courage. But to act as if the goal were achieved, to accept the mantle of a pastor—no, there is an arrogance in this." That's what he said. Then he added, "I fear for her soul." Darling. I do too! You are mocking the Church's authority from the pope on down. You are harming the very Church you love so much. You are giving scandal, and atheists are rooting for you in the hope you'll tear it down. Think, Macrina, what you are doing! Don't let all this star power go to your head. Step aside, please, step aside....

New York Times archives: The Womanpriest movement has gained its poster child. Still shy of 40, with a Ph.D in theology from Georgetown, three well-regarded books, and a broad knowledge of the world's major faiths, Professor McGrath, ex-Marine, now has a church. It doesn't hurt the cause that she is as charismatic as a rock star.

St. Augustine's is a church where history was made when it opened for business in 1819 for Boston's few Catholics. It is possible that history will again be made—this time for the world's Catholic Womanpriest.

Greg: I remember the picture of Macrina delivering her

first sermon to a packed little church. It appeared in every newspaper in the land, from the *Mobile Register* to *The New York Times*. Google's headline read "Has the Day Come? Cardinal Supports Macrina as Catholic Priest." The *Daily Beast* referred to her hilariously as "Father Macrina." A cartoon showed her playing golf with the President. A reporter asked who would pay her salary, and she said, "Hopefully the congregation." A week later she had received over a million dollars in checks made out to her name. With no Dad to force her to keep the money, she gave half of it away to her favorite charities. She found a two-bedroom apartment within walking distance of the church. Since the church lacked office space, she worked out of her apartment.

Boston Globe Archives: Rev. Macrina McGrath, Womanpriest, delivered her first sermon to an audience of Catholics and non-Catholics packed into storied St. Augustine's Chapel. "We are not a breakaway denomination," she sang out. "We are Catholics, united to its visible head, the Pope. We will send him the annual collection known as Peter's Pence."

She wanted to dispel the impression that she was leading a revolution. "Some people enjoy protest marches. They are excited by the prospect of overthrowing what is old to make room for the new. That is not my way. That is not the goal of us Womanpriests. Our goal is to pastor a Catholic congregation in the same way that men have been doing for centuries. Do not think of us as feminists. Think of us as priests."

She went on to say that future sermons would not beat the drum for female equality. "The fact that I am your priest will be drum enough," she said. "The Vatican will notice without my telling them to look. We'll win them over not by opposing them, but by serving the Church in love, the same Church they serve. In the end they will see the suffering that their anathemas have brought us and be embarrassed into good behavior. They will marvel that it took them so long to come around."

She promised to speak in parables and stories when she preached. She gave a short history of the Womanpriest movement. "All of us, nearly 480 spread out over the world, are empowered to consecrate the Eucharist and say Mass," she concluded.

"I'm a lukewarm Episcopalian," said Ellen Schreiber after the service, "but I'll be attending this church for a while. She's young and vital, and I want to do everything I can to support her."

An elderly man, unnamed, wasn't so sure. "She'd make a terrific pastor, but I can't get around the fact that she's been excommunicated. I don't stand with the Church in its treatment of women. But they make the rules."

Eight-year-old Pamela Dietze found it ridiculous that women shouldn't be priests. "She'd make a great pope. And she's pretty. Why can't women be popes?"

"Why indeed?" said her mother, Patty Dietze, with an approving smile as she stroked her child's silky brown hair.

Macrina, Journal: On September 3, 2059, I preached my first sermon at St. Augustine's. It was packed, and it went well. At least well enough without air-conditioning. My heart leaped for a moment when I saw Ezra standing at the back. Why was he there? Everybody wanted to talk to me after the Mass, especially reporters. By the time I got free he was gone. I've been texting him all afternoon, but he isn't answering.

Macrina, Journal: Walking alone through the neighborhood with my sun glasses and my drooping sun hat—my disguise— on a bright sunny but brisk autumn day, I discovered a woman's mosque, a humble, rather dreary looking place, and introduced myself to the imam. The recent bombing in Rochester left the nation's Muslims on edge. I wanted to do everything possible to assure her I didn't hold anyone responsible except that one fanatic. She had never heard of me and didn't seem surprised when I told her I was a Catholic priest. Her parents are Egyptian, so she is Sunni. Her name is Jamila Mansour. She appreciated what I said and invited me to a Friday service, where she would preach the sermon, or *khutbah*.

I took her up on it. She spoke in English except when she quoted from the Quran or the hadith, when she spoke in Arabic. Her topic was God's will and human accountability. Everything that happens is God's will, she said. That included the bombing in Rochester. But at the same time we are free and therefore liable to punishment for our crimes. She explained that God did not force the bomber's hand and that the bomber was therefore guilty of the crime of murder. God willed those twenty victims to die for reasons known only to him, but the bomber did not know it was God's will. He therefore had no excuse. The Quran forbids murder, and the bomber knew it.

I don't think this works. For the Christian, much of what happens on earth is decidedly not God's will. God has given us free will and wants us to use it responsibly and lovingly. When we don't, we violate God's will. God never forces us. It's a simple, straightforward concept.

Jamila surprised me by asking me to deliver a *khutbah* on any Friday I was free. I was shocked. I'd never heard of an outsider being invited to preach to Muslims. It's always we Christians who invited dialogue. Things must be changing fast. I'll have to return the favor.

Greg: I was fascinated when I read this in the Journal. It's long been known she preached in a mosque—she confirmed it many years ago. But she never made a big deal about it or told anyone what she said. Was there a record of it some place? She often wrote out her sermons word for word. I went back to that old thumb drive and searched for a long time to see if I could find it. And there it was. It's an extended parable, a story, like so many of her other sermons. It's so unusual that I thought I would share it uncut. Nowhere in her Journal does she describe its impact on the audience. One can only imagine.

Clearly, she had the Rochester massacre in mind when she chose her subject. But she placed the action in the world beyond death, what she calls the astral world, at a time when ISIS was at its height some 45 years ago. I think she did this because placing it in the present, in Rochester, would have been too jarring for her audience. Even as it was, her message might have been risky.

Macrina, old thumb drive: "Kasim was a Sunni Iraqi boy from Fallujah who left home to join the Caliphate when he was seventeen and volunteered as a suicide bomber. He died in Qamishli." That was all the earthly records said and all anyone could remember of him. But records in the world beyond death revealed more. Kasim's older brother had been killed by an American bomb, and this event was crucial in Kasim's formation. He ran away from home to join Islamic State and was never heard from again. The boy's grandfather was close to his grandson on Earth and died a few months after him.

A wise old spirit named Nahid was a counselor who lived in Paradise and agreed to meet Kasim in Astral Fallujah. Earth's Fallujah had been destroyed in the war, but Astral Fallujah, a neighborhood of Paradise, was a glorified version of what the city on earth had been at its height. Hovering overhead, Nahid saw in every direction palm trees waving in the warm breeze. Minarets and onion-shaped domes reached up into the vivid blue sky. Flower gardens grew between paved streets and pleasant homes, and streams of water wound between the buildings. Many homes had tiny ponds next to their gardens. Water gushed from fountains at street corners. Beyond the city's boundaries golden desert sands arranged in shapely dunes stretched out in all directions.

But Kasim had not seen any of this. He lived in an internment camp in the uppermost regions of Fallujah's Shadowlands. He lived with other bombers in a dormitory and was under guard. One of the guards led Nahid into the boy's room.

Nahid bowed to Kasim and introduced himself as "an outside counselor chosen by Islam's elder imams." He told the boy he wanted to help.

Kasim, thin-faced with a dark, close-cropped beard, looked sulkily down into his lap.

"Kasim, you have my word that all you tell me will be kept in confidence. My impression is that what happens here, if all goes well, will be a great help to you and your friends, and possibly to others in your predicament all over the Arab world. You and I are an experiment. Bear in mind that your body is astral and cannot be harmed. Physical torture is out of the question. Death is impossible. You have already died. Would you like to tell me how you died at the tender age of seventeen?"

Kasim looked up at Nahid and said, "You know how I died."

"Tell me in detail."

Kasim looked at Nahid as if surprised by his pleasant, encouraging voice. He studied the counselor for a few seconds, then looked back down into his lap without speaking.

Nahid waited immovably.

Finally Kasim looked up at Nahid and began. "They taught me how to drive a truck and told me I would go to Paradise if I died fighting the infidels. They loaded the truck with explosives and told me to drive it to Qamishli and blow up the Kurdish headquarters. This was in Syria, near Turkey. That's what I did, and I killed many people. I was proud of what I did. When I came here, I said, 'Where are my virgins? Where are my virgins?' I didn't understand why they weren't there to greet me. 'Where is Muhammad?' I asked. 'I want to see Muhammad.' But they wouldn't take me to see him. Finally I asked to see Allah, and they laughed. I asked to see Allah because I knew he would understand. But they wouldn't take me to see him. Instead they questioned me. They wanted to see how much I hated the infidels. I didn't understand. It seemed like they wanted me to say I didn't hate them at all. I was confused. It was crazy. It was like I was being tested. And I was failing the test. They finally brought me to this place."

"How have they treated you?"

"This isn't Paradise."

"No. But do they treat you bad?"

"I can't say that. But they tell me I made a mistake. That it was wrong to blow myself up and all the others. They say they made the same mistake."

"Do you believe it was a mistake?"

"I don't trust them. I see them as cowards. If they're right, my whole life was a mistake. The same for all my friends. It means my teachers back on Earth were wrong. It means hating the infidel was wrong. How can that be wrong? If you don't hate, how can you die? It takes courage to die. How can you be a hero for Allah if you don't hate?"

"Who are the infidels?"

"The infidels? The Kurds. The Yazidis. The Americans. The Shia. Especially the Shia. And many others."

"That's a lot of people to hate."

"It's our duty to hate them because Allah hates them."

"Kasim, have you ever hated your teachers back on Earth who taught you to hate and to kill? They lied to you about going to Paradise and finding all those virgins, right?"

He paused. "I don't know. Maybe I was intercepted on the way. I'm not sure."

"Intercepted? Does the Quran mention the possibility of a shaheed, a martyr being intercepted?"

Kasim squirmed, turned his head this way and that, then burst out, "'Remember, there are only two camps: Dar al-Islam, the House of Islam, and Dar al-Harb, the House of War, the House of Heresy, and it's up to you, each of you, to restore the House of Islam. If you do not fight to restore it, you will inherit hell!' Every day we recited this text. And we lived and died by it. How can it be wrong?"

Kasim's sudden eloquence startled Nahid. Hatred had found a sacred home in the heart of this boy. Nahid was beginning to understand why he was asked to counsel Kasim. He and Kasim would have been mortal enemies back on earth. He had as much to learn from this encounter as Kasim.

He remembered the boy's grandfather and asked, "I believe you loved your grandfather, am I right?"

"Yes, very much. And he loved me. I used to hang on his neck and kiss his cheeks when I was a little boy."

"He recently died. Did you know that?"

"No! Where is he? Can I see him?"

"He's out of reach for the moment. But I'm sure he wants you to leave this place. And I know he wanted you to have grandchildren of your own to hang on your neck and kiss your cheeks. This is my question: Do you really think Allah asked you to kill yourself?"

"Of course. That's what makes martyrdom so great. You have to give up so much."

"We'll meet again soon, Kasim. But meanwhile I want you to think about this question. And I want you to listen to your teachers over here with a more open mind. You have proof that your teachers back on Earth misled you. Are your teachers here misleading you? What proof do you have of that? Finally, I want you to prepare to meet your grandfather. He's waiting for you. But he can't come here. You must go to where he is. And there is one thing more." Nahid paused and leveled his most loving glance at the boy.

"What?" the boy finally stammered.

"I am an infidel, a Shia."

"Oh." Kasim shook his head, blinked his eyes until they fluttered, and said, "That's okay, I guess."

Nahid came close to the boy, gently placed his hands on either side of his head, and kissed him on the forehead.

Macrina, Journal: It's become clear that my little boutique church is simply too small, and there is no parking. I've begun to do my own searching—found a nice-size Catholic church for sale in Northampton. And I could buy it with my savings (if I can get past Dad). I hate to ask for more help from Stewart. How will he feel about my leaving Boston? Will he be able to sell St. Augustine's?

I'm going to drive over to see the church tomorrow. There must be something wrong with it. It must have rats.

Greg: It didn't have rats, but it did come with a condition. Paul Colby, the Bishop of Springfield, wasn't willing to sell to just anyone. Nothing that happened in the church or on the grounds of the church could be "inconsistent with the teachings of the Catholic Church." The Bishop considered her priesthood inconsistent with those teachings and rejected her request. Never a quitter, she asked Archbishop Driscoll for help. Being a cardinal, he used his influence to bring the bishop around, and Macrina bought her church for a cool $950,000. She described it as a "fire sale" in a community more noted for its higher population of gays and lesbians than Catholics. The church, unused for years, was in fair condition, and Macrina was ecstatic. It even had a parking lot lined for fifty cars. A bonus was its closeness to Amherst, just seven miles away on the other side of the Connecticut River. She could resume teaching if she wanted to.

Macrina, Journal: Mom, Dad, and Greg called me on my birthday, my fortieth, Greg said he and Sophie would come up and help me move into the church and set up the rectory, which will serve as my apartment. They wore ridiculous hats and sang Happy Birthday. It warmed my heart.

The call was expected, but another one wasn't. I hadn't heard a word from Ezra for almost a year and thought I'd never see him again. I was shocked when I heard his voice on the phone— he didn't risk a video call. My reaction was guarded, and he was obviously nervous and embarrassed. He began by apologizing for his disappearance from the church without a word. I told him I was sorry I hadn't been able to catch up to him after the service. I asked him if he had gotten tenure and married his Jewish bride.

"That's what I'm calling about. I thought that out of friendship I ought to show up for your big day in Boston." He said it occurred to him he might not see me again if I didn't come back to the college. He said he hadn't planned on the impact I had on him. He said he had never seen me "in action" and that he was "deeply moved." He told me how he met his bride-to-be, all 23 years of her, and how impossible it was that he could marry her. "What made me come to that conclusion," he said, "was thinking of you, thinking of you over and over, never able to put you out of my mind." He said he would prefer "a lifetime of friendship with me over marriage to her." He told his father he couldn't possibly marry the girl and set off an explosion in the home.

"You're what?" he said when I told him where I was. "You're in Northampton?"

I told him how delighted I'd be to see him. I suggested biking along one of the rail trails that wound through the Valley.

Macrina, Journal: Blessed Sacrament Church, built in 1899, sits on an attractive piece of property surrounded by handsome two-story homes with large trees and a high school off to one side. To everyone's astonishment, I paid for it in cash, which I owe entirely to Dad.

It seats around 400, not too large, not too small. A spacious office behind the sanctuary and next to the sacristy has built-in bookcases ready to hold overflow books from my school office. The Catholic population in Northampton is shrinking as older people die and the young go elsewhere Sunday mornings. They prefer meeting their friends over cups of espresso and café latte at Starbucks over the Eucharist at Blessed Sacrament. Who can blame them? I've got my work cut out.

Greg: Smith College is within walking distance of the church, and Macrina put out feelers to its students. In her Journal she writes that the school's Catholics were far outnumbered by its "nones." A few students who took her the previous year at Amherst and were aware of her growing reputation—Smithies could take courses outside Smith—asked her to guest-lecture on any topic she chose. They evidently did a good job promoting the talk, for she mentions the event was well attended—"unlike at the church so far," she adds rather dolefully. She chose as her topic, "Catholic Womanpriest: progressive or regressive?"

The talk and Q&A session was recorded, and Macrina saved it to her OneDrive account. One of the students asked her, off-topic, about the Church's position on homosexuality and whether she shared it. Her answer would be nuanced as she aged and matured further, but here it is, with minor editing:

Macrina and Smith students, One Drive account:

Student: I'm a lesbian. I know that the Catholic Church considers people like me abnormal, you might even say disordered. Where do *you* stand on this?

Macrina: I thought we were talking about the Womanpriest movement. Can you make clearer the connection?

Student: Well, aren't some of the womanpriests lesbian? If so, how could they fit in? The Episcopal and Methodist churches have had problems enough with this. And they're much more liberal than Catholics. So I'm wondering—

Macrina: I follow you now. You're wondering how a Womanpriest, and I'm assuming you consider us progressive, can fit into a regressive organization like the Catholic Church. Am I—

Student: I would add the word *repressive*.

Macrina: Okay. Repressive. (Pause.) First, can we agree that the primary reason for the sex drive is to propagate the race, to bring our species into the world?

Student: Sex is about much more than that.

Macrina: Of course it is. But the primary, the biological reason for it is having kids, right?

Student: Not anymore. The world is overpopulated anyway. There are already too many kids, wouldn't you agree?

Macrina: I do. The point, though, is that there wouldn't be any of us at all, or very few of us, if homosexuality replaced heterosexuality as the norm.

Student: So you are saying we are abnormal.

Macrina: You are moving too fast. Can you agree that a world without heterosexuals would lead to human extinction just as surely as a collision with a massive asteroid or nuclear winter?

Student: I don't think that's the point.

Macrina: I think it is. And in saying so, I represent the Catholic position. I'm emphasizing this because I would like all of you to grant the basic sanity of the Church's position. What I say next is open for debate. But this isn't. So let us give old Mother Church her due. Now — I'm sorry, what is your name? —

Student: Savannah.

Macrina: Savannah, I take it you don't like the word *abnormal*. If homosexuals aren't abnormal, then what are they?

Savannah: Normal. As normal as heteros. Normal in every sense.

Macrina: But the great majority of humans in the world have always been hetero, and that's true today as well. I don't like *abnormal* either. But I don't like *normal* any better. It masks a very real difference. Let's don't be shy or politically correct. Let's come up with a better word. I want you all to help me. Let me see hands. If lesbians are neither abnormal nor normal, what are they?

Student: Unconventional.

Student: Divergent?

Student: Exceptional!

Macrina: Good. Keep them coming.

Student: Atypical.

Student: Queer.

Macrina: Okay. Now come up with some words you might have heard but consider offensive.

Student: Deviant.

Student: Unnatural.

Student: Aberrant.

Student: Flawed.

Student: Freakish.

Macrina: Freakish? Seriously?

Student: Dyke.

Student: Bulldyke. (Laughter.)

Macrina: Wow, you Smithees are quick on your feet. Let's see now. Yes, let's try this. Do any of you know how Hindus account for homosexuality? (Pause.) They say it comes from a sex change between lives. Lesbians were males in their last life and had the usual habits of a male: they found women sexually attractive. Now that they're female, they still find women sexually attractive. The old habit has not been shed. Now let's return to that old word *abnormal.* If the Hindus are right, would you be willing to say that lesbianism is abnormal, or exceptional, or queer? Think a minute.

Student: I'm a Hindu.

Macrina: Really? What do you say?

Hindu Student: I don't have a problem with the word *abnormal,* because that's what it is. *Abnormal* doesn't mean inferior. It just means different from the majority, at least to me. But in another sense it's not abnormal at all. It's completely normal that such a girl would reincarnate with lesbian tendencies. It's normal in the sense that it's predictable, psychologically predictable.

Macrina: What is your name?

Hindu Student: Renu.

Macrina: Renu, what you are saying, and saying with

such great clarity, is that lesbianism is socially abnormal, but psychologically normal. I agree with you but still don't like the word *abnormal*. How about "socially exceptional but psychologically unexceptional"?

Renu: It's not as clear, but it would be more politically correct, I guess.

Macrina: Ouch! Well, maybe it's time to give political correctness its due. Can we all give Renu a hand? You were brilliant. (Applause.) Back to Catholicism — in case we almost forgot. (Pause.) The Church, of course, discourages belief in reincarnation, so there is no way it can call homosexuality normal in a psychological sense. Its official position is that gay tendencies are disordered and must be resisted. The tendency itself is not a sin, but acting on it is. The Church rejects same-sex marriages. Gays and lesbians are called to a lifetime of celibacy. (Booing is heard in the background.)

Student: But where do *you* stand?

Macrina: I think the Church should show LGBTQ folk the same respect it shows straights. It's not easy being queer in a society like ours, and we should extend to them our compassion, not make things worse by excluding them from our churches. We should include them in everything we do, even accept them in our seminaries. They are no less children of God than the rest of us. He made them gay and lesbian, bi and transgender. Many straights feel uneasy around them when they cuddle, or when movies show them making love, but that's no excuse for discrimination. Who knows? Maybe one day we'll have a gay pope. We've had a gay president, so why not a gay pope?

Student: Would you object to a *woman* pope?

Macrina: Not in the least. That would be a great day for the Church. But it won't happen in my lifetime.

Greg: Attendance at Holy Family was worrisomely small in the first weeks. She writes in the Journal how she had to almost beg for coverage in the local newspaper. The editor was a Catholic and seemed reluctant to promote a "lady pastor," as he called her. She got permission to write the article herself in a question-and-answer format—she both asked and answered the questions, which was to her liking. The article, placed on the back page, did help. She tells how it brought a few mothers with children to view the "experiment." One in particular, Page Preston, with her only son off to college, was looking for something to do with her free time and took over secretarial chores and even the gardening and some of the cleaning. She became a great support and friend to Macrina. Macrina also lobbied the Catholic organizations at all the colleges in the area, and this too helped attendance. She used social media: LinkedIn, Facebook, and especially Reddit, where she ran a subreddit group named Womanpriest. She posted a YouTube video of herself standing at the front door of the church describing the Womanpriest movement and inviting all to come and "make history." The congregation grew.

So did the work. The Journal takes on a completely new tone by late summer of 2060. It becomes an extended prayer in which she beseeches God, whom she usually refers to as Mother, or Divine Mother, or Heavenly Mother, or Blessed Mother, to come to her aid—as in, "I beseech you, Mother, to guide me in the choice of my assistant." This very issue led to her first of several clashes with the Womanpriest organization. Sister Carol had retired, and the new head assumed Macrina would choose one of their own. Macrina preferred a male. She wanted to show that men and women could work together running a parish, as Episcopalians had been doing for almost a hundred years. She was aware that a great pool of talented laicized Catholic priests who had married might be available and advertised the position. After much interviewing, she chose an ex-Jesuit named Bret Lambert. Macrina's new bishop was outraged at her "treasonous decision," but Macrina held firm. Fr. Lambert, a retired land surveyor, was thrilled to take up his duties and began at once to say the 7:30 daily Mass, relieving Macrina of a duty she had too little time for. Page and Bret were working for a pittance, virtually volunteering their time.

Those first months were not easy. She had to hire a lawyer in a fight for tax-exempt status for her "illegitimate church." The church's old LED screen malfunctioned and needed to be replaced at considerable expense. The high school marching band practiced in the field adjacent to the church when Bret was trying to say Mass. A rift over music developed between some of the older members of the parish and the college kids who came to church because "they loved me more than God," as Macrina wrote. In the Sacrament of Reconciliation parishioners sometimes described personal dilemmas beyond her ability to solve. One of them heard voices demanding that he kill himself, leaving Macrina feeling hopeless about what to do after the man refused to see a psychiatrist and Bishop Colby refused to lend her his licensed exorcist. These and other problems surfaced in the Journal.

She admits missing the orderliness and intellectual stimulation of life in the classroom. Amherst gave her a wonderful career, but Macrina by nature was a healer, and the Church, not the college, needed healing. She complained of exhaustion, and her entries became less frequent. But she never questioned her priorities, and her love of the Church, that imperfect vessel, carried her forward.

She managed to teach her Hinduism class in the fall semester but begged out of Buddhism the following spring. The college informed her that she would have to choose.

There were good times too, wonderful times.

Macrina, Journal: I visited Melanie Sampson in her home to give her the last rites—I'll never forget it. My oldest parishioner, absolutely fearless as her life ebbs away. Though 94 and Catholic all her life, she was thrilled from the start at her priest being a woman.... Bright in old age, facial skin almost transparent. Head slightly raised on her pillow. Eyes that look out as if half in this world, half in the next. Hospice nurse in next room, we're alone....

I bless the oil and ask if she wants to confess. Yes. In a faint voice she digs way back into her life, flushing it all out. I hold her hand and sing the beautiful hymn I learned so many years ago at Georgetown—"Be still, my soul! The hour is hastening when we shall be forever in God's peace." Eyes half closed, she is fading fast. I place my hand on her forehead and whisper her name. No response. Reading the prayer from my booklet, I consecrate the oil and bend over to apply it. Have I lost her? I apply it. She opens her eyes and, with mouth open, looks out at a corner of the room. Now she is strangely alert and whispers in a voice filled with awe, "Lovely brightness, wonderful beings." Then she says, "Oh, it's Father." I see nothing, but she does. Her attention is riveted. "He is so near. He looks so lonely. He wants me to come." She hesitates, as if uncertain what to say next. "Oh, there's Mother," and her face takes on the most incredible smile. She reaches out with her emaciated arms as if to embrace the figures that I cannot see. Then the arms drop, the face with its astonishing smile becomes motionless, as if in plaster. In that state she leaves the world. There is not the slightest struggle, no gasping for breath, no suffering, no fear, just a gentle liftoff of spirit from body. I feel for the pulse and close the eyes. I collapse on a chair and weep for joy. The gooseflesh covering my body subsides.

Greg: For all that's been written about Macrina, I've never read anything about her sense of humor. Dad is a bit of a jokester and especially enjoys a clever limerick, especially if it's a bit off-color. It's always amused me to see Mom, who disapproved of vulgarity of any kind, shake her head while Macrina and I chuckled indulgently after Dad hauled out his latest at the dinner table. "Oh, Clifford," she would say meekly with a slight titter. I think she secretly rather enjoyed it.

When we got older Dad started emailing us his latest limerick as a funny birthday present. Macrina grew to enjoy the special flavor of a good limerick and began composing them herself, though hers were never risqué. In fact they were usually quite Catholic. The case of the dueling limericks! — one off-color, the other sprinkled with holy water.

Macrina, Journal: Dad's naughty birthday limerick arrived today right on time, and I sat down to compose one for him myself. I actually composed two, one of them honoring my favorite Jesuit, the other my favorite apostle.

> When inspired, the saintly Ignatius
> Was very theologically loquacious.
> But when it came to vulgarity,
> He practiced austerity,
> And the worst he could say was, "My gracious!"

> My favorite apostle is Thomas,
> So famous for his doubting dramas.
> But did you know in the gloom
> Of that dark upper room
> He greeted the Lord in pajamas?

By the time I'm 90 I will have worked through a lot of saints.

Macrina, Journal: Ezra and I had a wonderful time hiking on a warm day in May through wildflowers on the Harkness Brook Loop. He knew how to distinguish periwinkle from lilac, nightshade from morning glory. Could heaven be more beautiful? We found a spot next to the brook away from other hikers. Sitting on a sheet under great trees two or three times our age, he told me about the Jewish blessings, six all together. After blessing the food we settled down to eat. For him latkes and kugel, for me an egg salad sandwich. We finished off a bottle of wine that he brought and lay back in a slight buzz. All things became merry, and we laughed and laughed.

We dozed off, then woke to a cool breeze. I told him about Shirley, my Jewish friend from Boston. She died suddenly of an aneurysm, and I paid my respects at a brief burial ceremony in a nearby cemetery. It was there that an old friend of hers told me she had no faith in a future life. He confirmed what I already knew: that not many Reform Jews give it much of a thought.

"I bet her rabbi didn't either," Ezra said.

I told him the rabbi, a woman in her fifties, referred to death as "our destination" and called it "our friend" because it forces us to enjoy life more fully and intensely due to its shortness.

I asked Ezra what he felt about that, and he threw the question back at me. "What do you tell the grieving family and friends at a funeral?"

I told him Catholics regard death as an enemy to be overcome and that heaven, not death, is our destination.

I asked him how so many Jews not only deny an afterlife but are indifferent to it. How could they see it as their friend? They are the wealthiest, most prosperous, best educated Americans alive today. Can they really be indifferent about giving the good life up and becoming nothing? Why doesn't the thought of losing it all haunt the Jewish soul more than any other?

Ezra had a lot to say in answer, more than I expected from a mathematician. I'll try to organize what he said.

First, the world to come is a relatively late Jewish belief, and that most Jewish scholars agree that the Torah makes no clear reference to an afterlife.

Second, from the Torah down through the Talmud down to the present day, Jews have been a people committed to the betterment of this world, and there is enough to be done in it to leave no time for consideration of the next.

Third, an underlying antipathy to Christianity leads many Jews to want to separate their religious beliefs from the dominant ideology, which decisively affirms an afterlife.

Fourth, the Holocaust has left many Jews asking how God could exist and let such a thing happen. He mentioned Elie Wiesel, a Holocaust survivor. Wiesel cried out in anguish that the Holocaust had murdered God and turned his dreams to dust. A heavenly afterlife was one of those dreams.

Fifth, Jews identify themselves with what they regard as an enlightened worldview, which includes the discoveries of neuroscience. They believe that the activity of the brain produces consciousness and that when the brain dies, they do too. End of story.

So they try not to think much about what death means—their own death, their children's death—and enjoy the present and only world as much as they can.

I was itching to know what Ezra himself thought about the question and feared what he would say. I very much wanted him to share my optimism—I thought it would bring us closer together. I finally asked him.

He said he was raised with a strong belief in the "olam ha-ba," or world to come, but lost his faith in it when he ceased being a religious Jew. "That was the greatest loss of all," he said. "I went from feeling like an eternal soul in a divine drama to a purposeless fungus destined to grow cold in the soil of the earth's crust." He put it something like that, but better. The point was that he suffered greatly from his loss of faith.

But a few years ago he happened upon a book written by a Chasidic Jew who collected stories of people claiming they remembered their previous life as a Holocaust victim, and it convinced him that life went on. "It was a huge awakening," he said. "It felt good to be alive again." He went on to say he thought Shirley "was eating leviathan and drinking wine from the time of creation," as the Yiddish folksong put it. "Where she is, there is no skull grinning in."

I was greatly pleased and a little surprised. What a precious friend he is.

Greg: It was as if a noose were tightening around her neck, she complains in the Journal. She had been getting more and more attention from the press. Interviews had become common, and Mount Holyoke College, followed by Barnard and Scripps, had invited her to give their commencement speeches, with nice honoraria thrown in. Many conservative Catholics bristled at the attention she attracted.

In her third year at Holy Family she gave a weekend retreat, advertised it broadly, and asked for a sizable donation. Unknown to her, one of the 50 retreatants was a mole—a frequent contributor, she found out later, to the prestigious, mostly Catholic, mostly conservative magazine *First Truths*. Macrina sometimes cut out articles and placed them inside her Journal. In this instance she included both the article and her reply, also printed in the magazine.

Tyler Kardaver, a professor of theology at the new University of Fort Worth, noted for its conservative Catholic faculty, skillfully summarized the multi-pronged argument against women priests in the Catholic Church. He claimed that all of Jesus' apostles were male, that among the countless female Catholic saints none had ever sought the priesthood and were "glorified by their modesty," that women by virtue of their capacity to bear and raise children were called to vocations different from men's, that women see things from more angles and find it harder to confidently come to a decision than men, that the motherly heart of a woman is "wounded" and "brutalized" by the tough decision-making a priest sometimes faces, that according to polls even women prefer a male to a female boss, and that God himself, the master of the universe, is a father and not a mother. These and other arguments of a more practical nature led him to conclude that women are called to a different but equally important and essential way of being in the world.

He then launched an attack against Macrina, "the leader of this unnatural assault on God's plan of salvation."

Tyler Kardaver, Professor of Theology, paper copy of article in *First Truths*: While attending a retreat Ms. McGrath was giving to a supposedly Catholic audience, I was exposed to positions that are not part of the Catholic tradition. One of the retreatants asked if it were equally true that God is our Mother, and McGrath said, "It is not required that you take God's Fatherhood as more true than her Motherhood. Whatever speaks to your sense of awe, beauty and wonder is a metaphor you should feel comfortable using, for in reality we know very little about God's ultimate nature." A little later she asked us to consider whether Jesus, if he were living today, would have described God as our Father instead of Mother. "Bear in mind," she declared, "that he lived at a time when women had little worth, and it wouldn't have made sense to his followers that God was Mother. Had he lived in our day, he would have referred to God as Father on some occasions and Mother on others." Somewhat later another woman asked if she could recite the Hail Mary substituting "Mother of Jesus" for "Mother of God" — as in "Holy Mary, mother of Jesus, pray for us sinners now and at the hour of our death. Amen." Without hesitation she gave it her blessing, adding that "mother of Jesus" has the advantage of history on its side, while saying nothing about the advantage Catholic tradition gives the original and truer formulation.

Greg: The professor cited "other miscues," but these were the main ones.

He ended by mentioning the cost of the retreat: $400 for two days of "highly unconventional teaching from a so-called priest excommunicated from the Church she claims to belong to."

Macrina counterattacked the professor by asking him to consider whether in his view God's nature was more consistent with fatherly or motherly qualities:

Macrina, paper copy of response in *Frist Truths*: Is God more a provider or a nurturer? A Father who governs the universe with his infinitely wise mind, or a Mother who responds to our prayers with her infinitely compassionate heart? To me God is both Father and Mother, not one or the other.... Words are feeble conveyors of truth about God. The great doctor of the Church himself, Thomas Aquinas, said that all language about God was to be understood as analogical, not univocal or literal. In other words, the best we can say is that some of God's attributes remind us of what fathers might be more likely to do, and others what mothers might. When the Church has forgotten this in the past, it has burned innocent Christian men and women at the stake.... About the Hail Mary, I am well aware that most Catholics, especially in the Global South, say the prayer in the old way, the way that tradition has passed down to us. But other Catholics prefer the more modest version—the one that Mary herself might have felt more comfortable with.... Unlike many Protestants, Catholics are not in the habit of tithing. My congregation does not meet the expenses needed to run the church, and the bishop and the Vatican are of course no help. The money I make from my addresses and retreats pay my staff, all of whom are underpaid by prevailing standards. We don't complain, but we certainly don't deserve a scolding. We live simply.

Greg: Macrina's old friend, sponsor, and cheerleader from her Boston days, Stewart Sheffield, kept in contact with her. He never stopped pushing her to think big. "Keep your sights on New York City, that's where you'll make the biggest splash." He even predicted that someday she'd be the dean of St. Patrick's Cathedral. Was he serious? As it turned out...

Stewart was on the lookout for a church in Manhattan that was for sale at a reasonable price. Over the previous twenty years, over ten churches had been put on the block; just as in Springfield, there were too few Catholics to use them. One of these was the Church of Our Lady of Sorrows, a 200-year-old building constructed by German Capuchins on the Lower East Side. A sculpture of Mary holding the dead Jesus in her lap surrounded by winged angels was mounted in a lunette over the entrance, and again over the central altar inside the church. Nevertheless, as churches go in New York, it was a less than splendid specimen sandwiched between apartment buildings occupied almost entirely by Hispanics, but it was twice the size of Holy Family. When Our Lady of Sorrows closed, Spanish was the dominant language. Masses in English were the exception. Many years ago it had renamed itself Nuestra Señora de los Dolores.

The Archbishop was happy to unload the building for $4.9 million, whether to a Baptist or a Muslim or even a renegade Catholic. Stewart came up with the money. He didn't tell Macrina where it came from, but she was sure that if it came from him, he would never feel it and would probably figure out a way to write it off on his income tax. Whatever the case, she wrote and called him her "guardian angel in residence." He had succeeded in placing the nation's poster child, now elevated to "poster girl," as her enemies dubbed her, to within two miles of St. Patrick's. In old age he had adopted her as his life's mission. St. Augustine's had been only the start.

It struck me as noteworthy that New York's Archbishop didn't protest Macrina's presence in his diocese. Did he secretly support her cause? I couldn't determine it one way or the other. Anyhow, she had no difficulty attracting a following once she arrived. This city of liberal and feminist causes received her with open arms. That she was a woman saying Mass in a historic church under the Archbishop's nose was enough for them, Catholic or otherwise. But for Macrina herself, Christ's message of love and forgiveness mattered more. That was the message she preached, with only occasional references to the Womanpriest movement. By now she was confident that if she lived long enough, she would see women say Mass with the pope's blessing regardless of any impact she might have.

Macrina, like perhaps most of us, led a life full of surprises, some good, some bad, many occurring at the same time.

Anna Onishi Cowan, email: Dear Macrina, I am your biological daughter, 23 years of age. For two years I have known that I was adopted. It was quite a shock, and I didn't want anything to do with you, not at first, no matter how much Mom urged me to contact you. Part of the reason was that I wasn't sure you would show any interest, and that would have been devastating. I have decided to take the risk.

I never guessed it. I knew Mom had a mysterious friend back in the States that she corresponded with because I once read one of her letters to you on her computer. I wondered why she went into such detail about me and why you would be interested. I guess it never occurs to a kid that they've been adopted.

Well, here I am, and I would like to hear from you. Mom tells me you are a nationally prominent figure but won't tell me more. She wants me to find out directly from you. I don't even know your last name for sure or exactly where you live. You are just Macrina to me. "Macrina, my biological mother." I would especially like to know why you gave me up. Was it a difficult decision? And where is my biological father?

I would be happy to hear from you.

Anna Onishi Cowan

Macrina, email video recording: Dear Anna, I was thrilled beyond telling when I read your letter. I dropped everything. First, here I am sitting at my desk after a rush to the bathroom to make myself look presentable. I wonder if you see a likeness;

I do. I'm 45 years old and have just moved into my new church in New York City. That's right, I'm a pastor just like your true mother, Grace. But I'm a Catholic, and as you probably know, women can't be legitimate priests according to the Vatican. I'm leading the fight against this discrimination in the U.S., and that's what your mother was referring to.

But enough of me. First let me say that your mom has sent me quite a collection of digital photos of you as you've matured over the years. You couldn't keep up with me, as your mother and I agreed, but I have certainly kept up with you, and I have hoped and prayed for this day. I can hardly believe it's come.

I am extremely curious to know all about you. I know you are completely bilingual and worked as a translator following graduation while you deliberated over what to do with your life. I was delighted to hear you chose medical school and that you thought you might go into ophthalmology. Grace wrote me that NYU was one of the schools you applied to, and they cover full tuition.

I hope you don't think of me as improper when I tell you what a pretty woman you are. Your dad was quite a handsome man, so I'm not surprised. I am eager to meet you in person.

But let's not restrict ourselves to writing emails. Let me call you. Let's talk. How does that sound?

Your loving Macrina

Greg: UCLA, NYU, and the University of Hawaii accepted Anna into their medical schools. She told me later that being near Macrina was not a factor in choosing NYU. It was just a coincidence.

Scandal surrounded Macrina within a year of opening her church in New York. She had been forced to seek new assistants when Bret and Page couldn't follow her, and one of them, a married priest with a long unblemished history (as far as anyone knew) who pastored a church in Queens before his marriage, seemed an ideal choice. His wife was a lawyer, so he was able to serve the parish fulltime for a relatively small salary. He preached well, said the midweek Mass, and taught catechism to the kids. He was willing to do marriages and funerals. He was good with numbers and, once having gained Macrina's trust, took over the books. It's not clear why he and the assistant, a retired dental hygienist, didn't get along. She caught him looking at child porn after-hours one evening during a snowstorm when he thought everyone had gone home. Someone leaked the story to the *Daily News*, which headlined the story "Macrina's Church Not Squeaky Clean."

She immediately fired him, then sent the newspaper the following:

Macrina, digital archives of the New York Daily News: I had little choice but to let Fr. Krong go after he tearfully confessed to me the incident. My decision was immediate. I knew that public opinion would demand it. But letting him go was not easy.

He was an able servant to the parish and was struggling, I later learned, against his addiction while in therapy. Unlike an active alcoholic whose work suffers, his did not seem to. He is a law-abiding citizen who was living a productive life on a small salary. With his permission I talked to his therapist, who described him as a solid treatment candidate not likely to re-offend. Occasional slipups, she said, frequently occur on the way to a complete healing, especially when unforeseen circumstances like a snowstorm break the routine.

There is a great difference between a child porn addict and a pedophile. This is not to condone his habit, but Fr. Krong is not a pedophile. His therapist told me that in cases like his the likelihood of developing into pedophilia is close to zero. She was saddened to see what happened to "such a good man who had come so far," as she put it. In a better world, therapy instead of a purely punitive sentencing would have closed the case.

How does a Christian respond to such a weakness in the face

of so much public outrage? I am reminded of the passage in which Jesus halts the stoning of a woman caught in adultery. "Let him without sin cast the first stone," he cries out, and the self-righteous crowd scatters. I have heard every imaginable sin whispered in the confessional. What hidden crimes might we all be guilty of? Let us be slow to condemn and quick to forgive. At the very least, let us be grateful that we didn't get caught.

I have read letters to the editor condemning me for hiring such a man. "It just goes to show that a woman has no business being a priest," one outraged Catholic wrote. Another called my church a "disgraceful fiasco" and called for the Archbishop to shutter it. Such words hurt; they are meant to punish. But they might also be well meant; they might have grown out of a love for the same Church that I love. We just love in different ways.

I am convinced that Fr. Krong is well on his way to a complete recovery. Let us all wish him, and all other frail men and women in the world who are addicted to one thing or another, Godspeed.

Greg: From about the time Macrina landed in New York, she kept a thumb drive best described as "personal." Apparently she copied her personal correspondence into it, then deleted it from her main drive, or at least the great bulk of it. This thumb drive is essential for a full understanding of how she evolved over the last eighteen years of her life. Quite a bit of it deals with her relationship with Ezra. In fact she refers to the drive as her "azure" file. I wondered what this meant for a long time before recalling how she sometimes playfully called people by their names rearranged. Is it an accident that *Ezra* is close to *azure*?

Ezra, email: Can you break away for Sunday afternoon after Mass? I could drive in, or you could meet me at our usual halfway point in Cheshire. I miss you almost frantically at times, especially at sunset as I look out my office window at the wintry landscape and recall our wandering like Wordsworth in those wooded hills....

Macrina, email: I am inundated with work. Next Sunday I'm ordaining 17 new candidates as womanpriests with much of the world watching, either praising or condemning. Please don't attend. I simply cannot give you the attention you deserve. Two weeks from now seems like a realistic possibility. Be content that you are in my thoughts every day. You and God keep me sane and (mostly) happy....

Ezra, email: It's maddening loving you so much but never being able to consummate the love. I am almost 50 and still not married to the woman I adore. You tell me that some of the women in the movement are married to each other. You don't object to that but do object to marrying me. This makes no sense. Why do you value celibacy so highly? Why not come out and tell the world we're planning marriage? Beatrice means nothing to me compared to you. For you to question my ability to be faithful to you because I slept with her when I was drunk is absurd. She is nothing more than an ornament to my desolation because you are not in my life....

Macrina, email: It's not just a Catholic thing, Ezra. The greatest saints of all religions, with the exception of Judaism, were celibate.... My celibacy has nothing to do with an absence of passion, as you claim. I dream of you, my love! In my dreams I do consummate our love! Why celibacy? Not just one reason. But the main one is the ideal of sacrifice. Parents make sacrifices for their children, and children recognize and admire this. For me to sacrifice married life tells my congregation that they come first. Spouse and family do not divide my concern for them. They respond to this sacrifice and perhaps borrow strength from my example to make the sacrifices they are called to make. In any case, my sacrifice gives me an authority that nothing else quite can. There are other reasons, but they are minor compared to this....

I understand your attraction to Beatrice, and I forgive you

the lapse. I shouldn't have questioned your ability to be faithful to me. I spoke out of my pain, I wanted to punish you....

I really don't know what to do about the situation, except for you to vanish from my life. I simply cannot give you what you want and deserve. Mulling over this distresses me....

There is another reason for my celibacy. Since I was consecrated a bishop in our movement, I see how one day I might regret marrying. In all the buildup to a married clergy, which is right around the corner, there is the clear assumption that if married men are allowed to be priests, they would never be allowed to be bishops. That has been the working assumption even in our movement. If I were to marry, I would be risking the authority the movement expects me to carry into the future. And when the day comes — and I don't think it's too far away — that women priests are blessed by the Church, I would not want to be kept back because I married. This might seem to you selfish, and in a way it is. But I also see how my staying unmarried would be for the good of the future Church. If I saw someone else capable of carrying the scepter of authority, I'd reconsider....

Can't we just love each other and enjoy it in its unconsummated beauty, at least until you find someone who better deserves you? I doubt that there are many married couples who love each other with any more intensity. Maybe that's because of the mutual sacrifice we make. Have you thought of looking at it that way?

Ezra, email: My darling Macrina, we have known each other for fourteen years. Do you remember our first real date, the night of the great snowfall? Do you remember how you assumed I would not call you again? Little did you guess what a deep impression you made on me. And do you remember our first bike ride a few months later — how our hearts and minds leapt as we peddled along side by side hour after hour, alternately laughing and turning serious as our words worked their wonderful mischief? And will you remember this moment many years hence—this moment as I pledge myself to you as angels on high nod invisibly—will you remember this moment with happy, regretless tears?

You have often said that our meeting seemed fated, that our meeting was no accident. You've said several times that it seems we've known each other forever, that God had at last brought us together after a long apprenticeship of loneliness and suffering. My darling, I am rich in love for you. If we marry, I will nurse you when you are ill and pick your spirits up when they sag. I will forgive, and ask forgiveness, as necessary. I will protect you, encourage you, and be faithful to you. I will listen to you and learn from you. I will meditate and pray with you. And someday, if it is permitted, may we be reunited in the Summerland of living Light, where all is vivid and clear and precise—just as you've always wanted things to be here, my dearest love.

Anna Onishi to Grace Cowan, her mother, email: Mom, I thought I would go into more detail about my impression of Macrina than I told you over the phone.

This morning I went over to what she calls her "rectory" in the basement of her church, and she fixed me a nice breakfast. She brought up the adoption and said it was an incredibly hard decision. I was very much hoping she would elaborate, but she didn't, and I didn't ask her to.

Did you know that just picked her as one of the world's most influential people for 2067? The magazine *Time* magazine was lying on her coffee table half buried by an open book. She didn't even bring it up, I did. You would never guess it by the humble way she lives. For all her fame, it doesn't seem to go to her head. If I hadn't asked questions, she wouldn't have said a word about herself. It was all about me. Be sure to watch *60 Minutes* tomorrow—or I guess that would be today for you. She's being interviewed.

I asked her if she could get in touch with my biological father, and she said she would try. She described him to me. I come from some very interesting stock. I began wondering what it might have been like if she had raised me on her own. I'm glad she didn't. Either she wouldn't have made enough time for me, or I would have hindered her advance.

Did you know she had a boyfriend? She told me about him after I asked—discreetly—about her personal life. He's a Jewish mathematician. She confessed that she didn't give him enough time even though she dearly loves him. That might have been my fate....

Video from CBS Television archives:
Lydia Wambach, interviewer: Here in New York, Macrina McGrath pastors what she calls a Catholic church on the Lower East Side. With a Ph.D. in theology from Georgetown and an academic background in global religions, she is taking on the Vatican as no one has, arguably, since Martin Luther. She believes that women should not only be deacons, but priests and even bishops. She is, she claims, already a bishop herself and is widely regarded as the leader of the movement to bring female equality to a resisting Catholic Church. The Vatican excommunicated her from the moment she accepted ordination 14 years ago while a religion professor at Amherst College, but she has remained undaunted.... Welcome, Macrina McGrath. Or should I call you Bishop McGrath?

Macrina: (laughing) I wouldn't know who you were talking to! No, Macrina will do nicely.

Lydia: Tell us a little about yourself. It's one thing to take issue with the Church on the woman question—as a Catholic woman I do myself—but quite another to lead a revolution.

Macrina: Is that what I'm doing? (Laugher.) It would be wrong to see me as having chosen this role. Years ago the

Womanpriest movement in America chose me as a possible future leader because of my youth and Ph.D. in theology. The movement's leaders thought I had the right pedigree. That led to my being adopted by a visionary Bostonian whom I regard as the father of what some call a revolution. Like me, he thought it was absurd that women should be excluded from the clergy. With his money he bought the three churches I've pastored. He gave me the impetus to fire ahead.

Lydia: I'm sure you give yourself too little credit. You've been called the Mother of American Catholicism and a new Joan of Arc; but also the "Catholic Medusa" by your foes.

Macrina: Yes, and a Siren eager to eat men! I hope I don't look like one.

Lydia: Well, you certainly have a bigger following among women than men, though even 30% of American Catholic males are rooting for you.

Macrina: The Vatican, of course, is unimpressed.

Lydia: Why is that? What is the underlying reason for their opposition? Help us to understand.

Macrina: Well, I can tell you what the opposition says, though there might be more to it. They say they have history on their side. All of Jesus' apostles were male, and they were the leaders of the new faith. Down through the centuries the Church has never condoned, or even seriously considered, a female clergy. In the early part of this century Pope John Paul VI reaffirmed the tradition. He also, let it be said, strongly affirmed the equality of male and female. He explained that it's not that women are less competent than men to lead. He said the Church might easily have assumed otherwise and gone with popular opinion. But God, the lord of the Universe, in his wisdom ruled otherwise, and the Church followed. Two-thousand years of history are witness to that wisdom. That's the reasoning.

Lydia: Many would say that history was witness to its folly and God has nothing to do with it.

Macrina: And I would agree, especially given the recent pedophilia scandals, which just keep turning up.

Lydia: Do you think that if women had been priests, they wouldn't have happened?

Macrina: In Anglicanism women have been priests for the last 100 years—I've never heard of one of those priests being involved in a sex crime. If women held the positions that our pedophiles held, think of the terrible harm that would have been prevented.

Lydia: Would you venture to say that women would make *better* priests? Is that where the evidence points?

Macrina: (With a pause and a look of momentary puzzlement.) Let me put it this way. A good man is every bit as good as a good woman. They often do more good. My male assistants have strengths I lack. My assistants have always been men—by choice. But bad men? I don't think that bad women do as much harm *generally* as bad men. That's across all professions and all cultures. Men are simply more given to violence, including sexual violence, probably due to their higher testosterone levels. And children are too often their victims. Women are desperately needed to counter it.

Lydia: Is it really as simple as testosterone levels? Are there other reasons for this sexual deviancy?

Macrina: Yes. This is the way I see it. Too many idealistic young men enter the priesthood before they know what they are giving up. Some are either afraid of sex altogether or afraid of their own homosexual tendencies and decide it would be best to go celibate. But when they leave the seminary and discover how exhausting and lonely a priest's job can be, their repressed tendencies break out. They seek vulnerable partners to give them the love they can't find anywhere else. And too often that's kids. But also their office assistants, or even nuns who cook for them and do their wash.

Lydia: Nuns?

Macrina: Anyone they can control. One more reason for instituting a clergy of women who know from the beginning that they are men's equals.

Lydia: Many of your supporters have argued that if Jesus had lived today, some of his apostles would have been women. They say the Church has victimized itself by imprisoning itself in the past. Do you agree?

Macrina: A century ago there were no women presidents of countries, no women CEOs, no women generals, no women playing in symphony orchestras, no girls playing intercollegiate sports. Go back another hundred years and you find no women doctors, lawyers, or professors. Now we find women at the top everywhere—except in the Catholic Church. At least half of Jesus' apostles would be women if he were alive today.

Lydia: Some people are drawn to the Catholic Church because it *doesn't* change. They like how it defies trends and fads and sticks to what it's always been. They don't want it to evolve. They see this as weakness. For them a woman priest is an assault on the faith. Do they have a point?

Macrina: Ideas evolve. If they didn't, we'd still have slaves. The Catholic Church must evolve or shrivel away. Judging by all the church closures in our country, they're doing a pretty good job of it.

Lydia: It's widely assumed that the Vatican is close to authorizing married priests. Would this stall the progress you women are making?

Macrina: Why would it?

Lydia: I imagine that men who used to be priests but then got married might be flooding back into the Church. Am I right about this? Would there be as much need for women?

Macrina: In the very last analysis, need is not my concern—though it might have seemed so from what I've just said. What I'm fighting for is simple justice. Women who feel a call to the priesthood have as much right to it as men. They have never been given the chance to show what they can do. Men are physically stronger and bigger than women, but those traits have no value in religion—except maybe for fighting a crusade, and I hope to God we're beyond that.

Lydia: Thank you. Let's move on to another issue that's troubled your critics: doctrine. Is it true that you wrote your doctoral dissertation on Hinduism?

Macrina: Yes, on a Hindu philosopher writing in Sanskrit.

Lydia: Some say you are too cozy with Hinduism and with non-Christian religion in general. To take one instance, you've been quoted as saying that if you had been born in India to Hindu parents, you'd be a Hindu worshipping Krishna and perhaps even a Hindu priestess. Yet you would be just as precious to God as are Christians.

Macrina: I've spent time in India and met many Hindus, even women who broke ranks with their tradition and now function as priests. They love Krishna or Shiva and feel loved in return. They make good people and good priests. Many men resent them, even dishonor them, but Hinduism has no pope to excommunicate them, as Catholics do. I feel no need to convert them to my faith. They are well served by the one they were born to.

Lydia: As I understand it, your critics don't condemn you for believing this; they only say that you can't believe this and call yourself a Christian. How do you respond to this?

Macrina: Let them go to India and see the saints that Hinduism has produced; then I will listen to what they have to say.

Lydia: Are you saying you could just as happily be a Hindu as a Christian?

Macrina: Not at all. I love my religion and cling to it as much as they do to theirs. Many years ago, when someone asked me what my religion was, I'd sometimes say I was a Hindu Christian. I experimented with meditation using a Sanskrit mantra. In the end, all that did was confuse me. It's hard to escape one's culture and start over, and it's not necessary. Better double down on your own, but never to the extent of forgetting all the beauty and majesty of faiths not your own.

Lydia: Some people call you radically progressive while others call you conservative. You've even been called a chameleon. What do you call yourself?

Macrina: I call myself a Catholic.

Lydia: Can you clarify for our viewers what kind of Catholic you are?

Macrina: I think what I've been saying would fall into the progressive category. That and my impatience with dogma, as if beliefs had much to do with making saints of us. But conservative? Well, I hold firmly to a personal God. Those who claim that we invented a personal God because we need a God who is like us miss the point. The reason we are personal is that God is personal. As the Bible says, we are made in God's image. At any rate, if I were God, that's what I would do. We are each of us as a tiny finite cell in God's infinite body. We have a divine pedigree.

Lydia: Anything else?

Macrina: Well, I'm not ashamed to admit that I'm otherworldly in my convictions. The kind of Catholicism that downplays the importance of an afterlife because it supposedly distracts us from laboring for justice in the here and now — well, I think that's a mistake. A proper grasp of the future life provides a powerful incentive for the sacrifices needed for justice-work; it could never lead to escapism, as critics like to claim. And, of course, my defense of celibacy as a high calling paints me as impossibly conservative to some minds.

Lydia: Is there anything else you would like to tell your audience?

Macrina: (Pause.) I'm deeply attracted to Jesus' religion, the religion he actually practiced in his ministry. I'm attracted to his emphasis on love and forgiveness. His great Sermon on the Mount is a call to heroic action unlike anything in the world's other scriptures. And his estimate of human evil, its enormity and destructiveness, reveals a realism that the world desperately needs to heed.

Lydia: Thank you, Macrina. By the way, as one woman to another, I've noticed how you accessorize in bright colors—your scarfs and shawls are quite a contrast to the priest's black robe. Are you modeling the dress of future women priests, or will you be wearing the traditional stole while saying Mass?

Macrina: (Laughter.) No, it's just worldly vanity, what I have left of it. My scarf and these bangles. (She holds up her hand.)

Lydia: It's been a delight getting to know you better. Good luck.

Macrina, email to Greg: Dear Brother, I appreciate your sweet concern for my legacy, but I'm sure you overrate it. I'd ordinarily write in my journal what I'm about to tell you, but I'll start sharing more with you.

I've received a lot of email since the interview, most of it positive. I even got three proposals of marriage—they must not have followed my remarks about celibacy very closely! Paper mail has been much less positive. "You're a charlatan," somebody wrote. "Satan has a mansion for you in hell!" wrote another. "There's only one way to salvation. You should know that if you're really a Catholic." A few lectured me on the Catholic faith—fair enough—but one demented soul threatened to blow up the church, and three others threatened my life. I notified the police, and they promised to guard the church on Sundays but said they couldn't spare anyone to guard me. They told me that death threats are the acts of cowards and that real killers almost never pre-announce. I've always believed that and was glad to hear it from them. But it's still frightening.

You know how I love to walk early in the morning. I do about two miles, sometimes longer, occasionally all the way down to the Battery, where they are building dikes against the rising sea. Sometimes I'm recognized and even have to pose for a photo, but mostly I walk the byways of lower Manhattan unnoticed. You know I'm not the fearful type, but I now carry pepper spray just in case. It's hard to pray when you know you're being followed. With pepper spray in hand, I confronted a stalker this morning. I was in for a big surprise.

He was following me about 30 yards behind. Two or three people walked between us. I took a deep breath, turned around abruptly, walked straight up to him, and caught up to him after he began retreating. "You're stalking me! Why are you stalking me?" He looked pale, even frightened, and stuttered incoherently. I could see he was no threat. I calmed him down and asked again why he was following me, and he said he wanted to talk. "Okay, but why didn't you make an appointment? You were waiting for me right outside the church."

We were next to a park, and it was already a warm day. We found a bench and sat with pigeons cooing around us. Walter, that was his name, told me he watched the interview and was impressed by my knowledge of Hindus. For five years he had been a missionary in a village in Tamil Nadu and worked tirelessly with his wife and three kids to convert the village's dalits to Christianity. The higher castes watched him succeed and told him to get out; they said he was creating disharmony in the village, and I'm sure he was. They finally had enough, burned his house and church down, and raped his daughter. They threatened the dalits with a similar fate.

On the evening before he left, leaving his flock high and dry with no leader to replace him, a 10-year-old boy, the son of one of his parishioners, found him in a tent and began cursing Jesus and spitting at him. "F--- your Jesus and his bitch mother, Mary! F--- them!" The boy repeated this obscenity again and again. Walter, a strong man, hit the boy with his fist so hard that he never woke up. Horrified and frightened, he carried his victim in the dark to a nearby river and dropped him in. He and his family fled the next day, and nothing has been heard of the incident since.

He is now teaching fourth grade in one of our public schools, and he "sees" — that was his word — the boy seated in his classroom with all the other ten-year-olds. He's had no peace ever since the murder. He wanted to know if I could help him. What should he do?

I asked him if he was a Catholic and wanted to confess — I was ready to hear his confession sitting on the bench with the world waking up around us. No, he was an evangelical — what I suspected. What would you have said, Greg? I began by asking if he would be willing to return to the village and confess to the killing, with a good bit of money thrown in. The boy was one of four children, and years had passed. Possibly his parents would see his remorse, take the offering, and forgive him.

He shook his head and said he'd thought many times about doing just that. "But they might kill me instead or turn me in. And I have a family to raise, three kids of my own. My wife is also a teacher, and we need both salaries. We barely get by as it is. And we've had to make sacrifices to save what little we have."

He is a man searching desperately for some way to atone for his sin and willing to make any sacrifice his family could afford. I told him to consider adopting a kid warehoused in one of those wretched Indian orphanages. "And bring him up Hindu," I added. He was appalled at the suggestion. "Then bring him up in your own faith. Either way, you'd be rescuing the child from a life of misery." He stared at me, then down at the ground, then back up and gradually broke into a half-smile. "I can do that," he said. It was a beautiful moment.

Before we parted, I asked why he thought those Hindus needed to change their religion. The answer was predictable, right out of Matthew's gospel: "Go ye therefore and make disciples of all nations, baptizing them in the name of the Father, the Son, and the Holy Spirit"—the "Great Commission," words that Biblical scholars are almost certain Jesus never spoke. I told him about the Catholic way of doing missionary work, the way of St. Teresa of Calcutta, the way of service to the poor and unwanted, Jesus' way. "You evangelicals rejoice only after a conversion, like linebackers marking their helmet with a sticker after a hard tackle. You could have spent your time making them better Hindus. That would have better served them." That's what I told him. I don't know what he thought, but he thanked me warmly. He wasn't waiting for me this morning.

Macrina, Journal: "My Hindu instinct tells me that all religions are more or less true. All proceed from the same God, but all are imperfect because they have come down to us through imperfect human instrumentality." So said Gandhi. My Catholic instinct tells me the same thing.

> This a Hindu, that a Turk,
> But all belong to earth.
> Vedas, Korans, all those books,
> Those Mullas and those Brahmins—
> So many names, so many names,
> But the pots are all one clay.
> Both sides are lost in schisms.
> One slaughters goats, one slaughters cows,
> They squander their birth in isms.

So said Kabir, the Indian poet claimed by both Hindus and Muslims as their own.

Is he correct? Am I squandering my life in an ism? Catholicism, Protestantism, Hinduism, Judaism, Buddhism, Sikhism, Marxism—on and on the list goes.

But we need our isms. They are the envelopes that contain

the message. What people do in their prayerful moments, those moments when they meet God face to face, is the message. That's religion at ground zero, the spark that jumps up when the match is struck. The Church provides the tinder. The formulaic prayers of the Mass, what to say, when to sit and stand, are comforting in their changeless reliability, the common language of the community. Then the sermon, always surprising if well done, arousing, challenging, individualized. Ritual and sermon, the yin and yang of Catholicism. This is the envelope. If I didn't believe it was necessary, if I believed people could generate the spark on their own, I'd give up this mad dash toward reform. I'd gladly hand over the mantle to somebody else.

Greg: Macrina's life following the *60 Minutes* interview went into warp speed. She couldn't begin to keep up with the mail that flooded in and regretfully turned over the weeding out process to her personal secretary, Glenda Roberts. She received invitations to lecture from all over the United States and Canada. Her Journal makes it clear how torn she was between advancing the agenda for Church reform and meeting the humble needs of her congregation. It also reveals a side of her that some of her critics have missed.

Macrina, Journal: This evening I sit at my desk following a hectic day deciding, with Glenda's help, which correspondence to respond to and which to ignore. I have this weird feeling of being unsuited to my task. I am a single, frail woman turned into a monolith. That so much responsibility should be placed on anyone's shoulders is unreasonable beyond imagining. Yet this is exactly what happens to anyone with authority over large groups of people, from presidents to CEOs to school teachers. There is no getting around it. But do they have the same feeling as I? As I look around, some seem to feel the opposite. They give the impression that they feel up to the task, some even that they always know best what to do, as if they were infallible. As for me, I never know exactly what to do, and yet my critics describe me as obstinately self-assured. The only thing I know for sure is the rightness of the goal I am working for. How to get there is not in the tea leaves.

Greg: Sometimes all Macrina had energy for was a prayer — in her own unique style, of course.

Macrina, Journal:

Heavenly Father, thank you for my life, the incredible gift of being human, made in your image.

Heavenly Mother, heal me in body, mind, and soul.

Divine Light, may your wisdom and inspiration shine through me.

Divine Heart of love, abide in me always.

Saints known and unknown, spirit guides and guardians, and any of you dear ancestors looking after me, thank you for your help, and keep it coming.

All you motherly spirits, bless my struggling congregants, especially Travis, Rebecca, Waverly, Blasco, and all the others, too numerous to mention.

And may the grace of heaven reach Anna this day, and all her days.

Greg: Soon after her popular *60 Minutes* interview, CBS asked Macrina if she would be willing to debate on Easter Sunday the conservative Boston College Catholic professor of theology Edward Litzinger. She replied humorously, "If you don't mind my losing." They didn't mind.

We'll get to it below, but first I want to spotlight Macrina as pastor, to which I have devoted too little time. Macrina loaded her sermons, hundreds of them, onto four thumb drives that have survived. One of the sermons struck me as "pure Macrina." To me it shows how she concerned herself with the spiritual lives of her charges, especially young people, even when it came to what many would consider small things. You might remember how she promised many years ago to preach in parables, and this one is typical. I haven't presented the sermon in its entirety as she gave it—I'm pretty sure she elaborated on what she wrote as she moved along. Most of her sermons weren't read, but almost all were accompanied by notes. This one was written out.

Macrina, sermon on the second of the surviving thumb drives: Little Marilyn had been preparing for her First Communion at St. Agnes Catholic School for the last month. Her mother, Sarah, had managed to store the very dress she wore 26 years before for just such an occasion. It was the usual white, the color of innocence and purity, and it came with a veil. The night before, Marilyn watched her mother iron the dress, then tried it on. It was a good fit. She was glowing with anticipation and eager to show off her dress to the other girls. She was sure the Blessed Virgin would lovingly look down at her when Father Braun handed her the sacred host, Jesus' very body, and she placed it in her mouth, as she had watched her mother and older sister do for as long as she could remember. Since making her confession the night before, she was feeling very grown up and very clean and very special to God.

Her father, Bryan, a screen writer and editor for Netflix, would even be attending, even though he hadn't been in a church since Aunt Minnie's wedding a year ago. She loved her dad not one bit less even though he wasn't a practicing Catholic, and even though he sometimes did and said things that hurt Mom. Marilyn never doubted his love for everyone in the family.

The altar was decked out in white lilies. Marilyn, a straight-A student, had been selected to read the epistle from Corinthians, and as she sat back down in the pew with her family, her dad nodded to her with pride in his expression. When the special time came, she processed up to the altar with the other children and received the sacrament. As she rejoined her family, she felt a warm glow. She remembered how her teacher told them at their practice the day before that the angels in heaven would be looking down at her and smiling.

A family party was schedule for that afternoon, but Bryan decided to celebrate early. They stopped at Mikey's for ice cream, and Marilyn chose a simple vanilla cup. As they were riding home, with Marilyn sitting in the place of honor in the front seat next to her dad, where Mom usually sat, she placed the cup on the dashboard of the car to remove her veil, and it slid off before Bryan could reach over and stop it. As ice cream spilled out over the hibiscus-colored mat on the floor of his new Tesla, he exploded, "What the fuck did you do that for?" (pause)

Dear friends, are you shocked? Much of the world would not be. After all, our Constitution protects free speech. Even the most obscene word in the English language when spoken in the presence of a child is protected. In our culture the f-word is pervasive. Even a priest might shout it at his computer when it suddenly goes down. And the word sometimes steals into our minds before we even recognize it's there—we're all infected by it. I'm not going to tell you it's a sin, but I am going to tell you it coarsens our culture.

Some of you might use the word habitually and thoughtlessly—like little Marilyn's dad. The other day on my morning walk I overheard a boy, he couldn't have been more than 12, use the word three times in a seven-word sentence. Chances are he'll carry the habit into his marriage, use it in front of his children, and abuse his wife with it when they argue. We don't get much help these days from the film industry. Movies on Netflix pepper the dialogue with a barrage of f-bombs. No, I am not asking you to think of obscene language as a sin, only to be aware of it, how it saturates our culture and our very lives if we let it.

Many years ago when I was a professor I had a colleague who used the word in class, and I called him on it. He said it was simply the *lingua franca*, just ordinary speech. As when a man says he and his wife had a good fuck. I told him there was a huge difference between making love to your wife and having a good fuck. I said the difference lay in the sacredness of making love to the one person you love uniquely and someone you hook up with on a Saturday night. The very reason the word is so degrading is that it degrades the sex act as it was meant to be practiced.

He is a clever man and put up a good fight. He told me he was a vegan but always ate the food his host served like an appreciative guest when he and his wife went out. He called me a goody-goody and compared me to a resentful guest. "Why get upset when people use the f-bomb?" he said. "Just do your thing and let them do theirs." He had a point, and I let him know it.

But I won't allow him the last word, and here is my response: The innocent Marilyns of the world deserve a childhood free of the everyday traumas of family profanity. Our Catholic faith reminds us that our world—not only a child's world, but all creation—is sacred space. Let's try to keep it that way.

Macrina, Journal: I might regret taking so much time off with the upcoming debate looming, but I couldn't resist. Ezra wanted to take me ice fishing in Littleville Lake in the Berkshires. We know it well. It's the scene of our meetings in Chester, but until now it had never been 16 degrees outside. I caught the Amtrak to Pittsfield and read most of the way while sneaking looks out the window at the snowy forests, so beautiful in the sunlight. He met me at the station and we drove the 20 miles down to the lake, thick with ice and covered with fresh snow from the day before.

Well, it wasn't like catching mackerel from the back of a boat in the Gulf of Mexico. All layered up and mittened, with a ski mask covering my head and sun glasses over my eyes, I shivered my way out onto the lake as Ezra pulled a small sled holding the equipment. Other men already had their holes dug and were shouting boisterously as they lifted trout and bass out of the water. Four groups—no women—were spread out over the ice. Each group watched their tip-up traps and rushed over to pull up the fish when it hit. Meanwhile poor Ezra was grinding away with his drill through ice a foot thick. There wasn't much I could do but watch and encourage. A red fox carrying a rabbit in his mouth trotted along the lake's edge.

A man from one of the groups noticed Ezra struggling and came over to offer help. Phil, that was his name, said he had a power augur that would cut through the ice in no time and wanted to know if Ezra would like to use it. Ezra took him up on the offer.

In his bright red coat and royal blue woolen beanie, Phil turned out to be a friendly sort of fellow and a real talker. He said he was surprised to find a woman out on the lake. "It's usually just guys hanging out together, drinking beer, seeing who can catch the most fish."

After he helped Ezra spud out the hole, and as Ezra busied himself setting up the trap with its flag jumping up and down, Phil asked about me. Were we married, did I have kids, what did I do for a living, was I religious? All those questions that would get you reprimanded or fired at a progressive college like Smith rolled out of his genial, well-meaning mouth. I confess to being rather intrigued and even charmed by his directness, and I answered his questions and threw back a few of my own. It turned out he worked for the Massachusetts Division of Fisheries and Wildlife and stocked the lake with trout the previous fall. It also turned out he was a Catholic.

The conversation got a little dicey, but also amusing, when I told him I was a priest—a Catholic priest. It went something like this:

"Oh, you must be one of those lady agitators. I saw something about the movement on *60 Minutes* a few months ago. Are you one of them?"

I noticed Ezra glancing at me with a big, impudent grin on his face.

I told Phil I even had a church of my own.

"But it's an illegal church, right? Do you say Mass and give out Communion?"

Of course I do. He scowled.

"I don't mean to be offensive, but that woman, I forget her name—"

Was it Macrina?

"Yes, that's it. I read something about her, and it said she had a Jewish boyfriend and believed in reincarnation and had been a Hindu at one point. I just can't believe she thinks of herself as a Catholic. Maybe you women will one day become priests, real priests, but this Macrina sure won't get you there. At least that's my opinion. I hope I'm not being offensive."

Not at all.

"The odd thing about her was that she said she values celibacy, yet she has a boyfriend. The whole situation just didn't add up. Do you know this woman? Have you actually met her?"

Yes, I know her, I said. I had met her. I was tempted to tear off my ski mask and lower my glasses but decided it would be unkind.

"Well, I'll be getting back to the boys. It's been really interesting talking to you. I'm not opposed to women, it's just that—by the way, I never got your name."

Macrina, I said. I told him I had the same name as the woman he read about.

"Well, I'll be damned. What a coincidence. Well, I'll be off." As we thanked him and wished him good luck with the fishing, he picked up his augur and crunched his way over the snow back to his group.

Ezra could hardly contain himself and took care to muffle his laughter until Phil was out of hearing. Finally he exploded, and so did I. "Why didn't you tell him?" he sputtered.

"I almost did. But it would have embarrassed him."

I'm sure I'll forget the fish we caught, but I'll never forget Phil. He taught me a painful lesson. If I am going to be a credible ambassador for the movement, I have to break off my relation to Ezra. Life can be cruel.

Greg: CBS was happy to provide me from its archives the Easter Sunday 2069 televised interview between Macrina and Professor Litzinger. I remember how nervous she was about the interview. Friends told her Litzinger played "down and dirty" and that he would leave her bewildered and embarrassed by the end. She ignored the advice and went to work watching him on YouTube batter his adversaries into submission. She told me she spotted a weakness in his methods and thought she could hold up. "It's not as if he has a monopoly on the relevant evidence," she told me. "Or on logical thinking." She said she owed it to the movement to take him on. She thought it would help the cause if a woman could match wits with a notorious bully—not win, just hold up. What follows is only a small portion of the debate.

Macrina and Litzinger, CBS television archives: Host Brent Cavendish: Good evening. CBS Television welcomes this chance to stage a debate between Macrina McGrath, former professor of religion at Amherst College and spiritual leader of the Womanpriest movement in the Catholic Church, and Professor Edward Litzinger, the noted Catholic philosophy professor at Boston College and one of the acknowledged American leaders of the movement to defend the faith against, what he calls, "fashionable mutations of timeless truth." The debate will be free-flowing. I will intrude only if it bogs down. In order to preclude audience participation and possible interruption, the debate has not been scheduled for an auditorium, as many of you had hoped, but is being held in a CBS studio here in New

York. Professors McGrath and Litzinger, welcome. [Each is eager to allow the other to speak first. Finally Litzinger begins.]

Litzinger: May I call you Macrina? It seems to be the name everyone knows you by.

Macrina: Certainly.

Litzinger: Let me come right to the point. As you know, I represent and speak for the present position of the Catholic Church, the Church you claim to love. Yet it is impossible for me to fathom how you can truly love it when you contradict it and trespass against its clear, unambiguous teaching again and again. Earlier this century Pope John Paul VI made it clear that women, by God's will, are not qualified for the priesthood. He did not qualify the claim in any way. He did not say that the claim would hold for so-and-so many years, or that it would be repealed when so-and-so conditions were met. He spoke apodictically. Can we at least agree that this is a matter of record?

Macrina: We can, but with a caveat. The pope did make such a claim, but he erred when he made it. He was in no position to speak for God and he knew it. He could have spoken *ex cathedra* but chose not to. He could have claimed infallibility but did not. He left open the possibility of further developments. Perhaps he even suspected it when the Church was more ready. Disagreeing with his position does not make me a bad Catholic.

Litzinger: You seem to be saying that because he didn't speak infallibly, you are comfortable putting yourself at his level. Behind him stand the entire College of Cardinals and tens of thousands of bishops and archbishops all over the world. You are the product of Jesuit schools—a plus. You got a Ph.D., no easy thing—another plus. You distinguished yourself as a professor at Amherst and wrote three books—all very commendable. But you also had a child out of wedlock—a serious mistake you have publicly acknowledged. In saying that, please don't think I am condemning you. I too have made mistakes, including divorcing my first wife. But here is the difference between you and me: I admit that I violated Christian teaching, but you do not. I admit that I fell short, but you continue to insist that Christian teaching regarding the priesthood is a mistake—not that *you* are mistaken, but that the Church is. That strikes me as arrogant.

Macrina: Give me a moment to digest what you are saying, one thing at a time…. First, didn't I just admit that my position contradicts present Catholic teaching? The point is that present teaching can change. It has in the past. It did last year when married priests were finally recognized—

Litzinger: But there was a precedent. After all, our first pope, St. Peter, was married.

Macrina: True, and, as I recall, you vigorously opposed that change. You seem to be opposed to all change. Which puts you, not me, out of step with the Church.

Litzinger: The point is that in this instance there is no precedent of any kind.

Macrina: Let me ask you this: why did you mention my child? What does that have to do with the question of women priests? You're a philosophy professor. Surely you know what an *argumentum ad hominem* is. It's a logical fallacy. Even I can spot one.

Litzinger: In a court of law a prosecutor is paid to identify character weaknesses in a witness. Once identified, the witness's testimony is weakened, sometimes even stricken from the record. I see you as a weak witness. I might compare you to an unseaworthy boat. Like water, the truth gradually leaks out of you. It's been doing that for a long time, so gradually that you now fail to notice it. It strikes me as remarkable that you don't see the absurdity of you, a single woman, defying 2,000 years of Catholic tradition.

Macrina: Dr. Litzinger, I was 22 when I made the mistake you mention. Today I am a year shy of 50. Do you really want to judge me on the basis of a youthful mistake?

Litzinger: You have a tendency to weaken Catholic teaching on a number of fronts—like a soldier who falls back in the line of fire. Take Catholic teaching about gay marriage. You've come out strongly for it. Yet Pope Francis fifty or so years ago condemned it. He wouldn't even allow priests to bless a same-sex union. He called intercourse between two men or two women a sin, an outright sin. Yet Francis is regarded as a relatively liberal pope. Despite his liberal tendencies, he strongly endorsed the Church's 2,000-year tradition. It has held ever since, but you would throw it away. So perhaps you see why I use the metaphor of a leaky boat.

Macrina: As you must surely know, the rank and file of American Catholics favor blessing such unions. A Pew poll put the figure at 63 percent. So I'm far from alone. Even a few bishops, especially in Europe, oppose the Vatican. And tons more would if they didn't fear for their jobs. Here is the basic difference between you and me as I see it: You favor a top-down approach to resolving doctrinal disputes, exclusively top-down. And I warm to a bottom-up approach. I think a billion Catholics need to be heard, not dictated to. Not exclusively, but taken into account. You call me arrogant, but I see top-down as arrogant. So does the rest of the world. And it's cost us. There are fewer Catholics in the world today than when I was born, when people were still driving cars and our coastal cities hadn't yet begun to build dikes. Much time has passed since then, and there are now 10 billion of us humans, but we Catholics are growing only in the Global South, especially Africa. Whites make up only 19% of the Catholic population. I find this distressing....

Litzinger: You mentioned earlier that we are not growing, and that's true. We make up only 11% of the world population. And why do you suppose that is? I am interested in hearing what you have to say about that.

Macrina: Well, there are many reasons.... So many it's hard to know where to begin. But one of them is the way we treat divorcees when we tell them they aren't worthy to receive the Eucharist when they remarry. They don't put up with this snub and go elsewhere, or they give up religion altogether. Another is our claim that our religion is the "one true faith." This only—

Litzinger: I think I know where you are going with this. You pluralists are so respectful of other religions that you give the impression that it doesn't matter what religion you profess. Who will take you seriously when you speak that way? If you don't represent the best, who will care?

Macrina: I wonder if you understand how young people think about religion. They are taught from junior high up that there are many ways of looking at things. Tolerance is the preeminent virtue in high school. Their teachers drum that message into them. Kids these days are impressed by more modest claims. They are distrustful of people who claim that their way is the best. The—

Litzinger: So do you tell them the Catholic Church is one among many options, all on the same footing?

Macrina: Not at all. Because that's not what I believe. I tell them to come and see. Or, more likely, others tell them to come and see. I never tell my parishioners that we are the one true church, but they find enough to like that they keep coming back. And they bring their friends. And the Church grows. I abhor such boasts as "we're number one." Leave that chant in the football stadium. Come to Church to sing that great hymn "Praise to the Lord." Rouse the saints in heaven with your voice. But at the same time rejoice that Hindus find God in their faith as much as Catholics do in theirs. All religions are bedazzled by their own revelation and are blind to the light shining forth from others. God does not have favorites.

Litzinger: That is precisely the attitude that is killing our Church....

Greg: This is a small sampling of the topics discussed.

Litzinger brought up abortion, birth control, physician-assisted suicide, premarital sex, life after death, reincarnation, mediumistic communication, war, and climate change—all in an effort to expose Macrina to ridicule, either by showing her ignorance of the subject, as in war, or her divergence from Catholic teaching, as in her openness to reincarnation. At the end she was exhausted and secluded herself for several days to recover. She told me she made a mistake by debating Litzinger. But the CBS call-in poll taken immediately after the program said otherwise. She and Litzinger finished in a 46%-46% dead heat, with 8% undecided. Mom and Dad were thrilled that their little daughter had become a big-time celebrity. Their pride knew no bounds. Nor did mine.

Ezra, email: Dear Macrina, This is a matter of such importance that I thought I ought to write rather than call. I want this to come out exactly right. Please accept my apology for being out of touch with you for the last two weeks.

I didn't travel to Israel to attend a conference on mathematical cryptography, as I told you, but to meet a woman I had begun a correspondence with two months ago. Her name is Libi Dayan, a divorced 34-year-old Israeli interior designer. She is completely secular, smart, personable, and she would jump at the chance to move to the United States. She is childless but wants a child. I think you would like her and see her as someone who is right for me. In any case, I am ready to take the plunge. Perhaps I should say that I am desperate enough to take it. I am profoundly tired of being single.

But I haven't formally proposed, and you could still intervene—in fact I hope against hope that you will. You know how I would love to marry you. That has not changed. I would even leave Amherst and look for employment in the City. But to speak frankly, I see you drifting away from me, even though you keep denying it. The truth is that your work, your mission, squeezes out the good times we used to have. Our hikes, our fishing trips, our having friends over, even our going out for a movie are just not happening. It's hard enough for you to make time for Anna. The only way to enjoy quality time with you is to come home to you every night, to be there for you as we tell each other about our day. And that's what I'd like.

I don't like doing this, Macrina. If you really do love me, if it would grieve you to lose me, then I am, in a way, forcing your hand, forcing you to choose. My suspicion though is that the choice would not be as difficult as I fear—your famous objectivity would step in and rule. You have always told me that a time like this would come and that you even hoped for my sake it would come, however much it would hurt you. Those are almost your exact words. Now the time has come, and I want you to have the chance to choose, to determine our fate. Libi is not so deeply involved—how could she be after so short an acquaintance?—that it would crush her. I have thought long and hard about my choice. I don't want to measure my life by halves: the half that included you, and the half that didn't. I don't want to divide my time in the way the world divides its: BCE and CE. I want to share your entire life, not just the first half.

Finally, I want to assure you I will be all right if you do what I think you must. You are a woman of destiny, and I don't want marriage to stand in your way. I know how compassionate you are and how likely you are to take my feelings into account. Don't do it. I have a backup. I will be okay. And we can always stay friends.

With all my love, Ezra.

Macrina, Journal: Ezra did for me the deed I didn't have the strength to do myself. I could never find a way to end the relationship. He did it for me. I am stunned.

Every now and then I hear of a Hollywood starlet who gives up her career for her man. I've always wondered if they regretted it. Would I?

I must think carefully. We could live together in a lovely home in the Berkshires. I could keep a flower garden, do a little teaching on the side, write the novel I'd always dreamed of, roam the fields and woods I love, and spend my days with my man. I would quickly be forgotten as a public intellectual and movement pioneer. The excitement and bustle all around me that I feed on, the fame that I enjoy as much as I dread, would dry up. The sun would shine down on me as it does on everyone else. The rays I cast on the world would cease.

Oh Macrina, what have you done? Aren't you allowing the world to use you? None of my admirers, none of those men and women who write me letters or invite me to give speeches or debate heavyweights cares for me as a person who loves and hurts and dreams.

But Ezra does. Even above a possible husband, he is a true friend, the most treasured I've ever had. I never have to fear being anything other than myself when around him. All the craziness that goes along with me he accepts. I can confess any fault or boast of any progress. I can share with him my heart's deepest secrets without fear of a rebuke. When he corrects me I don't feel pain, and when he praises me I don't feel flattered. How happy and carefree I am around him. What a terrible thing to lose all this.

Am I subverting the natural order by sacrificing the warm world of domestic friendship for the rising and falling turmoil of leading a movement? Macrina, you don't have to do this. You can send Libi Dayan packing back to Tel Aviv. You have that power.

But... no. I didn't come to earth to rest. I came to make a difference. I've known this since I was a girl. I just didn't know how it would happen, what I was supposed to do. It doesn't seem that I chose this particular path; it seems it was chosen for me. Resign from Amherst? Who in her right mind would do that? Yet that is what I did, or rather was prompted to do. Prompted by whom? By Stewart? No, it goes deeper than that, something more mysterious. Something or someone behind the scenes was prodding me.

I cannot afford to think differently. I must always feel, must work at feeling—and most of the time I do feel—that I am blessed and led by invisible powers, angels and saints, spiritual masters, God, that I am not alone, that they come to my aid to further the cause. But is the cause noble? Is it good, truly good, for the Catholic world to have women priests? Litzinger claimed it would smash a 2,000-year tradition, and he was right. Who am I to do this? I'm a tiny wren clutching a reed swaying in the breeze. It sings its monotonous song, the same one over and over—is it worth listening to? But when I think back to Okinawa, back to Grace as she baptized Anna, my courage returns. I have seen with my own eyes what women can do. I've seen with my own eyes, yes. Now it's time for the world to see. That is what I must believe to bend back this terrible temptation.

Ezra spoke of remaining a friend. I know better. This would undermine his devotion to his new wife. Even his friendship I must give up. If he reaches out to me, I must ignore him. No more phone calls, no more texting, no more—no more being held in his strong arms. No more looking into his kind eyes. No more entertaining his fun, crazy ideas.

Then there is Mom. She won't let up. Sometimes I hear her voice at night when I can't sleep. It haunts me. "Think of what you are giving up. You love Ezra, and he adores you. You are trading away happiness for—for what? Darling, you are likely to die before the Church comes around. You've always said it eventually would, but it hasn't. Have you confronted the possibility that it never will? That you will die excommunicated? What will all those Catholic saints in heaven think about you? How will you be received? And what will the world think? They will see you as misdirected, as chasing a dream, a chimera, something never meant to be. Darling, it breaks my heart to see you throwing away such happiness. You abandoned your first child, and now you are abandoning the possibility of anymore. What a tragic loss for a woman who loves children so much!" These are the words that rave inside my head.

Greg: Over the months following the breakup, Macrina agonized over Ezra's occasional emails or texts. I think he held out hope she would change her mind until the very end and that she knew it. But finally the day of the marriage came, and all communication ended—at least until the whole world wobbled on its axis two years later. In the meantime she made a new friend as lonely at the top as she was. Cardinal Joseph Cullen, Archbishop of the Archdiocese of New York, staunchly supported her cause and, in defiance of a papal order, invited her to preach at St. Patrick's. Their frequent emails suggest a warm but proper friendship, a camaraderie based on mutual admiration and trust. It helped Macrina miss Ezra less. It helped silence Mom's ominous warnings.

Greg: CBS was so happy with the ratings of her first debate that they asked her back. Would she be willing to debate the noted atheist Sam Hawkins in a free-flowing conversation? The topic would be the existence and nature of God. Hawkins, now deceased, was at the time a popular author with a huge internet following of mostly under-40 males who had contempt for theistic religions, especially Christianity. Macrina had watched him debate a rabbi on television and admired the way he kept to the topic. She wrote in her Journal that the philosophy of religion courses she took at Georgetown had stuck with her. She knew the arguments for and against God. She knew each side's strengths and weaknesses and wrote that she "might spring a surprise on Hawkins." She accepted. The date fell on All Saints Day.

The debate lasted an hour and covered much more ground than advertised. Those who have followed her later comments will be interested to see how her thinking developed. Her restless mind was always on the move. Despite what she said, she was no wren. What follows are snippets, kept short by the publisher's request for brevity.

I haven't said anything about her appearance for some time. One of her assistants, Vanessa Hamby, another woman priest, vividly recalled the debate and wrote me the following.

Vanessa Hamby, email: Regarding her looks, Macrina's philosophy was to honor her audience by looking good. I don't think vanity had much to do with it. She went to a hairdresser a few blocks away from the church about once every three months and wore her hair in a short bob. She wouldn't let anyone tint her hair. "I want to look my age, whatever it is." So there wasn't much else but white showing the night of the debate. But her hair was full and shiny and nicely framed her face. Her face was free of wrinkles of the easily noticeable kind. And her eyes shone with that incredible liveliness that drew people to her. She was a beautiful woman in a spiritual kind of way, a way that suggested she had suffered but had overcome it and grown through it, which she had. I think she had just turned 50. You were right about her having a lot of scarves. When people gave her a gift, it was usually a scarf. Yes, I do remember the scarf she wore on the night of that debate, a year before the Pandemic. It was a vividly gold, blue, red, and green collection of triangles, all melting into each other. It was her favorite, and it was gorgeous.

Macrina and Hawkins, CBS television archives:

Hawkins: Before we go any further, you might oblige me by defining what you mean by God.

Macrina: Define God? An impossible task. What we can do is use words that, uh, that could evoke a sense of what God might mean to us.

Hawkins: I'm listening. (Hawkins is wearing a brown jacket over an unbuttoned yellow shirt. His hair is full, longish, and wavy. He pushes back one of the curls from time to time when it obscures his vision. He looks to be about 65. He has aged well.)

Macrina: Words like beauty, goodness, power, knowledge, wisdom, compassion, joy. It might be helpful to think of God in those terms, but any word falls far short of who God truly is.

Hawkins: *Who* you say. That word seems to bring God down to our level. Is he a person? Does he by any chance have a gender—is he male—as I believe your creed teaches? Is he a father?

Macrina: It looks like you've caught me in a contradiction, but not really. One word comes pretty close to nailing down who God really is. God is personal. God is the supreme person. Those other words are his attributes. If we're ever privileged to know God as he truly is, we'd want better ones. But there is no way we can do without personhood and still have a God we can relate to, pray to, love and adore. God is not an It, a supreme It. God is the supreme person. And, no, he's not masculine in spite of the pronoun.

Hawkins: It seems to me you've conveniently designed a God whose essential nature is the same as yours—a boutique deity specializing in persons living on earth and even sharing their nature. A tribal God. Are you sure you want to drag the deity down to our level? If I were God, I might consider that an insult. (Enthusiastic applause and mumbling, mostly male in its resonance.)

Macrina: Very clever. Needless to say, God is a *unique* person. God is a conscious being. He has a sense of self. He thinks his own thoughts. He has his own life. That is what we mean by *person,* finite or infinite. No, he's not masculine. I use the word *he* because it's better than *it* and because I dislike saying *he or she* all the time, as if the woman in me requires constant reassurance. (A ripple of applause.) One more thing— and this is of the greatest importance. God watches us and loves us, as a good parent should. He delights in us when we love our neighbor and is saddened when we don't. He's vitally interested in our moral development and rewards us when we choose what's good over what's easy or convenient or downright evil. That's the kind of person he is. I know it seems prosaic to you, but it'll just have to do for the moment. Can we move on?

Hawkins: Does your God punish us when we choose evil?

Macrina: When we do it habitually, yes. That's what good parents do when their children mess up, right? But the punishment is always for instruction, never vengeance. Tough love, as we say.

Hawkins: So hell is not eternal?

Macrina: The will is always free. The door out of hell is never locked. And there are plenty of spirits ready to help those who are there. God is not in the condemning business. Everyone in hell chooses to be there. It's the place where God is absent. As bad as it is, that's the way some spirits like it. That's the way they liked it back on earth.

Hawkins: You seem to know so much about this fictitious being and even about hell. Anyway, I have a pretty good idea of his nature—I almost said flaws. How do you know there *is* such a God?

Macrina: Have you ever read Aquinas?

Hawkins: Not recently.

Macrina: Do you remember his famous five proofs.

Hawkins: Or five spoofs, as one of my philosophy professors called them.

Macrina: *Proofs* is too strong a word, I agree. But the argument from design has always struck me as, well, suggestive. Almost convincing.

Hawkins: I'm listening.

Macrina: I'll give a twenty-first-century version of the argument. Things of great complexity and magnitude, like a skyscraper or a jet plane or a Gothic cathedral or the latest super computer, require great power and intelligence to design and create them. I think you would agree. Now the universe is infinitely greater in complexity and magnitude than any of these. Whoever designed it must be proportionate in scope with it—or equal to the job, as we might say. That would be God—the cosmic designer of the universe. How does that strike you?

Hawkins: A fanciful hypothesis. All we know is that the Big Bang happened about 14 billion years ago, and the universe has been evolving ever since. You don't need an invisible, undetectable supermind to account for it. Your skyscraper can be built in a few years. If the universe is not in a hurry, it might have the power to evolve on its own—gradually, step by step. It's just something the universe does.

Macrina: But unless the universe has a mind of its own, it's hard to see how it could have evolved at all, however much time it took. If it's just mindless matter—isn't that what you believe?—how could anything so stupendous as a universe just happen? How could life evolve from nonlife? How could consciousness evolve from rock and fire? These are mysteries that your worldview doesn't touch.

Hawkins: I think of myself as a scientist, Macrina. We don't solve a mystery by heaping a second mystery on top of the first. Anything is possible, but an invisible, unknowable person dreaming up a universe and then pulling the trigger that ignites it strikes me as irresponsible nonsense. There is no evidence for such a being.

Macrina: I think you mean there is no physical evidence. Nothing you can see or hear. Nothing you can see through a microscope or pick up on a frequency analyzer. But dark matter has never been detected either, yet all scientists believe it's real. It's real because, they say, it's the only way to explain the way galaxies behave. You know this better than I. As I see it, God is like dark matter. God is undetectable but necessary to explain the behavior of our evolving universe. You know better than I that if the laws that govern our universe were in the slightest degree changed, it would never have existed. I think of God as its designer and overseer—a mathematician and engineer working with formulas of unimaginable complexity and precision. Everywhere there is evidence of intelligent design, a cosmic lawgiver. Every scientist should acknowledge this. The reason they don't is that they hate religion and will do anything they can to debunk it. There is a lot about religion that needs to be debunked, especially primitive views of God, and scientists like you are right to do so. But instead of giving God a redo, you throw him out. I think that's indefensible and, sorry to say, just a little stupid. (Booing)....

Hawkins: I have read that you strongly believe in the power of prayer. This is another instance of believing something on insufficient evidence. Surely you are aware that the great majority of prayers go unanswered. Think of the immense effort wasted on prayers for sick loved ones who end up dying anyway. Or the prayers for rain that farmers have said through the ages that have gone answered, with widespread famine the result. Or a mother's unanswered prayers for a child that never comes. Either he is deaf or he doesn't exist. Even if he did exist, how could you love him? Could you love a father who failed to feed you no matter how hard you begged and let you starve to death? To put it simply, how could a loving deity have created a world with so much misery in it?

Macrina: Not everybody will like what I'm about to say, but here goes. Life becomes meaningful only when we come up against difficult conditions and work to overcome them, and what brings us happiness is successfully doing just that. In other words, when we win. It might be as minor as arranging flowers in a vase or as weighty as building a startup into a billion dollar company. It might be fighting against a cancer or helping your child overcome an opioid addiction. The downside is when we fail. But without the possibility of failure, there wouldn't be any motivation for the work that's needed. There would be no upside. God know this, and that's why there is so much suffering in our world.

Hawkins: You've chosen easy examples. But many conditions are unwinnable; it doesn't matter how hard you try. A child born with Tay-Sachs, a beloved grandmother wasting away with Alzheimer's, a son whose legs are blown off by a roadside bomb, a whole city devastated by a deadly virus, a tribe wiped out by a rival tribe. Prayer has no impact on such cases. Yet people pray, and people like you encourage them to. You offer them hope when you know there is no reason to hope. Frankly, I question your integrity. (Light murmuring and a few gasps.)

Macrina: First let me say that it's hard to see how prayer harms anyone. At the very least it gives you hope. And it's a way of silently expressing love for the one you pray for. And to feel love is always a good thing, even if it has no impact on the one you pray for. But let's not be so quick to say that prayer never works. Anthropologists—and these aren't usually religious people—tell us it sometimes does, even though they aren't sure why. Ordinary people call such cases miracles. I don't think that's what they are. I don't think there is anything magical about them. I see them as healing energy sent down from heaven by spiritual beings who can impact our world up to a point. The more intensely and frequently we pray for help, the more likely we'll get it. It seems as if our efforts draw power from these heavenly sources, like a powerful workout routine builds muscles. There are no guarantees, but healings are reported everywhere.

Hawkins: But what about all those unwinnable cases I mentioned? You seem to have dodged the question. I think I know why. They can't be reconciled to the God you believe in. They are undeniably real, and your God is a mere possibility. When you can't have it both ways, the merely possible must give way to the certainly true. The only logical outcome is atheism.

(Light applause.)

Macrina: You make a good point, Professor Hawkins, but you overlook a key element of the Christian faith: belief in life after death. Your cases are unwinnable in the short run, but if death is not the final word, then they can be winnable in the long. I believe they are. This is not the place to go into the evidence for life after death, so I'll add only this.

A God who jumped in to solve all our dilemmas whenever we asked him to would enfeeble us. If God gets us out of all our scrapes, we'll never be motivated to do our best. And we'll never develop into better beings. Nobility of character does not come cheap. Unless morally challenged, we don't grow—just as spoiled children don't mature. God loves the good and hates evil. What's the meaning of our lives if we, like God, can't love the good and hate evil? What's worth doing if we live in a world where there is no evil to banish? For us to hate it and try to banish it, there must first *be* evil. And there is, plenty of it. And in hating it and resisting it and doing our best to defeat it, we become good. There is no other way. God values our goodness even more than our happiness. Goodness is fundamental. It's what God, who is perfect goodness, values above everything else. Fortunately, the more that people become good, the happier they become. Happiness is a side-effect.

Hawkins: You make it sound as if your God is a heavenly gym instructor. (Laughter.)

Macrina: That's not a bad analogy. I think God designed our world to be a moral gymnasium. We are souls in training. Some athletes like to play teams they can beat, but others prefer stiffer competition. If we're strong, we won't wilt when the "stiffer competition" blasts us–the rejection by the one we love, being passed over at work, the tumor—we'll just fight on. Trusting in God, we'll bear in mind that the greater the suffering, the greater the potential for growth. God has given us a world full of physical and moral challenge. We always have the freedom to choose the good over the bad. A saint is somebody who does it habitually, and I'm in the business of encouraging people, including myself, to become a saint. It's what priests do. It's not beyond even you, Dr. Hawkins. (Macrina, eyes flashing, throws Hawkins a wicked grin, which is followed by short-lived booing mingled with laughter and applause and a brief pause.) When we train well, we bring value and joy into our world. That is what God wants. It's what we should want too. (Light applause.)

Hawkins: I'm touched that you consider me saint material. (Boisterous, lingering laughter.) But one doesn't need to believe in God to become one, at least not the way you describe it. Christians don't have a monopoly on goodness.

Macrina: They certainly don't. But it helps to know that God expects it of them. Atheists don't have anyone pushing them. Most of us need a push. Criminals are usually people who need a push but don't get it. Perhaps you would agree.

Hawkins: I'm afraid not. Three objections stand out. First, what about the glaring differences in starting positions, with some blessed from birth and others cursed? What about all the people who didn't get the push you mentioned? Is your God arbitrary? Does he play favorites? Second, take another look at what you said about prayer. If God wants us to be challenged, if he sees the need for us to suffer for our own eventual good, does it make sense to ask him to remove the challenge, as even Jesus did the night before his death? Third, and most important, the degree of suffering is simply too brutal and horrible and too prevalent to sweep away. Can you put a smiley face on the starvation of children? Isn't that what you are doing?

Macrina (Looking down, not answering right away, praying?): No. But from God's perspective everything that happens on earth makes sense. From our limited perspective, the starvation of any child is a tragedy. But it didn't need to happen. Humanity has the means to prevent it. But it doesn't. And God won't micromanage us out of our self-made tragedies.

He leaves the solution to us. He doesn't intervene. If he did, the whole soul-building project that makes life on earth so challenging and ultimately rewarding would be aborted. God knows what he's doing. (Applause.)....

Greg: In the fall of 2070 Macrina came home for a 10-day visit—she called it a retreat. One of Sophie's friends owned a summer home on Mobile Bay not far from Point Clear, and she offered it to Macrina as a getaway. It came with a wharf that extended out into the Bay. Next door lived a three-year-old girl named Kikki. One day Kikki discovered Macrina sitting at the end of the wharf, and a friendship was struck. I imagine Macrina on a folding chair texting instructions back to Melissa in New York or perhaps just enjoying the sound of the waves slapping against the barnacle-covered piles as Kikki scampers up.

Macrina, Journal: Little Kikki has given me a wonderful topic for a sermon. Most of my story sermons are pure fiction like Jesus' but this one is fact. Connie, Kikki's divorced mother who lives next door, asked me to give her "some basic instruction in religion" if I had a mind to. "It's more than she'll get from me in a lifetime," she said with a laugh. Kikki didn't pick up the first syllable of my name and calls me Crina. I don't correct her.

We are sitting facing west under the open-air hutch at the end of the wharf. A break in the clouds reveals one of the most beautiful sunsets I've ever seen—orange, gold, pink, a streak of deep crimson, and a small patch of green. I can barely make out Mobile in the distance. A motor boat speeds by, and a man in a Hawaiian shirt waves.

"That's Mr. Clark," Kikki tells me. "He comes over sometimes. Mom likes Mr. Clark."

She scrambles over onto my lap and asks me to bounce her on my leg, which I do. She is the right age to be my granddaughter if I had one. She is a precious thing, all innocence, with long lashes sheltering her sparkling brown eyes.

"Kikki," I say, pointing west over the water, "who made that sunset?"

I stop bouncing her as she looks at the sunset. She turns sideways in my lap and says, "The sea goddess?"

"The sea goddess?" Amused, I can't hold back a chuckle. "Why the sea goddess?"

She looks up at me with a wondering, round-eyed smile. "Mom read to me about a sea goddess who killed the sea monster."

I look down at her and feel her love. It's been a long time since I held a child, too long. I feel faintly intoxicated, the way one feels after a particularly long and deep sleep while lying in bed remembering a happy dream.

"No, Kikki, God, not the sea goddess, made the sunset. Kikki, can you tell me who made your mother?"

She looks very puzzled. "Grampa?" She looks up at me with her hopeful, mirthful round eyes.

I stroke one of her loose curls. "No, Kikki, God made your mother too."

"Oh."

"Now, Kikki, can you tell me who made *you*?"

She fidgets with her hands and says nothing.

"Who, Kikki?" I coax. "Who do you think?" She smiles quietly to herself, and I think she might be losing interest in our little game. Then she says, "God made me."

"Yes! God made you. Good! Now, one more question. Are you ready?"

She nods her head somewhat dubiously.

"Who made God?"

She stares at me as if looking for a clue. Then, as if visited by a sudden revelation, she sings out, "You did, Crina!"

I quietly shake with mirth. (I think of Ezra and wish he could be with me.)

"No, Kikki," I say as I stifle a final giggle. "Nobody made

God. God always was."

For the next few days whenever Kikki caught up with me, she wanted to "play God." She learned to answer "God" to every question except the last. "N-o-o-o-body," she would say to the last, her tuneful speech suspended like a hammock. "N-o-o-o-body," I would repeat. And for a little while I would forget all my troubles. Forget that we are still so far away from accomplishing our goal. Dear God, give me patience!

Friends, let us make time to enjoy our children, our spouses, our parents, our relatives, our friends, and all the little Kikkis that drop into our lives.

Greg: None of us who lived through it will ever forget the N5N1 influenza virus that laid waste the earth beginning in February 2071. There were 10.8 billion of us at the time. Two years later only 8.5. I was born during the Lesser Pandemic. I almost died in the Greater.

I don't need to describe the horrifying details. I'll leave it to Macrina, who does it in her Journal and published essays. But a few facts for those too young to remember. The source was an international congress of ornithologists meeting in Bangkok who came into contact with infected birds and flew back to their homes carrying the disease. Overnight it began doing its work at eighteen epicenters all over the globe. The disease was much more virulent than the 2020–21 coronavirus, and it mutated like a thief who steals the young and healthy and leaves no time for mourning or even burial. Some governments had developed and stored broad-based vaccines to fight any virus that showed up, and these were helpful up to a point, but no vaccine could keep up with it. For the dead it was unstoppable. Sixty percent of the infected died. You had a better chance if you had been bitten by a rattlesnake.

Ten countries lost 50% or more of their populations. Overpopulated Nigeria and impoverished Bangladesh became great charnel grounds, with corpses lying densely over the earth as if a great battle had been fought there, with only buzzards and vultures to clean up after the slaughter. Japan and New Zealand, blessed by their island remoteness, lost only 6% and 7% respectively. The U.S. lost 13%, Britain 14%, Mexico 23%. The disease ravaged the obese of any country or race, but it did not spare the robust or even babies. It was like the wrath of God punishing a sinful generation. It changed everything, even the Catholic Church.

Macrina, Journal: After shutting down my church in New York, I came home to be with Mom and Dad and help them any way I could. But Sophie and Greg had already moved them into their own home, and that made six including the kids living under the same roof. People were dying all over Mobile and Prichard, and a call went out for volunteers to help any way they could. It was an easy decision. I told Greg how to handle matters back in New York in case I died. Bless him, he didn't try to dissuade me. At night I came back to my parents' empty house to keep from infecting them....

I remembered Anthony LaCoste, the pastor of Pure Heart of Mary, and went down to the church to see if he was still there after so many years and see if I could be of any help. No, he was long gone but warmly remembered by many, said Fr. Powell, who had never met him. Fr. Powell, a black man in his early 30s and a native of Mobile, was astonished to see a woman offering to go into home and hospital to anoint the sick and dying. "But you're a woman," he said, "and it takes a priest to administer the sacrament." I assured him I was a priest and pastored a Catholic church of my own in New York City. He stared at me unsteadily. "Are you one of those women priests?" I said I was, and he looked me over some more. "By God, these are desperate times." He showed me a list of parishioners and their addresses that he had to see. "Take the top four, I'll take the bottom." He handed me a backup prayer book, a few hosts consecrated by the bishop, and practically shoved me out the door.

Thus I began a ministry to dying African Americans in my home town.

Since the city's hospitals are overwhelmed with patients, I mostly go into homes. I witness horrific suffering, unforgettable struggles both physical and spiritual. Terrible attempts to breathe, 35 to 40 short breaths every minute, complaints of fire in the lungs, of breaths that feel like a swarm of bees stinging inside, or like air being sucked through mud. Terrible headaches that make sleep impossible, delirium leading to agitation, fear, and sometimes anger. Thrashing around or weeping helplessly. Deep depression with the feeling of impending doom. Cries like "I want to die," so great is the pain. The family's indecision over how to help. Their panicky efforts to learn the final wishes of the dying man or woman who left no will. Their confusion over what this white woman in their midst is doing, holds the dying person's hand, and reads from a book. I ask them to step back and ask the dying man if he wants to confess. I tell him I have holy oil to anoint him and the Eucharist if he can swallow. I anoint his forehead and hands with the oil and hold the bread in front of his face so he can see it. It calms him, and there is a hush in the room except for his ghastly rapid breathing as his lungs struggle for life. He can't swallow the host and it drops out of his mouth. A few minutes later he takes his last feeble breath and stares in terror up at the ceiling as bedlam breaks out. I say a prayer for the dead and in tears offer a hug to each of the family members, who by now accept me as some sort of Catholic minister, exactly what they aren't sure. But they are grateful and offer me a drink or a pastry. And I depart. Depart for the next address on my list.

This is the way it is. Except that it's much worse for a child. Especially when a television camera is poking its nose over my shoulder trying to record the doings of the local woman priest. I should never have allowed it though I'm glad I did.

I get a call from Connie, Kikki's mother, who had seen the interview. She says Kikki has caught the virus, and can I come quickly? How strange to see the I-10 causeway crossing the Bay so devoid of traffic. I wonder if my little girl is dying like so many of the others.

Connie's eyes are red as she greets me. She tells me the hospital is overflowing and leads me to Kikki's bedroom. She says a nurse came two hours ago. Kikki, now four, is lying in her bad with a favorite doll and stuffed animals all around her. Distress is written on her face as she coughs and gasps for air. Her eyes bulge with every gasp. I lift the cool cloth from her forehead and feel the fever raging. Her breathing when she isn't coughing is rapid and shallow. She is dying, but I don't admit it.

Her eyes focus on me and she almost smiles. I can tell she knows me. I hold her hand as she tries to tell me something. "God made me," she chokes out with a stricken look. "Grampa came," she whispers two or three breaths later. I look back at her mother. "He died," she mouths.

"Grampa loves you," I say. I hesitate, then add, "He is waiting for you."

"Grampa came," she repeats in a faint, shaky voice, followed by rapid, desperate breaths. I hold her hand and send her all the love I know how. She stares at me and sees the love. Then her face turns on her neck and shakes left and right, as if the effort will bring breath. But it doesn't. She sees the love, and that must be enough. She stares into my face and drifts away from her body. Her dark curls are as beautiful in death as they were in life.

Greg: Two months into her ministry Macrina caught the virus. She refused admittance to a hospital because she would not allow herself to take a bed away from someone without connections and because, as she put it, she was sure she "could beat it." When I reminded her that 60% didn't, she replied that the marriage of a healthy body and "a purpose worth living for"

141

would be sufficient. "But I will need your help." She added that she had suffered too little in life to understand the plight of the common man—"or for that matter Jesus." She felt she would grow from the experience. I told her she was crazy and begged her to reconsider.

She was deathly sick and suffered excruciating headaches. Her lungs were full of mucus and made her feel as if there was a band drawn tightly around her chest that dared her to breathe. She told how the feeling of wanting to die repeatedly tempted her to give up and how she fought it off by remembering the "purpose worth living for."

I washed her naked body, forced her to drink water, placed ice bags on her temple, and went without sleep for two days until the disease, like one of our Gulf hurricanes, finally spent itself. I read aloud passages from Tolstoy's *Confession*, The Epistle of James, and a short biography of St. Macrina, which somehow she had never gotten around to. She finally slept, woke up weak but refreshed, and told me she remembered a quote from Rumi.

"What was it?"

"When did you ever grow less by dying?"

Macrina, email to the Womanpriest Mother House and headquarters in Cleveland, reprinted in most major newspapers: Thank you for your prayers and cards, even from nine of you who have since passed on, God rest them. I am still weak but recovered, back in my parish in New York.

I received what felt like a revelation from on high while the fever was raging through my body. You are all aware of the devastation of our cities. Manhattan and Brooklyn have lost 430,000 between them with the Bronx and Queens not too far behind. You have seen how armies of corpses are being carried to makeshift trenches all over the city wherever unused land is available. You are no doubt aware of how the removal of bodies from homes and hospitals is being carried out. Powerful humanoid robots enter the buildings and pick up the corpses, place them on flatbed trucks, off-load them at the trenches, place them side by side or even on top of each other in the trenches, and cover them with dirt. Living persons are needed only to direct the robots. The whole process is efficient, impersonal, and profane. The city's services are so overwhelmed that this is the only solution. Everyone is horrified. No one has a better idea.

I propose that we sanctify this process. I imagine womanpriests turning these godless burial sites into holy ground. After the tractors and robots have done their job and covered up the hole, leaving behind only yellow barrier tape to mark the scene, let us take a stand. Let us put on our distinctive white bonnets over whatever clothing fits the weather and let the survivors know that their dead have not been forgotten. Let them see that 700 consecrated women are willing to brave the elements and offer prayers for the dead and their families as they stand over these godless places where their beloved dead lie.

I will take the lead in New York, but cities all over the country, even small cities, even towns, are resorting to trench burial. In a few places bodies are being burned en masse like so much refuse. I ask you to get involved wherever you are, all of you who have the strength. If others from other faiths join you, welcome them. And resist all efforts to segregate the bodies according to their religion. In our national cemeteries all are buried side by side, with no care taken to cordon off Christians from Jews or Muslims from Hindus.

You might say that you are needed to care for the dying rather than for the dead. I ask you to consider for a moment that caring for the dying, as I've been doing in Alabama for the last six months, is a most worthy task that goes unnoticed. Remember our goal: Let the Vatican see what we are capable of. Let them see what we have imagined but what our brother priests have not. Let them see our courage as we stand out in the rain or snow or heat. Let them see our rosaries. Let them see our Catholicism. Shame them into lifting the ban against us.

This might be our day, dear sisters. Many of the elderly cardinals have died, and we have a new pope, a young pope, Francis II, whose divorced parents have both remarried outside the church, a Franciscan looking for new ideas, a man looking for ways to stem the tide of defections from our religion. With so many priests all over the world dying, we are needed as never before. Yes, sisters, this is our day....

Greg: As we all know, an exhausted world rallied to Macrina's cause. Almost everywhere leading voices, both inside and outside the Catholic world, condemned the Church's misogyny. "Once upon a time we persecuted women because they were small and couldn't fight our wars, because they had been cursed by God with their menses, and because they couldn't pee standing straight up," wrote the outraged Archbishop of Munich, a newly appointed Cardinal. Caricatures of Vatican "troglodytes" and "ignoramuses" delighted the critics. Memes reached the Vatican in waves.

Pope Francis II declared that women would be trained for the priesthood beginning immediately and that women in the Womanpriest movement would be "outfitted" for immediate ordination at the discretion of their bishops.

The war had been won. Women all over the world marched and sang and gave thanks to God for the long-awaited miracle.

Snippet from an editorial in *The National Review*: What underlay the rather sudden but not altogether surprising elevation of women to the Catholic priesthood?

There can be no doubt that the activism of Sister (now Mother) Macrina McGrath's activism served as a prod. Without the Womanpriest movement that she led, it is possible, some would say likely, that the investiture would have been postponed until the next century. Why, then, did it happen now?

There come times in world history when events are so unsettling and uprooting that whatever is unprotected by universal custom is in danger of giving way. The pandemic that is at last behind us was such an event. We humans are not as a rule rational. When bad things happen to us, we look to the heavens, and the heavens in this instance seem to be punishing an institution that has been teetering for quite a while. The Catholic Church, stubbornly resistant to change, clinging to a revelation permitting no alteration in either doctrine or praxis, has been brought to its knees, though not in the manner it has long encouraged. It has lost 20 percent of its priests in America, both married and unmarried, to the pandemic. This high figure was largely due to the Church's perceived mission of caring for the sick and dying, as Christ commanded, but its heroism did not protect it from the ravages of the virus. In fact it abetted it. Why was this?

It is at this point that human irrationality intrudes. Very few Catholic prelates would claim that the pandemic was God's way of punishing his Church, as Yahweh punished the ancient Israelites when they disregarded his commands, or when he sent the ten plagues to punish the Egyptians. But sneaking unconsciously and irrationally into the picture is a suspicion that God has not been pleased with the Church's obduracy on the question of women priests. This suspicion has been just enough to loosen the Church's hold on its ages-old tradition of female exclusion. The average age of the cardinals before the pandemic was 74, and not all those years of sacred certainty could withstand the qualm, the queasy feeling that God has not been pleased. This uneasiness has cost the Vatican its misplaced confidence in its infallible good sense.There are of course more practical reasons for the Church's reversal. The influx of new married priests has helped to run the parishes, but not nearly to the degree expected. A recent estimate places the total at less than 10 percent. Women are needed to stanch the wounds of a slowly dying Church. Women are needed to baptize babies, memorialize the dead, officiate at marriages, hear confessions, counsel the grief-stricken, preach the gospel, and run the parish. They are needed to consecrate the elements and distribute them to the faithful at Mass....

Video interview on Star Power: Travis Ciccorelli, interviewer: In *The New York Times* you were quoted as saying you resorted to the rosary while doing trench duty in the heat. You said you were too exhausted to be more creative. Yet, you went on to say, you found the strength for one small creative act anyway. What did you mean by that?

Macrina: Oh, that. It's a trifle. I've never been a great fan of the rosary. It has done timeless service over the centuries for countless Catholics, and I always encourage it. But it usually doesn't fit me. During trench duty it did. That was because I lacked the stamina for a focused conversation with God or the saints. So I resorted to the rote prayers of the rosary, the same *Ave Maria* over and over. But I did find the strength to revise the prayer to better fit my needs. Instead of reciting, "Holy Mary, mother of God, pray for us sinners, now and at the hour of our death," I changed it to, "Holy Mary and all you saints, carry these souls into the light of heaven." That's all.

Travis: What about the first half of the prayer?

Macrina: Well, I left it intact. It establishes Mary's credentials as the mother of Jesus. No change needed.

Travis: But you changed the second half. That is quite a revision.

Macrina: I think you'd agree the situation was unusual. What's the point of praying for the dead at the hour of their death when that hour has already passed?

Travis: And you added a whole army of saints to the lonely Mary. She couldn't manage it on her own, I suppose? (Grinning) What is it you said? "All you saints"?

Macrina: That's right. This was my thinking. The dead came from all the major religions of the world, and then some. Would their saints respond to a call placed to a single Christian saint? This great throng of the dead from so many traditions needed all the help they could get. So I broadened the prayer.

Travis: If I may be a bit cheeky, do you actually believe there are saints who hear these prayers? Do Buddhist saints hear this prayer from a Christian priest? Or are all such prayers meant only for consoling the survivors?

Macrina: "A Christian priest." No longer a Christian "womanpriest." Those words are sweet to my ear, and I thank you for them. To your question, yes. Any prayer sent from the heart is heard by beings in the heavens. And now that you mention it, especially by Buddhist saints. Buddhists believe in a bodhisattva of immense power who hears the cries of all suffering souls. He even patrols the hells to bring relief to souls trapped there.

Travis: Your knowledge of traditions outside your own is impressive.

Macrina: I was once a professor of Asian religions. It's to be expected. Nothing special.

Travis: There is one thing more. You leave out a reference to Mary as the "mother of God."

Macrina: As I say, Mary's credentials are established in the first half of the *Ave*. She is the mother of Jesus.

Travis: But not of God?

Macrina: Theological niceties are not the point of the prayer. The point is to get help for the newly dead....

Vance Huskinz, email written to a friend and sympathizer: Macrina McGrath is a Trojan Horse in the City of God. Her good friend Archbishop Cullen said she was worthy of being a bishop, "the first in the history of the church." That would be the horse. The heresies that issue from her mouth would be the soldiers who sack the city, i.e., the Church.

Did you see her interview on Star Power? Ciccorelli was

brilliant. All he had to do was ask the right questions, and she destroyed herself with her own sword. Can you imagine desecrating the Hail Mary like she did? Doesn't that defy belief? She called the Mother of God "a theological nicety." She's willing to grant that Mary is the mother of Jesus, but waffles about her being the mother of God. What could that mean? Tell me, Kenny, what does that mean? To me it means she doesn't think Jesus is God. But she doesn't have the courage to come out and say it. Instead she covers up her blasphemy with that business about calling out to the saints. And that is the second horror. She calls out to the saints of *all* the religions, as if they're all equivalent to each other, as if St. Augustine is no better than that weird Buddhist whatever he is. Yet she thinks of herself as a Catholic. And a priest. And if Cullen has his way, a future bishop. God help us!

This woman belongs in hell, not in a diocesan cathedral. It's the likes of her that is destroying the Church. She's the kind that the good Catholic faithful should run from.

Have you read anything about what she believes on reincarnation? She seems to be buddy-buddy with Hindus, and you know what they believe. I would have no objection to the woman if she would just go away and start her own religion, but to claim she is a Catholic is an outrage. Confusing people with all her free-thinking rot—go away, witch, I say!

And God knows what she's got going with Cullen. And everybody knows she had a child out of wedlock. At least she admits that.

I love our Church, Kenny. You know how I love it. Where are the voices that should renounce this woman? I feel so helpless. Who will listen to me? I'm just a humble deacon in a rundown church in south Brooklyn. I brought up my concerns to the pastor and he counseled me to keep it to myself. And can you believe he's hired a female priest to beef up the membership among Hispanics?

Macrina, paper Journal: Come, Master, come, and fill me wholly with thyself. Still my mind, reach into my heart, change me. The whole universe is within you and you in it. In my very soul you dwell, yet I cannot find you. Why? You do not come and go. You are always present. Yet I do not feel your presence this night. I long to serve you, Master, to be cherished by you as your obedient, humble child. Nothing will give me rest and joy except the infinity that you are. With St. Teresa of Avila I yearn to "swim across the sea of life breasting its rough waves joyfully." But those same waves only buffet and toss me. Come, Master, come, and fill me wholly with thyself....

Greg: Vance Huskinz was more than a deacon working *pro bono* at a church that couldn't afford to pay him. He ran a prosperous small-business electrical appliance and repair store not far from the church. The message sent to his friend surfaced only a few months ago when investigators did a more thorough search of his email. At the time he was fresh off a third divorce and was in a custody battle with his second wife. He was 43 years old.

Somehow he learned that Macrina had scheduled a meeting with Archbishop Cullen at his residence next to the Cathedral and managed to talk his way into it. He guessed that the meeting would take place in the parlor, spacious and beautifully furnished, with valuable religious paintings hanging on its dark blue walls, and bugged it. The digital audio tape that follows was discovered at the same time as the letter above to his friend. Why Huskinz didn't reveal it to appropriate authorities remains a mystery to me. Did he have a change of heart? Was he moved by Macrina's humble earnestness as she poured out her heart to Cullen? We'll probably never know.

Macrina and Cardinal Joseph (Joe) Cullen, digital audio tape:
Joe: Wonderful to see you, Macrina…. (They chat about practical concerns: Muslims want to buy Macrina's church; Macrina can't afford to hire a second priest assistant; the Archbishop has just learned of a new sex scandal in the Albany diocese; they talk of taking a ride over the new Staten Island bridge just for the fun of it, etc.)

Macrina: Now that we've achieved our goal, I'm a bit at a loss. Most of my energy was given over to getting women ordained as priests, and now that it's happened, what next? When I next get invited to give a talk, what do I say? I could use some guidance, and of course I thought of you.

Joe: (Pause) Well, there's enough work right in your parish to keep you busy until the end of your days. You've won the fight, Macrina. You can put your sword back into the scabbard. You can rest. How does that sound?

Macrina: (Long pause) Frankly, it sounds boring. It's not me. That would mean accepting the status quo, and the Church needs changing. It'll always need changing, like everything else in the world.

Joe: *People* need changing. Let's not forget that. Sometimes they just want things to remain the same.

Macrina: Yes, they do. And for most priests that's enough. But not for me.

Joe: Okay. So you'd like to see some more changes. What would you like to see? You're known all over the world. You have a reputation that makes people look to you for guidance. What do you want to tell them?

Macrina: I don't know. That's what I'm asking you. What do *you* think needs changing? I have my laundry list but don't know how to get started. Actually it's more than a laundry list. It's closer to a mission statement.

Joe: Aha! So you *do* know what you'd like to do. Well, run it by me. Let's take a look.

Macrina: For me, ever since graduate school, three areas have stood out whenever you evaluate a religion: God, afterlife, and accountability. The closer to reality you get these, the more attractive the religion and the more likely it'll grow rather than shrink. And Catholicism has been losing its base for quite a while now, not only from the pandemic, which was bad enough, but from factors it can correct. God, freedom, and accountability — no religion has them all right, but some do better than others. On the whole Christianity doesn't do a bad job. More exactly, Catholic Christianity, the religion you and I love. But it could do better.

Joe: I'm glad to hear you say that. You're in a better position to judge than anyone I know. Very few of us can be objective. Mostly because we were born to Catholic parents —

Macrina: As was I. But anyone who knows history, especially ancient Roman history, won't miss the contrast between Jesus and Caesar. Thank God for Jesus!

Joe: Indeed.

Macrina: Let's get back to the Big Three.

Joe: Starting with God, I assume?

Macrina: Starting with Jesus. Or rather, both together. I'm not boring you, am I?

Joe: Good heavens, no. I feast on such questions.

Macrina: Is that your cat?

Joe: Yes, that's Gertrude. I think she likes you.

Macrina: Cats usually do. (Pause.) Anyway, Jesus. Jesus and God. I worry about how big or small God is — whether he's the creator of the universe or just, maybe, the guardian of our planet with a pipeline to the creator. After all, in Jesus' day God was tiny by our standards — it was much easier to think of God caring about every man and woman, especially every Jewish man and woman, and not much else. You could feel very special back then, but not now. Now it's hard. The universe is too big. Even the size of earth is enormous compared to the way the ancients saw it.

I have a hard time relating to the creator of the universe, and that's why I pray to the saints. I feel loved by a few of them. They have my back, so to speak. I go to them for help. But when I meditate, I like to think I find God in my deepest depths. I like to think I'm a spark or splinter or particle of God, and that the best prayer happens when I quietly sink down into those quiet depths. I know you use Centering Prayer, and so do I. That's when I make contact with the personal God that I am willing to consider the creator and master of the universe, a being both male and female, the eternal Mother as well as Father.

That brings me to the Trinity. If Jesus had lived today, do you think he would have thought of God as masculine only? Not in these times. Not a chance. And thank God! And do you think that the bishops of tomorrow would come up with the same formula they came up with back in 325 at Nicaea? Not a chance. They'd have come up with something entirely different. That's the Trinity we need today. Would you like to entertain one woman's crazy ideas?

Joe: (Laughter.) Sure. Why not?

Macrina: Sit back a minute and try to forget everything you ever heard about the Christian God. Forget you've been told that the primordial relationship is between Father and Son, the coequal creators of the universe. Think for a moment how strange that sounds. What has ever been born from the sterile union of Father and Son? If the universe had any parents at all, they must have been its Father and Mother, not its Father and Son. Think of them living in an eternal relationship of mutual love. But our Trinity makes no mention of a Mother—or a Daughter. How strange. How very strange, Joe. Do you see it? A revised Trinity would place the primordial relationship between Father and Mother.

Joe: And Jesus would be the third person?

Macrina: No. The universe would be the third person. Or

rather the Holy Spirit dwelling within the universe. Do you see how stupendous this would be? The whole material universe is the creation of the primordial Father and Mother, all of it sacred. Think of the Big Bang as the moment when the universe emerged from the cosmic womb. And, like all children, it's been growing ever since. It's been growing into the immense thing that it is, filled with little persons like you and me made in the image of their Mother and Father on planets too numerous to count. This is a creation worthy of an infinite deity. Nothing less will do in this scientific age. Imagine the reception it would get from thoughtful people once they got used to it. Imagine, Joe.

Joe: Interesting. Very interesting.

Macrina: Go even further. Think of Mother and Father as the soul of the universe. Think of the universe as the body of its parents, the literal body—an immense body housing an immense Being, a Mother and Father expressing themselves in us—as male and female made in their image, as the first book of Genesis says. Finite beings like us are spread out in worlds all across the universe. This indwelling activity is what we mean by the Holy Spirit, the Third Person. Father, Mother, and Holy Spirit, there is your Trinity.

Joe: Well, this is all quite wonderful; it's stupendous as an imaginative exercise, but where is Jesus in all this? Where is Christianity? We view Jesus as God's unique incarnation, not the universe.

Macrina: The universe would be God's first incarnation, Jesus the second. For us Christians Jesus is the grandest, the noblest, the best and holiest incarnation the planet has ever seen. You wouldn't get too much of an argument from our best minds on that score.

Joe: But he's not God.

Macrina: Why not? God dwells in Jesus, as in all of us, as I've said. But he is set apart from us because the Holy Spirit shines through him in a manner that's unique—think of his transfiguration on Mount Tabor. You might say he represents the planet's most advanced human specimen, humanity's supreme achievement. But he's the second incarnation, not the first. The universe is the first. We are right to celebrate his incarnation at Christmas and his death and resurrection on Good Friday and Easter. He has shown us how to live. He's made clear the price we must pay when we live well. Along with Jews, persecution has been our way for as long as the religion has existed. The greater the light, the deeper the shadow.

Joe: Though we've done our share of persecuting, sad to say.

Macrina: True enough.

Joe: So the First Person of the Trinity is the Father, the Second is the Mother, and the Third is the Universe. Is that what you are saying?

Macrina: The Holy Spirit *in* the universe.

Joe: (Pause Jesus, Macrina, do you want to put this out in public space for serious consideration? (grim laughter)

Macrina: I do, ardently I do. But I know I can't. I profoundly believe in this vision, this updated vision. This science-friendly, psychologically sound vision would make for a better Church in the long run, but I know the Church wouldn't be willing to consider such a proposal during my lifetime. If I were to publish it, I'd lose all the credibility I've built up.

Joe: You'd be persecuted. Most people don't like change. For them the humdrum sameness of our rituals is what they want. They prefer its beautiful banality to the dazzling experiment you offer.

Macrina: Those that stay in the Church do. What about those who flee its boredom—its beautiful banality, as you call it. They *do* want change. But you have a point. The unadventurous parishioner is our clientele, and it's with them we have to work. What would you advise me to do? What would you do if you were me?

Joe: I would keep it to myself. Personally I don't think it matters much how we parse the Trinity as long as we keep God and Jesus in it. Remember, you're a pastor first, then a theologian, or should be. You don't want to give scandal to your congregation.

Macrina: But—

Joe: It's not in your nature, I know, to follow a system that doesn't make good sense. I know that. And that's a great strength in the long run. The Church needs creative solutions, God knows it does.

Macrina: But you don't like this particular solution.

Joe: The Church isn't ready for it, Macrina. Go more slowly.

Macrina: I take it you wouldn't care to hear my views on reincarnation.

Joe: Sure I would. That's much more negotiable. Forty percent of our hispanics already believe in it anyway, or say they do in the polls. And the Church hasn't made an official statement about it since the sixth century. Let's save that for our next visit. I have to drive up to Albany Wednesday. Maybe we can drive up together. Can you get free? I'd like you to see what's going on in that hornets' nest and meet the retiring bishop....

Macrina, Journal: A hot, stagnant morning with the smell of soot in the air. I was walking my usual route toward the Battery when I noticed a policeman in the alley between two buildings looking up and talking to someone I couldn't see. His voice sounded like an appeal. My curiosity aroused, I couldn't resist walking up the alley to take a look. Standing a little behind him so he couldn't see me, I gathered what was happening. An elderly woman six or seven stories up had draped herself over the railing of the wrought-iron fire escape. One leg was hanging perilously over the railing. The policeman was exhorting her to step back; he told her she was in danger of falling (as if she didn't know) and that help was on the way. The woman did not step back. Instead she began bobbing left and right. I could tell she was trying to gather the courage to jump.

When he noticed me, he told me to back away. I told him I was a priest and asked him to let me talk to the woman until the right kind of help arrived. He hesitantly gave permission.

Different thoughts raced through my mind as I studied her. I looked at her, bedraggled and wearing her bed clothes, and imagined a woman unwanted by anyone. Maybe she was too frightened to come out of her apartment during the pandemic and lost contact with her loved ones, or maybe she lost them to death. I didn't have time to ask but used these thoughts to begin a dialogue.

"I want to know your story," I began as I craned my neck upward. "I want you to tell me your story. Can I come up? We can have a conversation. I have been lonely, and I'll tell you how I survived. Let me come up. Tell me the number of your apartment. Let's have a cup of coffee, a good long cup of coffee."

I thought about telling her I was a priest, even about what to expect if she jumped. But if she were not religious, that could be fatal. All I dared do was offer her my love. Give her my attention. Listen.

My strategy wasn't working. Now neither foot touched the ground. She had managed to get her whole overweight body on top of the rail and looked as if the lightest breeze might be enough to topple her over the edge. She reminded me of a nickel standing on its edge. I saw her eyes looking down at the concrete below, trying to find the courage to jump, dreading what it would be like if she did. I had watched countless people die, but never a suicide.

I decided to risk telling her I was a priest, even that I was Mother Macrina, when the policeman, who had left me, stepped out onto the fire escape and moved toward her. Just as he was about to grab her, she let go and wobbled over the railing. She fell without uttering a sound. Her body whomped onto the ground a few yards from where I stood. A wig lay on the concrete next to her smashed bald head, which had begun to bleed. In shock I knelt at her side and asked if she could hear me, which of course she could not. I had no oil to anoint her; all I could do was place my palm on her forehead and pray the prayer for the dead. I got up when two paramedics rushed up and brushed me aside. Nauseous, I left the scene and walked home, my thoughts filled with death.

I wonder what drove her to do it. The wig suggested chemotherapy. Or was it vanity? Had she fought hard to avoid a death sentence from the plague only to arrive at this? And what was she feeling now? And what will I be feeling when it's my turn, however I arrive?

And could I have saved her if the policeman had not intervened? I don't know.

Greg: This account of a suicide was written months after the scene about to unfold. I placed it here because it raises the question of death and afterlife in a dramatic way. You will recall that Macrina's visit with the Archbishop had been secretly recorded on an audio tape. The same tape ran for weeks before being detected and was full of extraneous conversation and noise in addition to the conversations we are interested in. Days or weeks after their first meeting they met again, apparently after they had traveled north together to visit the bishop of Albany, and the following conversation was also recorded. She is about 53 years old at the time. He is 75.

Macrina and Cardinal Joseph (Joe) Cullen, digital audio tape:
Macrina: I think we have to make peace with reincarnation. There is no good reason not to. Half the world already believes it. And there is empirical evidence that it happens. There are thousands of cases archived at the University of Virginia. Kids describe their previous life, and their memories fit specific individuals they claim to have been. There are well researched books I can refer you to. These cases don't suggest that everyone

reincarnates but only that some do. I have no attachment to the doctrine. It doesn't excite me to think I was my great grandfather Charles in a previous life, and I most surely don't want to come back for another life to relearn my ABCs and the multiplication tables. But evidence is evidence. We shouldn't be afraid to face it. We should make room for it.

Joe: To me it makes no sense to say I was someone else in a previous life. We are an incarnational religion and place emphasis on that single incarnation. The body counts; it has a lot to do with who we are; we are more than a spiritual soul.

Macrina: I agree that it's an odd fit. But if it were true, it wouldn't change Jesus' gospel at all. We'd still be required to love God with all our heart and mind and soul, and our neighbor as ourselves. If we didn't, we might have to come back to earth for another try, that's all. Personally, I prefer the idea of purgatory as the best means for readying myself for entry into heaven. But I'm not going to quibble with God if he has other ideas. Anyhow, if reincarnation exists, that doesn't mean purgatory doesn't. It doesn't nullify purgatory. Purgatory is either a preparation needed for entry into heaven, just as Catholics have always believed, or it's a preparation for the next incarnation. In both cases it exists, though I'd prefer to call it the World of Spirit or, more simply, the Spirit World. The only thing new about this way of thinking is that some souls are better served by a return to earth—you might say it gets earth's pleasures out of the way so they can yearn for something better. And it makes earth life essential, which I believe is God's plan. Reincarnation makes room for little children, even infants, who otherwise would escape life on earth with all its challenges. They would get another chance to experience all that you and I enjoy and suffer, and that is no small thing. Reincarnation introduces certain perplexities, I agree, but it removes others. Personally I think that what it removes is more important than what it introduces. Anyway, we can't escape the empirical evidence. The Catholic

Church must stop running from evidence it doesn't like.

Joe: (long pause) I think it weakens our belief that Christ is our salvation. We can't afford to waffle on that. To give souls all the chances they need to get it right trivializes Jesus' gospel. It suggests that given enough time we'll eventually get it right without his help. It takes away the urgency of getting it right here and now—in this one and only life.

Macrina: I think you make a good point. But it's not the last word. Take the example of marriage. More than half Americans fail at their first marriage, and many fail at their second or third. But there is always the next, and thank God for that. Most of us need more than one chance. The ideal is of course a single, long, happy marriage. Just as the ideal is a single life on earth followed by a brief stay in purgatory and then heaven. That's the ideal, but what's the reality? What's the reality for most of us? I see reincarnation as God's mercy flowing down upon us. We even get to forget all the stupid things we did in our pervious life. Those terrible memories don't haunt us—except in the cases of those little kids, most of whom remember how they died. What a blessed arrangement for most of us!

Joe: So you don't grant me the point that reincarnation trivializes Jesus' mission?

Macrina: For me, *trivialize* is not the right word. I would say that the possibility of reincarnation—of second, third, and fourth chances—tempers it, softens it, you might even say humanizes it. If you don't do this, what do you end up with? We well know. We end up with eternal hell for a single serious screw-up. We end up being crippled by a religion of fear, the religion my great grandfather grew up with. That puts too much urgency on getting it right the first and only time. Eternal hell is an inhuman doctrine. I see reincarnation as a liberating alternative. It makes God more merciful; it loads up Jesus' teachings with mercy, and that isn't bad. It's not my first choice, but I'd love to see the Church lift the edict against it.

Joe: (long pause, followed by a chuckle.) You've almost convinced me. But you'd never convince the Vatican.

Macrina: I don't hope to convince them, just make them think. Maybe go back and take another look at that sixth-century edict and stop making arbitrary claims it can't support. I'm not saying the Church ought to turn Hindu and adopt reincarnation as an official position, only that it ought to allow the faithful to believe in it if they find it plausible. How stupid would it be if we told all those Catholics who already believe in it they are no longer Christian and ought to hunt for another religion? What, after all, does believing or not believing in reincarnation have to do with loving God and neighbor and forgiving one's enemy? Joe, in the final analysis, all I want for the Church is to stop making claims it can't support and that even fly in the face of evidence. I want it to be truly catholic, eager to discover truth from which ever direction it cones, ready to change when it must.

Joe: Be careful. You might end up with nothing left standing.

Macrina: I think we'd end up with the essentials standing.

Joe: Macrina, I would never try to silence you. But I must ask you to be realistic. We don't usually get all we want in this life. If you're going to make changes in our hoary old Church, you must go slowly. You must tiptoe into the shallows, not rush into the breakers. The Church could use you—it already has—and it could accept further guidance if you don't rush. In fact you can do great work in the Church if you practice patience. (Pause.) Macrina, I brought you up to Albany for a purpose. I intend to nominate you as its next bishop—the first woman in the 2,000-year history of the Church—but I must be assured that you will move ahead cautiously. And that means softening your views—not bottling them up, but softening them—on reincarnation especially.

Macrina: (Pause) Wow! (Further pause) Wow! Joe, I am profoundly honored... I... forgive me. (sniffling, weeping in background) I... I am overcome. (Further sniffling)

Joe: Take your time.

Macrina: I don't know what to say.

Joe: How about saying you accept the nomination?

Macrina: Yes, of course I do. Nothing could be better for the cause of women than this. I thank you over and over. Not just for me, but for all women. It's unbelievable.

Joe: Did you not guess what I brought you up to Albany for?

Macrina: Not at all.

Macrina, Online Journal: Arrived in Osaka a week ago with Anna to hike the Kumano Kodo, the ancient Buddhist and Shinto pilgrim trails through the rugged mountains in the peninsula south of Kyoto, and visit her parents. July is not the best time to visit these regions. The climate is hot and steamy, like Mobile's. But at least we have these beautiful forested mountains to ourselves—one day we came across only three other hikers. And on the third day it rained all day long—a warm rain that drenched us to the bone and left our soggy maps almost unreadable. But we welcomed the cool.

Anna usually took the lead. We didn't say much since the trails were usually too narrow to permit us to walk side by side. And that was the way we liked it. I tried to imagine the thoughts of those ancient monks as they trudged along with little to guide them except the stars, or small wooden shrines devoted to a particular deity, or stones piled up to commemorate the spot where a fellow monk succumbed to sickness, starvation, or bad weather. Now we have milestones and even steps to help us navigate those slopes. We carry food prepared for us at the inn we stayed at the night before. But the trees, especially those massive cedars that watch over us, are the same. The ancient Japanese imagined gods, or kami, everywhere, each tree alive and attentive. And I could almost feel the activity in their ancient souls as the wind whirred gently through their upper branches.

The wildness of these mountains felt visceral. I thought of Ezra and how he would love it.

On the fourth and last day as we arrived at an overlook after a long climb, we sat to rest and eat our lunch. We gazed out at rank after rank of mountains to the north, the most distant ones vanishing into the hazy purple distance. My heart swelled with the grandeur of God's world. I tried to describe my feeling to Anna, hoping she felt the same, but the conversation took a surprising turn.

Sparrows chirp in the twilight as we rest after our meal in this family-run ryokan, which we have all to ourselves. Anna is reading in the next room. I don't want to forget what she told me, as much in her own words as possible. I must take it to heart and reflect on it. I must never forget it.

It began with what seemed like an innocent remark. "Mother, everything about you is so grand, so big. You are happy with broad vistas."

"Of course I am."

"I like these mountains too, but you get more out of them. There is something about you that makes me think of eternity. You are a little scary."

"I am all ears."

"I can't imagine you tying yourself down to raising a kid. I can see how you gave me up for adoption. I finally understand it."

I told her once more that I did it for her, that I wasn't ready to marry, that I wanted her to have a father, that I would stay in touch at a distance and not let my love get in the way of loving her adoptive parents. It had nothing to do with bigness.

"I've thought about this a lot. There is something about this that doesn't make sense. I don't think you've faced up to the real reason. And I can't quite forgive you until you do."

I listen in alarm and rising anger at being so grossly misunderstood, even by my own daughter. I have tried so hard. I have always done what was best for her. But now this. I notice a dragonfly buzzing around my head. The mountains are forgotten. I don't interrupt.

"What motivated you to give me up? I think I know. Yes, the reasons you give are all true, but they all take a back seat to the one thing that underlies them all. Ambition. You're an ambitious woman. You need to be noticed, praised, even lionized (that was her exact word). You gave me up because you knew I would get in the way of your ambition. I want you to look into your heart, deep into your heart, and acknowledge this. And I want you to apologize to me."

I let her go on. Her face is red with emotion.

"Yeah, I'd like an apology. I was raised on a small island overrun with American troops and humble Japanese people famous for their long lives and not much else. My life would have been so different if you had raised me. You would have found a way to make it all come out right—for both of us."

I tell her I seriously doubt that.

"Even if you hadn't, even if your ambition was thwarted, even if you suffered because you had to settle for an obscure career as a teacher or something else, isn't that what Christians are supposed to be good at? Christ's life is all about rejection, suffering, and death. You haven't tasted any of the agonies and tragedies of life. There is something hypocritical about your climb to fame."

I defend myself. I tell her I never sought fame. Fame just came my way. And now that it's come, I use it to further the cause of female equality in the Church.

"You're a month or two away from becoming a bishop. You should turn it down and be a humble parish priest. Just sink into obscurity and serve ordinary people. There is nothing I would admire more. That would amount to the apology I seek. Your suffering would atone for the suffering you brought me."

This comment hits me in the gut. She actually wants me to

suffer, my only child wants me to suffer. I face more honestly the truth about what I did. I rejected her, the fruit of my womb. I rejected her. Why did I do this? Was it really that I wanted her to have a father? Or was it something else? Was it that—I hate to admit it—that she would get in the way? In the way of what? Future fame? No. What then? Just whatever opportunity came along, whatever it might be? I don't know. But I suddenly feel the enormity of what I did. It wasn't a purely noble act but was laced with selfishness. What suffering have I brought to this child of mine? What if my mother had done this to me? I still think her conclusion misses the great complexity, the tortured analysis that went into my decision, but this was no time for fine points.

"Anna," I say, "I understand. I never thought of it this way. Thank you for making me understand." Seated on the straw with the mountains witnessing the moment, I take her hand and ask her forgiveness. She pulls it away and looks out over the vista with lips drawn tightly.

On the way to the Coast and Nachi Falls, Japan's tallest waterfall and the site of unnumbered suicides down through the centuries, the trail widened. As we walked side by side down the steep slope, I tried to reason with her further. I told her I couldn't give up my life's mission, not even for her. She asked if in my opinion Jesus would have allowed himself to be a bishop. I used his ride into Jerusalem on a donkey to argue that he was not opposed to leadership. Anna answered tersely that he was only bowing to the wishes of his followers.

Greg: I was determined to learn how Macrina's appointment went, and Archbishop Curran was my most helpful source. About two months ago he gave me an interview. He overcame his scruples regarding confidentiality because of its historic importance—in his opinion the public had a right to know.

Curran was shocked by the resistance to her nomination, which he personally put forward and argued strongly for.

He said he misplayed the entire process, which he descried as a debacle. The retiring bishop's highly regarded personal secretary, Father Herb Constantine, was the clear favorite of the bishops making up Curran's province, and they expected him to get the nomination. When Curran put forward Macrina's name, his bishops were reluctant at first to object, but they gathered courage as one, then another, questioned her credentials. No one dared say what really concerned them: that she was a woman. Their main expressed objection was that she had no experience outside parish ministry; therefore she couldn't be expected to know how to run a diocese. When Curran replied that he didn't see that as a deficit, but an asset, they objected that she had no training in canon law: she hadn't gotten her graduate degree at the North American College in Rome, but at Georgetown, where her primary training had been in Asian religions and Sanskrit, not Christianity and Latin. Others questioned her orthodoxy, especially her "irresolute position" on Mary's virginity. When one bishop questioned her "unusual personal credentials," which everyone understood to be her child out of wedlock, Curran exploded, yelled out "you fucking Pharisees!" and walked out of the meeting.

The bishops thought it prudent to add her name to the *terna,* the mandated three names sent to the papal nuncio, from there to the Vatican's Congregation for Bishops, and then to the pope for ratification. They ranked him first and Macrina third, giving their reasons in detail.

When Macrina returned from Japan, he despondently told her that the Catholic Church was not ready for a female bishop and that she should seek a position outside the archdiocese where she was "less misunderstood." He imagined her as bogging down in some large parish church where her exceptional leadership skills would be untapped and history set back half a century. He regarded the Church's failure as a crushing blow and took it personally. He later admitted there was nothing he or anyone else could have said to change the rankings in the nomination.

What happened next was utterly unexpected.

Pope Francis II, electronic news release from *Vatican News*: These are unsettling times for the Catholic Church and indeed for all peoples of the earth. The pandemic cost our planet 21% of its human population, and the Church has suffered a similar loss. The last three years have been a time of tumultuous reexamination. What do we need to do differently, not only in preparation for the next world catastrophe, but in all things? That was the question we asked ourselves.

We are all aware of the revolutionary leap forward in our Church regarding the ordination of women as priests. St. Francis's beloved companion, St. Clare, must have danced for days in the lighted halls of heaven when she saw what the cardinals dared to do. The proudest moment of my reign was its ratification.

Every day I am asked to ratify the nominations of bishops — such is the number of new appointments from all over the world, last year almost 400. Much thought, collaboration, and prayer go into the process, and in almost every instance I accept the recommendations as they are presented to me.

Two weeks ago in the archdiocese of New York, a vote was taken for the position of Bishop of Albany. Our sister in Christ Macrina McGrath was among the three nominated for the position. As many of you know, she led the struggle for female equality in the Catholic priesthood. That struggle has already borne much fruit, with more of the faithful retuning to our Church where women are in charge than where men are. Consequently I was more than a little curious when the nuncio presented me with the bishops' recommendations. To my surprise, I found that Mother Macrina was ranked last.

When I was a young Catholic boy growing up in England, I was delighted that an Argentine had won the papacy. His devotion to St. Francis led to a similar devotion in me, and that is why I chose my present name. One of the most memorable points that the first Pope Francis made, one that struck me as unquestionably correct when I was a little older, was that the Church's shepherds should carry the "smell of the sheep" with them wherever they go. He meant that a priest's first job is always the care of souls. That care is achieved best at the parish level.

In the analysis presented to me by the nuncio, the main argument against Mother Macrina as bishop of Albany was that she had no experience at the upper levels of Church administration. Instead, her ministry had been spent entirely at the parish level. In other words, she smelled like a sheep. Rather than a weakness, I viewed that as a positive strength—a strength missing in most of the cardinals I work with.

It is time for a change in our beloved old Church. For as long as I am pope, no priest will be appointed bishop unless he or she has spent a minimum of three years at the parish level caring for souls. The same goes for archbishops and cardinals. If I live for another ten years, that minimum will be raised to five. As a first stab at this much needed reform, I have appointed Mother Macrina McGrath Bishop of Albany. I look forward to her installation at the Cathedral of the Immaculate Conception in Albany sometime early next year.

Greg: A snowstorm kept the attendance down for the installation, but every news outlet was present. Archbishop Cullen, the main consecrator, gave a history of the cathedral from its beginnings more than 200 years ago, when the original building rose to meet the needs of immigrants fleeing Ireland's potato famine. He then launched into Macrina's accomplishments, highlighting her crucial contribution to the Womanpriest movement. Then followed the nine questions to ascertain whether the candidate was qualified for the job—a formality. I wondered how she interpreted the third of the questions: "Will you maintain without change the deposit of faith passed down from the Apostles?" She was certainly no conservative! Meanwhile snow beat down in clumps on the stately Gothic church, its gorgeous warm interior holding out against the elements rattling the stained glass windows situated between the buttresses. Did the weather symbolize the heavy challenges that would face her in this secular post-Christian city where "spirituality" polled high and Catholicism ranked near the bottom?

The motto of her ministry came from St. Paul's letter to the Corinthians: "from glory to glory." Her coat-of-arms showed a quarter of the sun with rays shooting out in broad streaks, with the motto emblazoned at a slant on one of the rays. The miter covering her head was not the traditional red hat worn by bishops-elect down through the centuries but the white bonnet she and her fellow womanpriests wore as heretics standing sentry at the pandemic burial trenches just four years ago. The symbolism was not missed by the press. It was a spectacular moment for Catholic women and for women generally.

There was work to be done. Within the first week she scanned the unabridged ledger of priests in the diocese accused of sexual misconduct. Dealing with this issue would become her highest priority, followed closely by her outreach toward men, especially young men who had left the Church or never thought about joining it. She consulted with me often during her ministry in Albany. We grew closer.

In her second month she traveled to Kerala in India to recruit womanpriests for her churches. A stopover in Ghana led to an African hire. She chose more men than women to work under her as assistant priests at the cathedral.

To protect herself and the diocese against lawsuits, she recorded conversations she had with priests accused of misconduct, four altogether. Three she had to denounce and let go after their offenses and their implausible denials were exposed in the *Times Union*, Albany's newspaper. She reached out to the Vatican for help, and the Vatican sold off still more of its art treasure to cover the sins of its disgraced American sons that insurance would not cover.

The fourth priest presented her with a painful moral challenge, one that cost her much sleep. In what follows we see her heart colliding with her sense of duty. I've changed the name of the individual and made other slight alterations to disguise his identity. But the nature of his crimes and Macrina's deliberations remain unaltered. As you might imagine, it wasn't easy gaining access to this information. I'm not exactly proud of what I had to do.

Macrina and Fr. Wilbur Quiñones, voice recording:

Macrina: Wilbur, I, uh, I've called you in to discuss your crimes—you admit to them, and I thank you for that—and what we're going to do about the situation. I should tell you straight out that I haven't made up my mind. Twelve years have passed since the last of them, or at least the last I know of, and you've performed your duties commendably, or at least without anyone's complaint, since Bishop Clyde moved you from your former parish to your present. As far as I know, we are lucky, extremely lucky, that no rumors have been floating around between the parishes, and very little even in the parish where the damage was done. Most important, the press hasn't picked it up. Are you aware of this?

Wilbur: Yes, that's my understanding too.

Macrina: First of all, I want to describe the crimes as they've been documented in the records. Feel free to correct or elaborate.

Wilbur: Okay.

Macrina: It says here that your victims were two altar boys and a friend of one of them. Is that right?

Wilbur: Yes.

Macrina: The acts took place in the sacristy after Mass, one child at a time. Though in the case of the friend, you met with him at other times, but always in the sacristy. The kids were never together. In fact the two altar boys knew nothing of what was happening to the other. Apparently they were too embarrassed to talk about it.

Wilbur: Yes, I'm afraid that's correct.

Macrina: One of the fathers overheard his son, about 18 at the time, now in his early 30s, reminiscing about it with his friend. They were in the garage trying to make sense of it. That's when he called the Bishop. And that's when the cover-up started.... I want to read to you what you wrote for the record. This is how you summarized what you did and what later happened. You also wrote a brief summary of your early childhood. We'll start with that. I want to make sure it's accurate, that you don't need to make a change.

Wilbur: Okay.

Macrina: You wrote, "I was sexually molested by an uncle when I was five or six, and I watched my father brutally beat my mother. This led to her being placed in an asylum and me and my brother and sister being taken to an orphanage run by nuns. While there I learned to love the beautiful Mass and Benediction services. At 18 I entered the seminary and was ordained nine years later. By then I realized I was gay but didn't tell anyone. I hardly admitted it to myself. I've served in two parishes since then, the last as pastor."

You then describe your crimes.

"It began with innocent tickling and then progressed to touching, rubbing, and massaging. These were lewd acts, but the boys didn't seem to mind. They were just innocent kids. They hadn't reached puberty and didn't really understand what was going on. I stressed how important it was not to talk about it to anyone and that it would be a serious sin if they did. I started giving them little gifts and money to keep them coming back and keep them quiet. When nothing seemed to go wrong and they didn't seem to mind what we did, I moved ahead into more serious play. I dared to go so far as oral sex. It never progressed beyond that point. After about six months I had a crisis of conscience and never repeated those abominations. I realized I had thrown my faith and the very foundation of all I'd considered to be my spiritual self-identity into a cavern deep within the recesses of my frozen soul. A truly frightening realization came over me that I was not really who I thought I was; that I should never have become a priest of the Church of our Lord Jesus, and that I was not what I had hoped to become and never would be. I felt that I was nothing of worth. I sensed that I had no special qualities. My ministry had been an utter and absolute failure, the priesthood entirely a mistake. I was scared to death because I was lost and I knew it. I was horrified by what I did and afraid I would be found out. I seriously considered the possibility that I was being manipulated by a lewd spirit." Does that correctly sum it up?

Wilbur: Yes (spoken in a voice broken with remorse).

Macrina: Wilbur, look at me. Have you ever repeated those acts over the last 12 years?

Wilbur: No.

Macrina: Not even once?

Wilbur: They're completely abhorrent to me. I've knelt many long years in my room contemplating the darkness of my crimes. At one point I vowed to God that if I ever did slip up, I'd walk out into the wilderness in a sweatshirt in sub-zero weather and die of exposure.

Macrina: That is quite a vow. Were you ever tempted?

Wilbur: Twice. But I fought against it as if I were dueling with the devil himself, and I won. That was more than eight years ago, and since then I've devoted myself to the Lord's work. I'm as celibate as they come. Prayerful and content.

Macrina: This is what I don't understand. You knew from your seminary training what disastrous consequences fell upon the Church between 2020 and about 2025—the loss of parishioners; the loss or weakening of faith in the members that stayed; the dramatic drop-off of converts into the Church; the closing of churches; the selling of Church property to meet the cost of lawsuits, a barrage of them; the near bankruptcy of the diocese. You knew all this yet committed the very crimes that brought disgrace upon us fifty years ago. You told me over the phone you love the Church. Wilbur, I just don't understand.

Wilbur: I don't either. I'm just a rotten human being, I guess.

Macrina: Let's not rehearse that. I want to know what drove you. What deep-down emotion drove you?

Wilbur: I was lonely. I didn't feel love coming my way. I was desolate.

Macrina: So why didn't you reach out to an adult for love rather than a child?

Wilbur: I am ashamed to say. It was too risky reaching out to an adult. They might report me. But a child wouldn't.

Macrina: So it wasn't that you found children more to your liking?

Wilbur: I wouldn't say that. Innocence is a beautiful thing to behold. To touch and be touched by a child felt good. I won't deny it.

Macrina: Hmm, what do you think I should do with you?

Wilbur: I have no idea. I understand your position. I don't deserve to be a priest.

Macrina: Yet you run one of the best parishes in the diocese, you and Mother Christa. I take it you're gay?

Wilbur: Yes.

Macrina: You get along with her?

Wilbur: Very well. I've always gotten along with women. They make great friends.

Macrina: I met the parents of those kids over the last week, and they are understandably outraged. The boys vary in their reaction to your crimes. One laughs them off. Another says he was so traumatized he's never known whether he is gay or straight. He's asking for damages into the millions.

Wilbur: I deserve to be sacked, I know that.

Macrina: That's true. But we're Christians, and Christians know how to forgive. We believe in second chances. I see your contrition. I see no evidence you'll repeat—unlike the other three. I'm tempted to leave you where you are. Unless the word gets out, and it might at any time. In that case you'll have to look for another career. No sin in the world excites such condemnation as what you did. A mother once told me she'd rather her child be murdered than be victimized by a pedophile. Do you know how universally loathed you'd be if your victims talked? I hope it doesn't come to that. I don't think it will. Even if it does, even if the world won't forgive you, God will. You are a good priest, Wilbur—at last. And we need you.

Wilbur: You have no idea how sorry I am, how much I want to make it up to the Church I love—and to you.

Macrina: I've decided to let you have that chance. I'll be watching you like a hawk, and so will Christa—you can be sure of that. And if you slip, I'll accompany you to the wilderness so you can put an end to your miserable life. I am taking a risk in giving you a second chance, Wilbur. Don't let me down.

Wilbur: Not a chance. I solemnly promise. Please don't worry. And thank you. Thank you so much.

Macrina: Here, take my hand. Let us pray....

Greg: For the next four years Macrina labored as Bishop of Albany. She managed to save the diocese from a second bankruptcy but watched some of the smaller churches and two of the diocesan elementary schools close their doors forever. Her goal of placing a full-time pastor at each of the churches proved too costly, and mergers of churches into a single parish remained in place. She once told me that if she worked 24 hours a day she wouldn't begin to provide the oversight needed to run the diocese as she had hoped. For the most part she could only watch as the 100 or so active priests, as many deacons, 500 nuns, 16,000 school children in diocesan schools from kindergarten through high school, and her own staff did their jobs. She could guide and inspire, but not do their jobs for them. When there was an illness or a pregnancy or a death or a drinking or narcotics problem or even embezzlement by a member of her staff, and the work did not get done as it should, she tossed and turned in her bed and wondered how she could have prevented it. But the 111 parishes spread over 14 counties did not feel her pain. The seasons of Advent, Christmas, Lent, Easter, and Pentecost with their respective colors rolled on by as they always had, and Archbishop Cullen praised her for actually growing the diocese by 14,000 souls. She even got a letter from the Pope noting her "revolutionary advance in Church history."

She found happiness in spite of the work load. She joined the Cathedral choir and sang at the 11:00 Sunday Mass like an ordinary chorister while an assistant officiated. She preached at the 5:00 pm "Men's Mass," so-called because she chose a male, usually but not necessarily Catholic, as the subject of her sermon, this in an effort to attract men back to the Church. She took pleasure in what she called her "little experiments" — for example, spiritual readings at Sunday Mass from outside Christianity in place of the Old Testament — Dostoevsky, Gandhi, the Dalai Lama, and so forth. She hiked and canoed with high schoolers during summer camp at the beautiful Pyramid Life Center in the Adirondacks.

And she — but I'll let her tell the story in her own words:

Macrina, Journal: A week ago we hired a new groundskeeper, and we happened to meet one morning when I was out in my grungies trimming the roses and picking cherries from our little grove. I was standing on a low ladder when a voice called out from behind, "Lady, do you have permission to pick the cherries?"

Amused, I turned around and said, "Not exactly. I just thought they looked like they wanted to be eaten."

"This is private property. Do you work here?"

I stepped down off the ladder. "I do. You must be the new groundskeeper. I don't think we've met." His bronze features were handsome, his shoulders broad and strong, and he talked with an accent—maybe Haitian. He looked like he was in his mid-40s. "What's your name?"

"Étienne, but they call me Flapjack."

"Flapjack?"

"Yes, ma'm, I ate up all the flapjacks before my little brother could get to 'em, so Mama called me Flapjack. What's your name?"

"Macrina."

"Macrina? Macrina? Isn't that the name of the boss lady? You not the boss lady out pickin' cherries?"

I chuckled.

"You pullin' my leg, ain't you?" He laughed good-naturedly as if at a joke. "You almost had me. Sheee-it." And he laughed some more.

"Are you married, Étienne?"

"I ain't free, if that's what you're gettin' at." His eyebrows shot up as if he were giving me a warning not to get too close.

I smiled. "No, no, I just like people. Like to know their histories. Sorry."

"Got a daughter named Maizy. How about you?"

"I've got one too—Anna."

I often run into him mowing the lawn or trimming the bushes, and he always calls me Macrina to carry on the joke, not guessing who I really am. Or does he? Is the joke on me? I don't know.

Greg: What happened to Fr. Herb Constantine, the previous bishop's personal secretary and the clear favorite as his successor? Losing the position to Macrina had been a bitter pill for him to swallow. Archbishop Curran transferred him to the Buffalo diocese, as far away from the smell of humiliation as possible. Working under her was out of the question.

I can't see what he personally had to gain by what he did. His loss was final. Whatever his motive, he began keeping a record of all the faults he found with her administration and more especially with her beliefs. Was he driven by resentment or by a genuine concern for the future of the Church? I cannot say.

Fr. Herb Constantine, paper copy of a letter he sent to Archbishop Curran:
- Without authorization she substituted at Mass readings from non-Christian sources in place of scheduled readings from the Old Testament.
- Without authorization she welcomed all in the Church to receive communion "at Christ's table," whether baptized or not.
- In her sermons she strayed from factual truth by telling stories—she called them parables—taken from her own imagination, thereby suggesting that the events really happened when in fact they did not.
- At a retreat for high school seniors she shared the story of her fall from grace when having a child out of wedlock as a "prudential error" rather than a serious sin.
- In a catechism class discussing the ethics of abortion she said it was not clear when the soul entered the fetus.
- In public debates she had claimed that such a fetus might better be considered a potential person than a real person.
- She implies that abortion might be permissible when a nonviable fetus could not live outside the womb if expelled.
- She declared that Catholic divorcees who remarry outside the Church should be granted the right to receive

communion.

- In one of her TV debates she said that reincarnation could serve the same purpose as purgatory and that the Church would be wise to reconsider its position on "multiple lives."
- She wonders if homosexuality is not a perversion of the natural order but a natural result of a sex change between lives.
- On many occasions she has gone public with pronouncements that salvation is available to ex-Catholics and even atheists.
- She leaves out the reference to Mary as "Mother of God" when saying the rosary.
- She implies by that exclusion that Jesus is not God.
- She says that God is not offended when Buddhists leave out any mention of him in their teachings.
- She says that it is impossible for humans to know God as he is and that the formulas adopted by the Church Fathers at Nicaea in AD 325 were "the best they could do at the time."
- She says that God is as much a Mother as a Father and that her exclusion was due to the Church Fathers' low estimate of women.
- She claims that hell is not necessarily eternal and that souls who repent their sins after death can leave hell and enter heaven.
- She says that souls choose hell over heaven because God is not there; in other words, God does not damn them, they damn themselves.
- She views purgatory as a relatively friendly place where souls are cleansed of their selfish habits rather than a frightening place where suffering is intense and a place to be avoided at all cost.
- She challenges the Church's claim to know when a soul in

purgatory can pass into heaven via plenary indulgences.
- She encourages the faithful to pray to their saintly relatives in addition to or even in place of the Church's canonized saints.
- She says that Jesus' death on the cross was not required by God to atone for the sins of man but showed by his example how we can expect the world to condemn us if we follow his example.
- She questions whether God "micromanages" events in life by answering prayer.
- She distorts statistics when claiming that churches in her diocese fared better under the leadership of women and married priests than under celibates.

Greg: Archbishop Curran told me that Fr. Constantine sent him the above list of grievances against Macrina and asked that it be forwarded to Pope Francis. Curran did not honor that request. He sent it to me when he heard I was writing this book. I wonder what would have happened to Macrina — and the Church — if he had.

After four years as Bishop of Albany, Macrina got another of those surprises that seemed to follow her wherever she went.

Archbishop Curran, phone conversation: The Church moved the age of required retirement for bishops from 75 to 80, so I lasted an extra five years, but now it was upon me. I always had in mind Macrina as my successor, but I was afraid she'd turn it down. She disliked administration. She had had her fill of it in Albany. When Francis told me he wanted her in Rome full-time as one of his cardinals in some administrative post, I told him it would be a hard sell. Frankly I hated the thought of her slogging through all those committee meetings with withered old men like me.

Pope Francis II, Photo of a postal letter sent to Macrina at her Albany address:

Dear Macrina, this is a follow-up from our conversation yesterday on the phone. I listened carefully to your objections and am trying hard to balance your personal needs with the needs of the greater Church. This is not an easy letter for me to write.

First, let me remind you that your commitment to ordinary parishioners is dear to my heart. You are the very opposite of a lazy careerist. You are the very sort of priest I need to govern the Church at the highest level. You are a priest for the people who understands their needs, a woman who mothers her flock.

I am asking you to think big. The *Church* is sick and dying. When you were born, Catholics numbered 16% of the world's population. Now it's down to 11%. The reason is that we have been stuck in old ways that no longer work, especially for men. I need you to help reform the Church, to show the world that this old organization can be the best the world has. We are caught up in old dogmas that deflect attention from its mission. To keep it simple, our mission is to make good men and women who will lead the world back from ignorance, greed, and hatred. The materialist culture that rules the world is our enemy. The allure of the internet that leaves no time for serious reflection is its accomplice. The relativism that tells our young people there is no higher authority than the whim of the moment is the result. As Catholic Christianity recedes, makeshift boutique spiritualities arise to take its place.

Macrina, I am surrounded by men who do not know how to fix the Church. They think the Church is losing members because it has drifted away from the old ways—it has betrayed its charter, they say. I am certain they are wrong. If you agree with me, please reconsider your decision. You take joy in helping moms and pops, aunts and uncles, the homeless and the addicted, the sick and the dying. You would be in a position to help millions of everyday Catholics. I repeat: Your flock would number in the millions.

You need to consider other factors too. Think what this appointment would do for Catholic women at every level. As you say in America, it would level the playing field. It would lead to many more appointments for women at the highest levels of Church governance. Even if a more conservative pontiff were to follow me, it would be too late to turn back the clock. Did you think your life had been crowned with success when we opened the priesthood to women? Did you think you could finally rest on your laurels when we made you a bishop, as if anything more were unthinkable? Think what the red hat would do for women everywhere!

We lost 36% of our cardinals to the pandemic, and I've been scouring the planet in search of worthy replacements ever since. At the moment we have only 156. Entire Congregations and Papal Commissions are functioning at half-mast. Think of what you could do for Interreligious Dialogue. At present we don't even have a competent Bureau Chief for Islam. Or think of the impact you would make as a fresh voice in the Congregation for the Doctrine of the Faith, an area in special need of a complete overhaul. More to your liking might be the Congregation for the Causes of Saints. I hear that you follow the Master in the way you preach. You use parables. Our inventory is full of contemporary good Samaritans. You would be tasked with uncovering new examples of holiness—men and women of heroic virtue being considered for canonization as saints. I would place you wherever you wanted to go. But as a member of the Curia you would have to live and work in Rome.

Macrina, I love this Church, and I know you do too. You must trust me when I tell you you can do more good in Rome than in Albany or even New York. Help me wake up this hulking old behemoth....

I'm convinced that we must conduct Church business in English. Latin is archaic, and few of our new cardinals know Italian, but everyone knows a little English. I'm going to need a little help selling that to the Curia. Will you help?

Cleona Morris, *Mobile Register,* **Online Edition:** Earlier today, as St. Peter's bells rang out the news over Rome's piazzas and palaces, Pope Francis II elevated 23 bishops to the College of Cardinals. Mobile's own Macrina McGrath was among them.

The English Pope wore a smile that no one standing near could miss as he placed a red hat, a cardinal's insignia, on her head as thousands filling the cathedral looked on in solemn silence. She is the first female cardinal in the Church's storied history, just as she was the first bishop four years earlier.

Following the ceremony the crowd applauded and let out a few whoops and whistles, and the new red hats were guided by Swiss Guards to their respective rooms to celebrate with their families and friends. I, the pesky hometown journalist, came loaded with questions.

"What did you feel when the Pope placed the red hat on your head?"

"Astonishment that it was happening, not just to me, but to a woman."

"Will you be living in Rome?"

"Yes."

"Where?"

With a laugh, "At the end of the hall with my own separate bathroom."

"Seriously?"

"On the other side of a wall," she said with a prankster's smile as the little crowd burst out laughing.

"What will be your job?"

"Fixing the Church."

"I hear your new title will be 'Your Eminence.' How do you feel about that, Your Eminence?"

"That's one of the things that needs fixing."

"What do you mean?"

"We should be encouraged to think of ourselves as pastors, as servants, as aides."

"To the Pope?"

"To the people."

"How do you feel about Mobile, your old hometown? Do you still think of it as home?"

"I do. It's where Mom and Dad and my brother and his wife and children live. It's where the roots of my faith were planted. It's where I served the dying during the pandemic. It's where I almost died myself. (She pauses.) It's the place I retreat to when God seems distant."

"Mobilians know what you have accomplished and are very proud of you. You've put this sleepy Southern city on the map."

"Fifty-six years ago it put me on the ground. I guess that makes us even."

I turned to Greg, her twin brother standing next to her, while phones flashed and cameras clicked. I asked him what it's like having such a famous twin sister.

"Memories. Paddling a canoe up the Mobile River at flood-stage. Playing games in the cemetery across the street. Feeling proud when she played Dizzy Fingers at school on her clarinet. Grabbing for candy thrown from floats at Mardi Gras. Serving Mass together at St. Ignatius. Little things that stand out in my memory, things I should never let die."

"That's the real me," Macrina said almost in a whisper as she leaned against Greg's shoulder, her eyes moist with love....

Greg: Following his retirement at age 84, Francis was eager to cooperate with me on a biography of Macrina. He cut through a lot of red tape and put portions of the Vatican's archives at my disposal. I had to swear before God and in writing drawn up by one of the Vatican's lawyers that I wouldn't remove any of the documents from the room where I did the research. I lived at the Vatican for a month. Every three or four days I would take a helicopter out to the Apostolic Palace of Castel Gandolfo where Francis lived, show him what I had written, and consult with him. Much of what I hoped to share with the world he discouraged, but enough he supported to make my stay in Italy indispensable.

In the four years she spent in Rome as a cardinal, she divided much of her time between the Congregation for the Causes of Saints and the Congregation for the Doctrine of the Faith. In this work we see the two sides of this complex woman: her deeply conservative spiritual instincts next to her progressive theological agenda.

In going over the various histories of beatified men and women who fell short of the finish line as a certified Catholic saint—dozens, some stretching back centuries—one stood out. This was the case of a Canadian nun who had been earlier married and had three children, all lost to disease before she reached 30. Her name was Emelie Gamelin. Why this woman? I think I know and that you might easily guess: like Macrina, Emelie was no virgin like most nuns and had children. She understood the flesh firsthand. Macrina identified with her.

Why was this holy foundress of a Canadian religious order not canonized as an official saint? The problem was that only one miracle could be attributed to her intercession, and two were required. Macrina kept researching her case, looking for that evasive second miracle. She never found it. She told me she felt like a trial lawyer who knew her client was innocent but couldn't convince the jury. Meanwhile she prayerfully asked Emelie for help in healing the rift between herself and Anna.

She had better luck with Doctrine. Much better. As I read over the minutes of the Committee meetings and talked with three of the cardinals who served with her, the impression I got was that her presence was almost seismic—"tornadic" one of her rivals put it. Was it her sex among so many old men that gave her such clout? Did they feel guilty in front of her as the representative of a spurned or even persecuted minority? Was it the breadth of her worldview, nurtured by a knowledge of religions as far apart as Buddhism and Mormonism? What could these narrowly educated cardinals say to contradict the comparisons she came up with? Was it her personality, unflappable in the face of heated debate or even ridicule? When one of the indignant men told her to "go take a walk," she took no offense and only solidified her support by her composure. Was it the freshness of her arguments when she confronted traditions that had ossified over the centuries into fossils that no one except her dared to challenge? Or was it the dismaying responsibility that these old men felt for the Church's shrinking membership? Whatever it was, she had many of the cardinals in her hands.

One of the discussions recorded in the minutes dealt with clerical sexual abuse. She has written at length on the subject, and her views are widely known, but it's worth bringing up here to show how she maneuvered her colleagues into following her lead. The meetings are conducted these days in English, with translations available in Italian, Spanish, French, and German.

Voice recording of the doctrinal committee of the Curia, aided by English translation where necessary:
Macrina: We've come a long way since the scandalous '20s, but out of 460,000 priests worldwide, we're bound to have some bad apples, and we do. Like me you are all bishops. You've dealt with the problem first-hand: priests preying on children, especially vulnerable altar boys. It's sickening to think about. We've heard Cardinal A emphasize forgiveness and rehabilitation. Cardinal H recommends a two-year suspension of priestly duties with counseling. Cardinal M says that whatever we do, keep it hush-hush, keep it in the Church. If reparations to the victims are required, so be it. But work to keep the victims from going public. We don't want our priests going to prison. Does that sum it up?

Cardinal A: Forgiveness is paramount. It's what we Christians are urged to do. Yes, I know that children are victims. Of course it's a terrible sin. But I want to emphasize mercy, whatever else we decide on.

Cardinal M: I agree. Children are more often victims of their fathers, yet their fathers are seldom punished. At most they lose custody or visitation rights. And bad priests don't batter their victims like bad fathers. I'm just trying to put things in perspective.

Macrina: You make a point. But what do you propose we do?

Cardinal M: I'm not sure. But don't forget what pressures priests are under, especially celibate priests.

Macrina: So much pressure that we should overlook the trauma they cause?

Cardinal M: Of course not. They need to be punished.

Macrina: How?

Cardinal O: In Nigeria I knew such a priest. He was in my diocese. I turned him over to the authorities. They didn't do anything. They didn't want to deal with it. Though he did show up with a swollen face and a black eye.

Macrina: It sounds like he got away with a beating. What did you do with him then?

Cardinal O: I made him one of my assistants. He kept the books. He said Mass in private. He didn't get anywhere near a kid.

Macrina: Good for you. But what's he doing now?

Cardinal O: Holy Mother of God, I'm not sure.

Macrina: Are you still the bishop of that diocese?

Cardinal O: Yes, but as you know, I spend most of my time here.

Macrina: My God, man, I hate to think what he's up to.

Cardinal O: I'll take care of it. I just forgot about him.

Macrina: That's one of the problems. We don't take that man's crimes seriously enough. We forget about them. Other things are more pressing. But, dear brothers in Christ, *nothing is more pressing*.

Cardinal M: Do you want to expose them to the world outside? Put them on trial? Put them in jail? For God's sake, they're one of us. They're not criminals.

Macrina: That's exactly what most of them are. They're not that different from scammers and murderers-for-hire. They committed a terrible crime, and that makes them a criminal. They should be put on trial with few exceptions. Nothing less than that will stop these deviants. Nothing less will restore confidence in the Church.

Cardinal M: It's not what Christ would do.

Macrina: Really? For every verse in the Bible that shows his mercy, I'll find one that highlights his sense of righteousness. In the parable about the greedy rich man dressed in purple and poor Lazarus with all his sores, Jesus leaves the rich man in hell. There is a great lesson in this. At the very least it applies to pedophiles, wouldn't you agree? Remember what Jesus said about those who drag the "little ones" into evil? "Better for them if they had drowned in the sea with a millstone tied around their neck." Jesus was no wimp on crime, especially involving children. If we are his followers, we shouldn't be either.

Cardinal M: He also told us to be slow to judge: "Judge not lest you be judged." I see in you a judgmental attitude.

Macrina: Thank you, João. I love you for your consistently sweet nature. You grew up in São Paulo. You've seen how circumstances turn innocent boys into brutes—or perverts—or even demons. I accept your correction. There are times, though, when we must judge. We cannot make exceptions for bad priests—or bad bishops—or even bad cardinals.

Greg: Cardinal Z was the only other American in the Curia. His unusual pedigree is out in the open, so I am not revealing secrets. His parents were drug addicts, and he was shuffled from one group home to another. The woman who mothered him between his sixth and thirteenth years was a devout Catholic and by all accounts a saintly person. When she closed down her home following a heart attack, he kept her memory alive by attending the same church she took him to, and where he served Mass. As he tells it, his Catholic faith kept him sane and was the only thing that made his world bright. The pastor of that church noted that faith and guided him toward the local Catholic high school and from there the priesthood. "He had a mind like a trap door," the pastor, now an old man living in a retirement home for priests, told me over the phone. "And he was stubborn. He would have made a great lawyer. I'm glad he went on to better things." He graduated first in his high school class.

It's unclear whether he was gay or straight. The people who knew him best, especially his fellow seminarians, agree that he was sexually inexperienced, probably a virgin.

Video recording of the doctrinal committee of the Curia, aided by English translation where necessary:
Cardinal R (seated at one end of a long table in a room surrounded by art treasure on all four walls): Most of us come to this discussion with minds made up. Let's give the other side the Christian charity that the subject requires. As you know, our sister in Christ, Cardinal McGrath, our own esteemed Macrina, if I may refer to her in so intimate a manner, though that is by her request—as you know, Macrina has asked since she arrived at the Vatican ten months ago that we not shy away from this momentous subject, namely the nature of Christ. So here we are. Macrina, I turn the floor over to you.

Macrina (seated at the opposite end of the table): Thank you, Your Eminence, or, as I would prefer to call you, my brother in Christ. Let me say at the outset that I don't expect to make converts of you. I only want you to listen to what I say. And I look forward to hearing your replies.

As I suspect you all know by now, I am at heart a reformer, not a traditionalist. I have long believed that the Church is stuck in old ways that are leading to its slow demise, as the polls have been showing us since the turn of the century. On this particular subject, Jesus' divinity, I have not spoken or written with the candor that you will hear from me now.

You might say, why should we debate this? Since Nicaea the Church's position has been crystal clear: Jesus is the coeternal, coequal son of God the Father. He is God in the fullest sense. But he is also man in the fullest sense. Over 300 bishops have said so, and they were guided by the Holy Spirit. Fully God and fully man—that is the formula. Seventeen-and-a-half centuries have passed since then. At the time those who disagreed with it were classed as heretics and often condemned and persecuted, even unto death. Nowadays we just think of them as non-Catholics and bless them as they go their separate ways. That in itself is a great advance over the barbarity of the past. But we must advance further if the Church is to grow. Let's look afresh at this formula. Nothing prevents us from doing so. Let's start by going back to the beginning.

Let's begin with the famous account of Jesus' meeting with the rich young man. In the Gospel of Mark, as you all know, the young man says to Jesus, "Good Master, what must I do to inherit eternal life," and Jesus answers, "Why do you call me good? No one is good but God alone." What could be clearer? Jesus is putting a great distance between the goodness of God and the goodness of himself. This is not the language of a man who knows he is God.

Cardinal Z: So you are actually going to question the divinity of Christ? You are actually coming out and saying this? I just want to be clear.

Macrina: Jesus actually came out and said it for us. We just didn't listen. It's time we listened.

Cardinal Z: This is preposterous. You are denying the one thing that makes us different from every other religion. This is the grossest heresy. And have you forgotten John's gospel where he says he is one with the Father? What could be clearer than that?

Macrina: One in mind, one in purpose, not one in nature. Jesus makes bold statements throughout his ministry. He tells us to pluck out our eye if it leads us into sin. Did he mean this literally? Of course not. Did he think he was God, the creator of the universe 14 billion years ago? How does this sound to the rest of the world today? It sounds like a sacred superstition. It chases away educated people, the people who keep drifting away from the Church as soon as they begin to think for themselves. We need these people. "The Father and I are one" is one of his boldest statements. We have to interpret it in light of his other claims, especially the one about God's unique goodness. The early Church fathers did not do this. In their eagerness to deify him they failed to see his intent. They failed to see it as another of his bold statements, the boldest of them all, the one that directly led to his death.

Cardinal Z: What distinguishes you from the Jews who picked up stones to kill him after he made this momentous claim? Apparently what sounded like blasphemy to the Jews 2,000 years ago sounds like blasphemy to you today.

Macrina: Not at all. The universe was tiny in his day, a disc with the Mediterranean at its center, its age a few thousand years. The Creator was also small. So it wasn't hard to imagine a man being one with a God so small. But today we measure the universe in light years and galaxies. Claiming that any man who walked this tiny planet is the same being as the one who created the universe 13.8 billion years ago sounds like lunacy. No, I don't think of our position as blasphemous, only as ignorant. And easily explainable if we remember the times Jesus lived in. But we don't live in those times anymore, and we have to do better if we are to grow.

Cardinal Z: If you throw out Jesus' divinity, you are left with nothing but Judaism. There are fewer than 15 million Jews in the world today and a billion of us. And you speak of growth? You think downsizing Jesus would lead to growth? It would lead to a global catastrophe. It would lead to the end of Catholicism as we know it.

Macrina: You have just said it: "as we know it." But what you see as a catastrophe I see as a radiant new birth. A rebirth of the religion that Jesus stood for, not the religion of dogma and heresy-hunting that the all-male bishops at Nicaea left us with.

Cardinal Z: And what, in your singular wisdom, is that?

Macrina: A God worthy of the best that humankind can imagine. A morality of universal love that Jesus preached in his great sermon on the mount. A spirituality of prayer and meditation directed to God and the saints. A delight in the world that God has given us and a responsibility to cherish and sustain it. Accountability for the decisions we make and an afterlife based on it. A never-ending ascent to diviner worlds for those who choose and deserve them—what St. Gregory of Nyssa called rising from glory to glory. That is Catholic Christianity in a nutshell. It has much in common with its sister religion, Judaism, but in many ways it's different. And none of it depends on Jesus being God.

Cardinal Z: Very bewitching. But how can we know any of it's true if Jesus is merely a man? Men are prone to error. Or haven't you discovered?

Macrina: Jesus was an inspired man, a rare man, a great spiritual master. He stood up for the common people against the domination system of the day and lost his life defending them. We're incredibly lucky to know of him. But his claims are subject to reason and evidence, and so are the claims of his followers.

Cardinal Z: Reason and evidence, the slippery tools of science and philosophy. They'll lead you to atheism and nihilism, the utter destruction of everything we stand for.

Macrina: Not necessarily. Let's not be deceived by the bullies who rule out certain kinds of evidence from the start. There are evidences of the heart, of the soul, that they ignore. We don't ignore them. We bring them into the light and let them carry us into faith. There are no guarantees we aren't deceived, but there are many hints we aren't. Many indeed. So many that, at least for me, my doubts have settled into a heap—like dead algae at the bottom of a pond.

Cardinal Z: You are eloquent, you are sincere, and you are a woman. You are easy to like. But you are wrong, terribly wrong. The teachings of the Church have weathered centuries of examination. They have been scrutinized by many of the world's greatest minds and not found wanting. The Holy Spirit has kept them from going astray. It's that Spirit that we should put out faith in, not the so-called hints you speak of. Think, Macrina. How likely is it that you, all by yourself, have solved the riddle of how to save the Church from its decline? Think how much more likely it is that this decline is caused by radicals like you who confuse the faithful with strange new teachings that undermine, no, that contradict the deposit of faith laid down by your worthy predecessors, and that you swore to uphold when consecrated a bishop. My God, woman, think of the damage you would do if your private infatuations, your obsessions, were to gain currency. It's not new ideas the Church needs, but old ones, the ones that brought forth martyrs—

Macrina: —And persecution of innocent women as witches, and wars of religion that put to death whole towns of Christians whose only fault was that they were Protestants, and wars with Muslims who condemn our understanding of Jesus as God. I apologize for cutting you off. What were you saying?

Cardinal Z: Catholics hate change. They want stability. They want timeless truths. And that's what we've always given them. Can't you see this?

Macrina: You can't build stability on a false teaching. Eventually it will turn on you. Of course Catholics resist change. We all do. But it's up to us to get the teaching right. Then stability will endure.

Cardinal Z: You are shameless!

Macrina: We've become a house of pre-furnished ideas. Rigid ideas turn young people off. We should encourage them to question and wrestle with their doubts. We should show them they aren't that different from us, that the Church is big enough to include those who believe like you and like me, both of us.

Cardinal Z: Do you see this ring? (He holds up his fist, displaying his golden cardinal's ring.) Do you see it? It's too bad you didn't live 500 years ago. Then we'd have known what to do with you!

Cardinal R: You've gone too far… this isn't Christian love. I suggest you apologize. I demand… (The cardinals in their red hats and vestments are visibly agitated.)

Macrina: Please, I need to be clearer. I'm not saying you have to think like me to be Catholic. All I'm saying is you *can* think like me. You can be a traditional Catholic like the Cardinal or a—what's the word?—a different kind of Catholic like me. Maybe I should say a renewed, or a reformed, or even a green Catholic. But Catholic any way you call it. Why not? Why all this emphasis on exclusion? Let's look at all the ways you *can* be Catholic. What a novel approach for us red hats. Why not, I ask. And let's not stop here. Catholic doctrine claims Jesus is really present in the bread and wine, so much so that they cease to exist after consecration. They are just Jesus. If you can believe that, fine. But if you can't, if you just see the elements as symbolic, like me, that's okay too. You can be a Catholic in good standing either way. Let's put an end to all this excluding. And let's stop telling people they can't receive the elements if they're in a gay relationship, or if they got a divorce and remarried outside the Church, or if they condone abortion, or if they question their gender, or if they're in an adulterous relationship, or if they're not even sure they want to be a Catholic, they're just experimenting. Would Jesus refuse to allow them a seat at his table? You know the answer. Let's open our arms so wide that no one is excluded who loves the gospel Jesus preached, no matter how far they fall short of practicing it. Especially if they fall short, for they are the ones who need it most. That's the way to grow the Church, brothers. That's the way to do it. And let's get started now. Let's don't leave this business to the next generation. Let's not be bystanders. Let the future enter the world through us.

(Following this call to arms, her colleagues react in a stunned, stony silence, hard to interpret. Cardinal R hastily brings the meeting to an end.)

Greg: Our usual way of communicating once she arrived in Rome was by phone, but occasionally she used email. This one covers a lot of ground.

Macrina, email: Dear Big Boy, it's been a crazy day at the Vatican. Zamora is organizing a cabal against me, but the Pope encouraged me to overlook it, to keep talking, to bear in mind that there are others who want me to prevail, no matter how heterodox or inflammatory my views. Like them, he doesn't subscribe to everything I say, but he wants it all to come out. Clearly he wants to shake up the Church. He sees it as suffering from exhaustion, as lacking the vibrancy to carry out its mission. He knows it has to change, and unlike every pope before him, he's courageous enough to see it through—he's a new John XXIII, only 50 pounds lighter. He doesn't have a clear idea of what needs changing, but I have his ear. Sometimes I shudder at the thought of how much power I potentially have. Believe me, I pray daily for humility.

I have no bigger supporter than Cardinal Iglesias. This dear Spaniard (I call him by his first name, Santiago) is totally behind my push to open the Church to a "green" option. Nearing 80, he endeared himself by telling me he loved me as a daughter. I could see in his eyes a sadness; this was a man who should have married and had a family. He is one of the lonely casualties of the Church's teaching on celibacy. What a wonderful thing that priests can now marry! One of the reforms I'll be pushing for is married bishops. You will remember how I used to oppose this. But why? Is Santiago a better bishop because he didn't marry? All I can see now is that he would have been a happier bishop. But a married cardinal? I think that's going too far. What do you think?

I have other followers. My enemies call them "Greens" — a word I first used at a meeting on Doctrine to suggest a spring-like rebirth of the Church. For them it's a term of disrepute, an insult, but for my allies it's an emblem of progress. Can you guess what my allies call the traditionalists? The "Browns," the color of autumn, a lovely but slow decay. If the standoff were not of such huge importance, I would find this amusing.

Please keep me informed about Anna. Is she still visiting? Sometimes I wonder if she is losing her sanity, if the strain of her internship is more than she can bear. She emailed me the other day that I was an addict and that we couldn't have a relationship unless I acknowledged it. She called it "tricky" if I didn't. An addict — can you imagine? By this she means that I always think I'm right: I'm addicted to feeling that my opinions are superior to everyone else's and telling them why. Truth to tell, I sometimes do feel this way. That's what makes me a reformer rather than a follower. But the deeper truth is that I constantly strive for richer, more comprehensive, more inclusive perspectives and am willing to do the work to arrive at them — the habit of any competent professor. This calls for an antecedent attitude of modesty and caution, and this is an attitude I am very familiar with. In fact, it predominates until I've done the necessary research.

But she has a point. In the past I have given her more advice than she asked for or even wanted—all with an eye to helping her avoid mistakes I made. How hard it is to remain quiet when a parent sees a child about to wade into quicksand! I see this now, but it might be too late for her to trust me again. She called my advice "invasive," that was her word. When we were traveling together in Japan, I put many questions to her because I wanted to get to know her better. As she looks back, she sees them as an attempt to control her. That's not how I see it at all. I merely wanted to know the child I brought into the world at a deeper level, not control her. I did, however, give her advice unsought. And that was, apparently, a mistake, however well intended.

Remember me telling you about Emelie Gamelin, the saintly French Canadian nun needing a second miracle to earn her canonization? I've been asking her to work a miracle in my daughter's heart, but so far it hasn't worked. Who knows if such prayers ever reach the intended target, or how much influence the saint has over conditions on earth even if they do? But it's worth a try.

We have a meeting next week on the afterlife. It's a subject about which the Church sometimes says far too much, at other times far too little. Some of my red-hat colleagues take their cue from St. Paul and the theology arising from his speculations in I Corinthians 15. Or they speculate about what the world will be like when Christ returns and the dead come out of their graves, or how to interpret the Book of Revelation when it tells of God seated on a throne with Christ at his right hand. They've never heard of the testimony of spirits, many of them Christians, describing through respected mediums the fascinating world they live in. Most of them have given little thought to the crucial doctrine of purgatory (an unfortunate name) that the Church has championed almost from its beginning. Or if they bring it up, they ignore the evidence suggesting what it's like. I've asked them to come prepared at a future meeting by delving into this research. We'll see what comes of it.

An anonymous note scribbled in Latin on a piece of computer paper, translated by a friend of mine at the Vatican: Francis is ailing, and there is talk of his retiring and returning to England where he chooses to die. I hear rumors that Macrina McGrath could be his hand-picked successor. Can you imagine? Seriously, can you imagine this? This must be faced at once and stopped. The Pope, of course, has no control over succession, but his recommendation could influence the process in her favor. The witch's power of persuasion must not be underestimated. The Greens are a minority, but their number is growing. and two of them, you can guess who they are, have turned activist and are stumping for her behind our backs. We'll meet tomorrow night at 8:00 in the Raphael Room to plan a counter-offensive. Please attend.

Greg: Macrina is vacationing with Sophie and me in a cabin high above Grindelwald in the Swiss Alps. I had to twist her arm to get her here, but she is loving it. We hiked all day yesterday, and today we are resting. We're on our third of four days. The low-roofed cabin, 180 years old, sits on the side of a mountain over the town. We are sitting on an outdoor balcony with a view of two massive snow-capped mountains standing guard over the village at the bottom of the valley and vivid green meadows covering the slopes surrounding it. A glacier, what's left of it, straggles down between the mountains, one of which is the famous Eiger. A red umbrella—what other color would you expect?—blocks out the sun on this mild, cloudless July morning. I'm drinking tea, the girls coffee. We're all wearing sun glasses.

I've asked Macrina for permission to record her voice. "Why?" she asks. I tell her I'm not sure but want to do it anyway.

Macrina, Greg, Sophie, voice recording:

Greg: Last night you said life at the Vatican was like the canoe trip we took many years ago. You didn't elaborate.

Macrina: Oh, that. It's not the best metaphor, but, well, do you remember how hard we had to paddle against the current to keep from being swept downstream into the Bay?

Greg: Unforgettable.

Macrina: The old men I work with are like that current. Exhausting work.

Greg: Yeah, but we beat the current. Are you winning?

Macrina: I don't know. Maybe that's why it's a bad metaphor. (Laughter) No, I'm not, at least not with the majority. They're like a weather vane turning this or that way with every gust. One day they seem to be persuaded, the next day I have to start all over again.

Sophie: Have you been appointed their teacher? It seems like you are. How did that happen?

Macrina: You might call me the Vatican gadfly, and they are obliged to listen. Francis urges them to. He thinks that something constructive will come of it, though he's not sure what. It's not like they don't present worthy rebuttals that sometimes take me by surprise and knock me off balance. Most of them are, after all, very bright men. Some are holy men. So they can be my teacher too.

Greg: Can you give an example of how they teach you?

Macrina: Well, I never thought I'd hear a defense of the Atonement Doctrine that made any sense. One of the cardinals said that God sending down his son to die for all our sins was a "true myth." Dying for others out of love is the noblest, most heroic deed imaginable, he said. And a father sending his son to do it is more heartbreaking for the father than the son. Far from God appearing monstrous, God appears lovable. It doesn't make God despicable, but worthy of adoration. That was his argument. Another cardinal added that a suffering

God, whether father or son or both, makes the Christian God stand shoulders above any other. He went on to say something I've always believed: that God suffers when he watches a whole planet go seriously astray when its inhabitants misuse the great gift of free will God gave them and start killing each other by the millions.

Sophie: How did you reply?

Macrina: I thanked them for opening my eyes.

Greg: Really. What was their reaction?

Macrina: I think it helped them trust me.

Sophie: So you won their hearts by losing.

Macrina: We all love displays of genuine humility. So I guess you could say that.

Sophie: Wow, what is *that?* (Pause in the conversation as a supersonic Swiss fighter plane roars over the valley.) I thought Switzerland was a neutral country.

Greg: They are. But they'll defend their country if attacked.

Sophie: So those old men changed your mind?

Macrina: Not at all. But they argue well if you grant their starting point.

Sophie: And you don't.

Macrina: That's right.

Sophie: What don't you grant?

Macrina: That someone's death is needed before an offence can be forgiven. I don't believe in atonement at any level. It's the most unchristian concept I can imagine. Forgiveness takes its special character by being freely given. It's never the result of a transaction.

Sophie: Hmm. How did they take that?

Macrina: I haven't troubled them with it yet. I will when I get back.

Greg: God help them!

Macrina: How is Mom taking all this?

Greg: With amazement and, I'd say, fear. She reads

everything she can get about you. It's her hobby. She read there's speculation about you possibly becoming pope. She's never gotten used to you becoming a bishop, not to mention a cardinal. "With all those old men," she said in dismay. On one level she simply can't get over her baby girl becoming something as high as a pope. On another she shows real insight into your character, though you might disagree with her. She's sees you as having a God complex—

Macrina: A God complex? Really? What do you mean?

Greg: As having this extraordinary confidence that you see things right, see things as they truly are. See what must be done. She sees this as a weakness. She looks back at your decisions and questions them.

Macrina: Like what?

Greg: Well, your decision to enter the Marines, to give up Anna, to travel in India by yourself, to give away your money, to walk away from Ezra. She has always thought you lacked common sense. And she genuinely fears you would mislead the Church. She loves you, as you know, without reservation. But she worries about you and worries about the Church. In a sense she worries about her own legacy. The thought that she brought into the world a soul that did more harm than good troubles her.

Macrina: Mom actually said that?

Greg: No, it's just a hunch I have.

Macrina: Do you think I've gone off track? Tell me honestly, Greg.

Greg: I think you're a little impulsive, not off track. I share your vision.

Macrina: Thank God. I don't know what I'd do without your support. And I'm not as confident as Mom thinks. In fact, I'm not even certain that God exists. Faith—at some point we all have to admit that faith is different from certainty. Faith is a choice. I make it without the least hesitation and wish the world would make it too. And I wish with all my heart that the Church would help it to. That's what I'm all about, Greg. But let's not confuse faith with a logical syllogism. But impulsive? I don't feel I am. Maybe I appear that way because I think quickly. About most things I've already thought them through.

Sophie: Your mother's just afraid you'd make a mistake, that's all.

Macrina: Really, this is all just so much make-believe. I'm not going to be the next pope. All I'm going to do is try to influence him, whoever he is.

Sophie: Would you *like* to be the next pope?

Macrina: Like? All I know is I wouldn't be worthy of it. Then again, no one else would be either. The responsibility is too much for any single individual. It's a tremendous burden. For me sleep would be difficult, next to impossible. But I would accept it if it came my way. I wouldn't feel I had a choice.

Greg: As Francis' resignation neared, what once seemed preposterous suddenly seemed less so. It's hard for me to know whether it was her "mesmerizing" personality—one of her adversaries used that word—or the skill with which she argued for her reforms that helped turn the tide.

Anonymous two-page flyer placed in the Vatican mailboxes of resident cardinals:

As you are all aware, the faction pushing for Macrina McGrath's election as Bishop of Rome and sovereign shepherd of the Holy Catholic Church is gaining traction among our brother cardinals. This extraordinary, unimaginable event must be firmly opposed. In fact it must be stopped if our Church is to survive. The direction of world history as God wills it will depend on our success. We must use every means at our disposal. We begin by examining her personal history.

No one could have imagined how a devout Catholic girl from a respectable American Catholic family could have risen to such a height, even less how she could have evolved into the heretic she most certainly is.

We must begin by pointing out that her early life as a teenager was marked by a personal tragedy that probably traumatized her and enduringly left its mark on her character. I refer to the loss of her boyfriend, a Notre Dame student, in a drowning accident. Up until then she had been planning to attend Georgetown University and major in theology on a scholarship. Instead she imponderably signed up for a four-year stint in the United States Marine Corps as a clarinetist in one of their bands. While stationed in Okinawa she had an affair with the band director, an atheist, and got herself pregnant. Instead of keeping her daughter, which she had the means to do and which her parents urged her to do, she gave the baby up for adoption and dismissed her from her life until she turned 21. We have it on good authority that the child, now in her 30s, wants nothing to do with her mother.

From there she seems to have returned to her good senses and attended Georgetown, but quickly fell away from her goal of studying the history of Christian theology for a future career as a specialist in non-Christian religions, especially Hinduism. A trip to India placed her under the influence of a Hindu holy man, who convinced her that Hinduism was a religion no less loved by God than Christianity. She claimed that she was a Catholic rather than a Hindu by accident of birth. Ever since, she has been lobbying for the Hinduization of Christianity.

This revolt from the well-trodden paths of the Catholic Church reached its climax when she joined and soon became the U.S. poster child for the outlawed Womanpriest movement. Although excommunicated from the Catholic Church, she led a revolt against it by acting as pastor at several disaffiliated churches that were once Catholic. For years in this capacity she dated a Jewish man and took no care to hide the impression that she was his lover. During the pandemic she achieved notoriety by praying for the dead at burial sites, one of her few noble enterprises that were not self-serving, but insulted the Virgin by removing reference to her as the Mother of God while saying the rosary. When appointed bishop of Albany, the first thing she did was ferociously hunt down "bad" priests without so much as allowing them a fair trial. She has a heart of stone, lacking compassion. And since joining us in Rome, she has wormed her way into Francis' heart, no doubt hastening his decision to retire. When he does, he will leave the Vatican in an uproar.

In a few weeks we will have a new pope. Please consider what the world would see if she were elected by a horribly misguided majority of us: A woman distinguished neither by exemplary morality nor fidelity to Church doctrine, an unstable nonconformist and provocateur who pictures herself as a reformer and savior. Note her legions of adorers: atheists, Marxists, radical feminists, "nones" — the entire post-Christian secular world — who would like nothing better than to see our beloved Church crumble and die. We are not accusing her of consciously engineering this descent into oblivion, but the outcome would be as if she had. She is neither a devil nor a lunatic, but a domineering autocrat who fancies her vision of change as God-ordained. Think carefully about what is at stake, brothers. If you elect her, defections will multiply. It won't be long before there are more Muslims in Europe than Catholics. We need a powerful defender of the faith at our head, a staunch guardian of its doctrines, not a theological daredevil who claims she once had a close encounter with a UFO.

St. Augustine wrote, "If you believe what you like in the gospels, and reject what you don't like, it is not the gospel you believe, but yourself." This description aptly applies to Cardinal Macrina McGrath.

It has been with deep sadness that we write this. As Christians we are required to love our enemies and not to judge. We do not stand in judgment of Cardinal McGrath's soul, which is known to God alone. But the future is approaching us with potentially cyclonic force. We must seize it, control it, and fashion it.

One-page flyer with 54 signatures placed in the Vatican mailboxes of resident cardinals: We have read the jeremiad representing Cardinal McGrath as unfit for Church leadership at any level, especially the See of Rome. Before defending her against such scurrilous and unworthy attacks, we point out that she has never sought the position. We see our colleague as a woman who arrived in Rome seeking nothing more than to rouse the Church to new life. Like the rest of us, she hated what was happening to it, but unlike us, she had a fresh vision of how to save it. Is this so damnable a trait? Should we disown her because she aims high? On the contrary, we should bless her and give her a chance. We don't agree with everything she represents, but we see in it a possibility for a different kind of Church, one more prone to include than exclude, connect than isolate, reconcile than condemn, serve than rule, love than fear. What cannot be denied is that she has a genius for bringing people together, for winning them over, for ignoring and forgiving the sleights of her enemies. She can work wonders for this tired old bastion of outdated dogma and undeserved self-regard. She reawakens in us the memory of what we love about it: the heroic example of its saints, the magnificent music and art and architecture it inspired, the retreats into silence when our spirits sag, the stories about Jesus at Christmas and Easter, the prayers we learned as children, generous service to the poor and forgotten, and the sheer joy of all that drove us to dedicate our lives to it. It is true that she calls for change, but she is no reckless buccaneer, as you depict her. She has a keen sense of what is worth preserving and the charisma to attract the world to doing it with her.

Every Wednesday morning you can see her walking along the Tiber in street clothes to say Mass at Santa Dorotea, her titular church. On her first visit she arrived unannounced and wasn't at first allowed in the sacristy to vest—no one knew who the strange lady was. A month later the news had spread. "This is that famous lady cardinal, and she is ours!" She won the hearts of the parish with short homilies in her broken Italian. Wednesday attendance rivaled Sunday. This is the real Macrina, not the parody of misrepresentation circulated by her adversaries last week.

Will she end by succeeding Francis? This is unlikely. It took 260 years before America was ready for a female president, and we would be foolish to expect so dramatic an elevation for our friend. But we are not closed to it.

Ezra, email: Dear Macrina, It saddens me to tell you that my marriage to Libi has failed. This is no place to go into the reasons, but they have much to do with you. Throughout our marriage I could never put you out of my mind. There was no comparing the fun we had or the sheer sense of being with the one right person in the whole world that you represented for me (excuse my goofy prose). Do you remember our first bike ride and picnic in the woods or the time we went ice fishing? Thank God (though I'm still not quite a believer) for those memories.

This letter is what you would call a Hail Mary. I've been following your adventures in Rome as you try to reform that hopeless church you somehow find the heart to love. Or do you? Are you stuck in a rut? I find it hard to believe you're enjoying life in the way you and I did. And isn't that what life at its best should be all about? You are only 60, so there is still time.

I read that it's rumored you might be the next pope. Is this really possible? If it should happen, at least I would gain a little more respect for the institution. But this must be one of those ridiculous rumors that journalists like to spread to justify their existence. My guess is that you will end up stuck as a cardinal, chaste and browbeaten, until the day you die. I know how hard it would be to betray the "cause" of women equality and empowerment in the Catholic Church, but the only thing you haven't achieved is the papacy, and if that's denied you, what else is there to do? Your life would flatten out. All the acclaim and popularity, pretty heady stuff, would fall away. You'd just be another of those silly cardinals dressed in pinafore and elf's hat.

Please consider carefully what I offer — what we offer to each other.

Ezra

Macrina, paper Journal: I got a letter from Ezra today as if from another world — a world of the past, a world that somebody else not quite me used to live in. I could walk away from the Curia into that world, into his arms. That is what he wants. That is what he offers. What a thought.

He tells me I'm stuck in a rut, and he is right. But it's a rut I rather like. It's called the Catholic Church. Now, against all odds, I might be on the cusp of making history. He knows I could never duck out of such a responsibility. But if it doesn't happen, what then? If the Church just rolled on like it always has, could I happily go back to being the bishop of Albany? Or continue here as the Vatican's lunatic laureate? I would never give up the priesthood, but why not as a humble priest in a Massachusetts parish with Ezra to come home to every night? I almost get starry-eyed thinking about it. But if elected, well, if elected — what a thought — my God, I could still have it all. Not as his wife, but his friend. What a thought. But, no, that would give scandal. I would have to put all thoughts of happiness aside. I would belong to the Church, my life ruled by it. My life would not belong to me. My conduct would have to be irreproachable. Could I sneak in a phone call? Could I even travel incognito to see him? No, every move I made would be studied, and we would be discovered. I would have to find happiness of a different kind — one I already know a little about. The happiness of being loved by Greg and Sophie, by Mom and

Dad. But also by the whole world as a celebrity, a middle-aged, clerical version of Princess Diana, a shallow love that in the end disappoints, like melted ice cream.

Suddenly how frightening the thought of being pope, like a fly stuck to a gluey surface. But I shouldn't exaggerate, I shouldn't pity myself. My dear friends the saints will always be near when I call out. And God is always there when I hit rock bottom.

What a ridiculous meditation. Wouldn't it be enough to see the Church change? Power wielded well has its satisfactions. And the people I would meet along the way: acting presidents, living saints, scientists, inventors, philanthropists, Olympians, crippled children notable for their courage, lepers needing a hug, even penitent criminals. The whole gamut of humanity. Perhaps one would become a true friend. Someone to replace Ezra, to subdue the ache in my heart? No, I don't think so.

Macrina, communiqué in paper addressed to the College of Cardinals by request for a clarification on her position on abortion:

Dear brothers in Christ, some of you asked me to be more clear about where I stand on abortion. I believe in transparency and am happy to share my view.

In my early twenties I got pregnant by a man I loved but later realized I could not marry. I was a U.S. Marine at the time, as was he. What I chose landed me in temporary disgrace and wounded my family, especially my mother. Why not abort? I might be deceiving myself, but it had nothing to do with Catholic teaching. For one thing, I wasn't sure that the Church was right in holding that a fetus is a person and that aborting the fetus would amount to murder. On the other hand, I couldn't say with certainty that it wasn't. That doubt settled it for me. I had to be certain before proceeding, and I wasn't. A lesser consideration was the certainty that the fetus was, if not a living soul, at least a housing for that soul. It represented, you might say, a trajectory toward life as a human person. Violently removing that housing would, for me, amount to a roll of the dice I was not willing to do—not murder, but an action with profoundly serious consequences. I brought the baby to term and, as you all know, put her up for adoption with a couple I befriended and chose for my baby girl. I've never second-guessed that decision even though it has brought me great grief.

I think the Church's present position is indefensible. No one can know the exact status of a young fetus, and no one should pretend to. I understand the argument that the Church is playing it safe, but it is also misrepresenting the facts; namely that it is possible to know exactly what happens at conception. In doing that it outrages those who think otherwise, ranging from physicians to Protestant theologians.

So what should the Church's position be? Because we do not know with certainty that the fetus is not a person, we should avoid abortion: We are not justified killing something that might be a person, or even something that might lead to being a person. On the other hand, we should not condemn women who choose to abort if their consciences tell them the fetus is not a person, as do many God-fearing mainline Protestants. As for pregnant Catholics who come to us for advice, we should explain the position I've just outlined, urge them to keep the baby with our full support, and leave the decision up to them. If they choose to abort, we should refrain from condemning them and encourage them to attend Mass and receive Communion as Catholics in good standing. We should also make it clear that the sacrament of Reconciliation is always available to them if they should feel the need of it later on, as many no doubt would.

As in other matters dealing with doctrine, for example, the Real Presence of Jesus in the bread and wine, or his exact status with respect to God, we should not confuse what we would like to believe with what we know to be true. Refraining from exaggerated claims about what happens in the womb will attract sturdy minds and good hearts. Scientists and philosophers will look at us, and religion in general, with new respect. They will see that we represent the moral high ground but without the arrogance that once characterized us. Also, the best of our young Catholic men and women will take a new look at us as they consider a career in ministry. As for the uninstructed laity, the fine points of doctrine that get us so worked up will pass them by. They will follow our lead.

I hope this helps.

Quotations from postal mail addressed to Macrina (unreachable by email):

...you have the full support of the Sisters of the Sacred Heart. Go gal!

...you are no better than a trashy prostitute. You would disgrace the papacy. For God's sake, woman, where is your modesty?

...you compare yourself to Augustine because he, like you, had a child out of wedlock? What!

Your hometown and the whole state of Alabama is totally behind you. Roll, Tide! Roll, Macrina....

...we are praying for you. You have done wonders for the Church. Wonders more are coming.

If you get yourself appointed pope, we will kill you. I swear to God we will kill you.

...Pauperize the Vatican. Get rid of all that pomp and ceremony... feed the hungry. Then I'll be your biggest fan.

...I always knew the Anti-Christ would be a woman.

You're a *one* on the Myers-Briggs personality test. Just wanted you to know.

Hindus are offering pujas for you. You must have been Hindu in previous life. Jai Macrina!

...atheists are praying you'll be pope. They are your biggest fans. The wrecking ball is hovering over St. Peter's.

...big donation to Catholic Relief Services if you are elected. Very BIG!

Greg: Picture the cardinals in the Sistine Chapel as they gather to elect the next pope. Two rows facing two rows are seated in their red robes under the famous frescoes on biblical themes by Michelangelo. When the cardinals look straight up, they see God touching Adam and bringing him to life. They see Adam and Eve's expulsion from the Garden of Eden and Noah's drunkenness. At the far end of the room Michelangelo's fresco of the world's end and final judgment reach to the high ceiling. This famous chapel is the place where the voting is done. Referred to as the conclave, it is the place where the College of Cardinals will lock themselves in until they have a new pope. The date is January 1, 2081, the day after Pope Francis II resigned. Only the cardinals who haven't reached the age of 80 can serve as electors, 127 in total. All are male except for Macrina. All take an oath to maintain secrecy over what happens during the process, though in past elections leaks have surfaced. The Chapel is swept using electronic devices, and Wi-Fi access is blocked. High excitement pervades the enclosure. This is a great moment in the life of every cardinal, electors and non-electors alike.

A two-thirds majority is required before a pope can be named. Speculation about who would be chosen came from all over the world. Polls in the U.S. showed that 79% of Catholic women rooted for Macrina, 43% of men. On December 28, Maria Evans, an American Catholic divorced from her billionaire husband two years earlier and said to be worth $53 billion, vowed to give Catholic Relief Services $12 billion if Macrina were elected. Opinions were divided on whether this would help or hurt her chances. Many pundits thought that being American was harmful enough since a link between the world's superpower and the Church suggested an unholy entanglement with the interests of the rich rather than the poor. Others felt that Macrina's "softer sex" would rebalance the anti-American bias. Did the electors consider such factors? Judging by the extraordinary events of the conclave that were about to happen, apparently they did.

On the little desk in from of each elector's seat sits a ballot with the words in English and Italian, "I elect as Supreme Pontiff," and then a space for the elector to write the name in his own handwriting. He then rises and approaches the urn placed on the altar next to the scene of the Last Judgment and says, "I call as my witness Christ the Lord who will be my judge that my vote will be given to the one who before God I think should be elected." Each elector approaches the urn one by one in this way. After all have placed their ballots in the urn, the ballots are tallied and the names called out. This process is repeated four times each day until the new pope is elected. Black smoke rising out of the little chimney above the Chapel signals to the faithful gathered in the Square that no one has the necessary two-thirds of the ballots. They wait with nervous expectation for the white smoke and the announcement, "We have a pope!"

At the end of the third day and twelve elections later, no white smoke showed, and the crowds in the Square drifted away and waited for the news on their televisions. "What in the world is going on?" the world wondered. No one alive could remember a process so dragged out. There had been so much black smoke that the chemicals needed to make it gave out, and the announcement had to be made to the Square by a long-range acoustic device (LRAD).

What *was* going on inside? If Pope Thomas II hadn't later permitted the cardinals to break the oath—that was his right— it's likely we never would have known. Even at that, I was extremely fortunate. The proceedings were videotaped, and I was given access to the tape—the first outsider so blessed, no doubt because of my tie to Macrina. Thomas' thinking was that if the cardinals knew what happened, why shouldn't the rest of the world? What was there to hide? Further, ugly rumors that had surfaced almost from the beginning would be put to rest.

At noon after lunch or at night after dinner, it was the custom for the cardinals to cluster in the hallway or at an open door leading into a bedroom to discuss the election with close friends. Consensus building in this manner led to the dropping of nominees who had too few votes; an unusually high number, 20, had received at least one vote in the first round. After the morning rounds of the second day, only four names remained: an Italian, a Brazilian, a Chinese, and an American. At the end of that day, after eight failed attempts to name the next pope, two remained. Neither was Italian, not even European. One was the Chinese archbishop of Shanghai, Xao Huang Chai, the other Macrina. By now China had more practicing Catholics than France, Germany, and Italy combined. Xao represented the new China, the Christian China. A weakened, frightened Communist Party embraced Catholicism in order to survive, and churches were allowed to spring up all over the nation. Macrina could claim a growing renewal of Catholicism in America under her influence, but Xao, or rather Xao's followers, could counter with a similar claim for China. The electors had gradually been won over by the growth argument and fell into one or the other camp. It was either Macrina or Xao. Once there, growth quickly became irrelevant since both could claim it equally. The emphasis shifted: Xao represented the conservative red faction, as it became known, Macrina the progressive green. It was a classic, timeless standoff between two different kinds of political systems and ways of seeing the world. The two superpowers had grown closer since the pandemic humbled both equally, but the gap between them had not closed. Many electors were appalled to find themselves having to choose between candidates they distrusted equally, but choose they did. And for them the line between them admitted of no compromise. As a result, vote after vote in the next four rounds showed little movement. By the end of the third day, the cardinals went into retreat for one day to rest and pray.

After two more inconclusive rounds on the fifth day, as the world continued to wait and speculate wildly, and after one of the electors went into convulsions and dropped to the floor as he approached the urn with his ballot, even the holiest cardinals found their impatience wearing thin. The custom over the centuries had been to reserve the Chapel for voting, not for presenting an argument or attacking an opponent. But the utter frustration on both sides burst the dam. Cardinal Zamora stood up and asked Macrina if she thought she was worthy of being pope. But before she could answer, one of the other electors rose and tried to silence him. Zamora only raised his voice. "What do you say for yourself? I have no objection to a woman. But you are a woman with a history. You are no martyr and no virgin like thousands of our saints. My mother, God rest her soul, is named after one of them, Catherine of Siena. What will the faithful think? Don't you see the scandal you give? You drag down every Catholic woman to your level. By your example you tell the world it's acceptable to sleep with a man not your husband and have his child. Why can't you see this? Your brothers in Christ will never give you the final votes you need. They would rather die first. Withdraw so we can bring this agony to an end." By now outraged voices had begun yelling at Zamora. He began reciting her doctrinal deviations, but the voices drowned him out. The room was erupting into bedlam when Macrina calmly stood up, raised her arms, and called for quiet.

Unlike any of the cardinals in that sacred setting, she was battle-tested to a degree that they had never known. In no other way can I explain her uncanny calm. And that calmness had a magical effect on that holy mob. More than anything she said, I believe, it was her composure that turned the tide in her favor. "Brothers," she began, "Cardinal Zamora has a point. He has spoken out of fervor for the Church he loves as much as I. In the eyes of God he might be one of God's special angels—who else would dare do what we've witnessed? But in his zeal for our brother Xao, instead of presenting his excellent traits, and there are many, he has chosen to list the faults of his opponent. This is not what our good brother Xao himself would have wanted, for Xao knows he has faults too—but they are unknown, whereas mine are evident to the world. Xao no doubt knows of the great Confucian philosopher and general Wang Yangming. Wang never chose an officer to serve under him unless that man had first lost a battle. That loss, he said, taught him more than any training exercise. It taught him how to win a war. Like Wang, I lost a battle." With that she sat down, and for a few seconds there was stunned silence. Then the applause came, and it grew, and it grew, and when the vote was taken after the dust settled, Macrina was close to the two-thirds necessary. On the next round, the last of the day, the sixteenth overall, as the evening shadows darkened the square outside, there was just enough light to discern white smoke rising from the chimney. Then the announcement came from the LRAD: "We have a pope! We have a pope!" Someone in the small crowd waved a big American flag.

The next morning crowds surged onto the square to see Pope Thomas, the name Macrina chose, address the city and the world. In Catholic churches from Buenos Aires to Warsaw special Masses were said for her guidance and protection. In New York City crowds of mostly women marched in triumph down Fifth Avenue to Times Square. In her hometown, bells over the Cathedral of the Immaculate Conception chimed all day long. Everyone, from wall-eyed atheists to contemplative nuns to teenagers who had never set foot in a church, talked about the "woman pope."

Macrina, Journal: I am the pope, the leader of a billion Catholics. This is an indisputable fact, but it's not sinking in. I hardly slept last night. This morning—it's 5:40, and Mass is at 7—I feel a kind of delirium, as if I am living in a dream. It's all so astonishing. I shake my head, look up at the crucifix on the wall above my desk, finger the keys on my laptop. The dream does not vanish. This is reality. And it's exhilarating. I thank God for it, not only for what has happened to me, but for women everywhere.

Last night I talked to Mom and Dad. Even Mom was happy. She tells me she'll never stop praying for me, praying I'll make good decisions for the Church. And Dad came through, at age 89, with another of his ridiculous limericks:

An American girl named Macrina
Became the Vatican's top signorina.
A cardinal named Zamora
Couldn't live up to his aura
And took flight like a laughing hyena.

It wasn't really that funny, but I couldn't stop laughing. It was my way of releasing all the tension that had been building up over the election.

Prayer, Mass, breakfast, the gym, a walk in the garden, then the business of the first day, in that order.

Greg: Every newspaper columnist suggested what Macrina's triumph meant for divorced or gay or transgender Catholics. Within the first week three billionaires, former Catholics, united to set up a fund to pay married recruits to the priesthood a living wage through seminary training. Such was the enthusiasm unleashed by her election.

But the doomsayers were rattling their drums. Three cardinals writing in *Vatican* magazine implied that she used American wealth to buy the papacy. A Catholic think tank in Germany predicted a transformation of Catholic doctrine from timeless truth to "mythology," with Mary's virgin birth the first casualty and Christ's second coming the second. A conservative Catholic magazine published in Dallas called Macrina's choice of

Doubting Thomas as her papal name a conscious assault on the faith, a "novel interpretation" encouraging young Catholics to doubt Church doctrine. When the *Washington Post* rhapsodized over the election, comparing its retreat from "implausible dogmas" to the demolition of the Berlin Wall, skeptics warned that it was the Church itself that would be demolished. On social media sites all over the world, opinions flitted or raged back and forth.

Macrina and Paul Cabendish, excerpts from a television Interview on BBC World:

Paul: It is the highest honor for me to welcome you as the new pope. Congratulations on your election, Your Holiness.

Macrina: Macrina will do nicely. Or even Thomas, though the world seems to have forgotten that.

Paul: I've noticed. Could it be because Thomas was a man? It did take most of us by surprise. Especially after what you've done for women.

Macrina: Yes, everywhere I'm being called Macrina. There is no fighting it. At least it's a good saint's name.

Paul: Why did you take Thomas as your papal name?

Macrina: Well, for one thing, I like men. (Both laugh.) No, it's not really that. Not at all. I chose it, first, because there had never been a Pope Thomas. I found this amazing. I think he deserved some air time. The real reason, though, was my long-time admiration of him. He remained skeptical until he had evidence. He had to see the risen Christ for himself. I've never faulted him for that, but the Church has—always has. And I'm faulted for the same reason. I require evidence before I can believe something that on the surface seems outlandish.

Paul: You mean, like Mary giving birth to Jesus while still a virgin?

Macrina: Or believing that the world will end when Jesus comes back to earth rather than when we destroy it with our own madness. But, yes, Mary's virginity is a perfect example. We know that Jesus had quite a few siblings. His brothers are actually named. Even the Bible tells us Mary was not a virgin. Yet the Church claims she was. Why? Because sex was regarded as impure, and Jesus, being God, couldn't have been stained by such an ordinary origin. So the rumor got started, and we've been stuck with it for 2,000 years—all of which makes us look ridiculous in a scientific age. Such beliefs chase educated people away from the Church, and that's a tragedy. It's a situation I'll be working hard to change.

Paul: I notice you're wearing a dark green robe, not the usual white we expect of a pope. Or a red. Any special reason?

Macrina: If you look closely, you'll see brown thread woven into the green. Symbolism is important. I feel white suggests a purity that angels have and I don't. As for the red, some say it represents the blood of martyrs. I think it represents vanity, showiness, self-aggrandizement. It calls attention to itself. This earthy dark green, the color of spruce, of earthy vigor, better fits our vocation. We are meant to be servants, not masters.

Paul: There is talk of substituting robots for the Swiss Guards. Where do you stand on that?

Macrina: Yes, this has been grabbing headlines lately. Well, the Curia are quite divided on the issue, and I can see why. I've finally come to a decision after mulling it over for weeks. Robotic technology has come a long way. We've consulted a manufacturer who assures us they can perfectly duplicate a Swiss Guard in full regalia, right down to the friendly directions they give to tourists. These robots are expensive, but they don't eat, sleep, bathe, go to the toilet, change clothes, or need any more housing than a closet. And they don't get bored or tired or fractious. They're machines. In the end they cost less than the corps of living Guards we maintain, so there is a lot in favor of the robots. So for me this has not been an easy choice, but I oppose the change. We Catholics value the spiritual soul above all else. The soul is the seat of consciousness and free will, God's greatest gift to us. Humanoid machines have no more awareness than furniture. Keeping company with machines acting like humans has no spiritual value. We can talk to them, and they will answer skillfully, but they will have no idea what they are saying. They're like dolls you wind up and play with and then set aside. They could become a distraction, in time even a nuisance—like something you can't help seeing but wish you didn't have to. But I've made a concession. The guard standing at my door to protect me through the night will be a robot.

Paul: A novel solution! But are you opposed to robots in general?

Macrina: Not at all. They buried our dead during the pandemic, and they can perform all kinds of services that for humans are degrading or dangerous.

Paul: On another subject—I daresay a more important one—your sharpest critics grill you on the question of Christ's nature.

Macrina: Yes, this is the issue that excites the most passion. Even more than abortion and pedophilia. It's also behind most of the death threats I get.

Paul: Death threats. Really?

Macrina: I'm afraid so.

Paul: Where do you stand on the issue?

Macrina: I've written a great deal about it, so what I say here is a very short version.

Paul: Don't hold back.

Macrina: Well, world history is full of examples of cultures divinizing the founder of their religions. It's natural for us humans to do that. That's what happened to Jesus over the first 300 years after his death. Jesus himself was a God-centered man who related to God as his Abba, his loving Father. He didn't claim to be God. I accept and love Jesus as my savior, but not because he died on the cross for my sins. I love him because he showed me, showed all of us, how to live. If anyone can be considered the world's great spiritual master, for me it's Jesus. Even all those liberal atheists who write for *The New York Times* and champion human rights have Jesus to thank for their philosophy.

Paul: But are ordinary Christians, the moms and pops in the pews on Sunday, are they ready for this?

Macrina: I don't think Christianity will decline further if we humanize Jesus. What makes him so special is all he did *because* he was human. We Catholics have had Jesus' divinity pounded into us since we were kids, but future generations will be luckier. They won't be forced to squeeze the designer and master of the universe into a Galilean who lived 2,000 years ago on a planet called earth, however great he was. Let me add that I have no objection to Catholics believing in Jesus' divinity if they must. The whole Green program is about making room for both traditionalists and progressives. The Church's doors should be wide enough to accept both.

Paul: But wouldn't unity be better?

Macrina: Yes, it would, but we're not there yet.

Paul: The Catholic Church has been mired in scandal ever since I can remember. I know that you're concerned about this. Where do things stand today?

Macrina: We've made great strides forward in the last ten years. Women are now priests, even bishops. Catholics no longer have to choose between the priesthood and marriage. Married men and women are pastoring parishes all over the world. Older celibate priests who fall in love are now allowed to marry and keep their profession. On the other hand, celibacy is still held up as a special calling for monks and nuns, and this is good; such self-denial if freely chosen makes a very different kind of person, one that Jesus himself was. All of this has led to a huge reduction in child sexual abuse.

Paul: It sounds like you've reached you goal.

Macrina: We'll never reach our goal.

Paul: You're making your first trip next week—to China. You'll be paraded through Beijing's streets as if you're a rock star. It sounds rather exciting.

Macrina: I don't like being made a fuss over. I'm just a white-haired, middle-aged woman playing a role. But when I see all those smiling faces, I'll warm to the task.

Paul: I hear you'll be out in the open, not behind a bullet-proof shield.

Macrina: Life is risky, always risky. There are many ways to die. One of my favorite authors, Tagore, said that after we die we'll discover that life was like a "slight, momentary dream."

Paul: Hmm. I hear that back in your home town they're making a Mardi Gras float about you.

Macrina: Yes, isn't that hilarious? Mobilians love their Mardi Gras.

Paul: And their Macrina.

Greg: When Macrina called home, she was upbeat but seldom effusive about the progress she was making. Nothing she said suggested being dazzled by the fame the world showered on her. Sometimes she complained of being overwhelmed by work. Catholics were being slaughtered by radicalized Muslims while worshipping in their churches. Dioceses were still being sued by victims of pedophilia. Priests preferring Latin refused to say Mass in the vernacular. Penniless Peruvians wrote to her in broken handwritten Spanish asking for money to feed their children. Ghanaians hoped she would consecrate their new basilica. And so on. She usually called us around 9 p.m. Sunday (her time) just before her struggles with sleep began. Mom and Dad were often with us. I recorded those calls.

Her days were taken up with meetings with Curia officials, visiting bishops, heads of state, and representatives of other faiths. Every day she had to appoint new bishops, just as she had been appointed by Francis, or move Vatican diplomats.

On Wednesdays she delivered the traditional message to an audience of thousands in the Square. Mail, often handwritten, reached the Vatican, too much for her to read all. She depended on her secretary to sort it out, then asked to read at random two of the rejected letters. "It left me a little autonomy," she laughed. She had to read drafts of major documents and speeches she had to give, making changes as needed. She might make a phone call to someone who was ill or needed special encouragement. Then there were the complaints over the changes she proposed, the opposing points of view she had to consider and respond to. There was enough work to "keep ten popes busy," she said. Her insomnia worsened. "Sometimes I find it impossible to stop my mind from worrying about all that's wrong in the Church." But her spirits didn't sag.

She followed the example of the first Pope Francis by shunning the lavish Apostolic Palace and lived instead in the Vatican guesthouse, Casa Santa Marta. She began her day with centering prayer, then reached out to her favorite saints "for any help they can give." She continued to ask Emelie Gamelin for help with Anna. Past popes had always said a private Mass every morning with invited guests and Vatican employees attending. Macrina broke with this tradition by sometimes asking one of the guest priests staying at Santa Marta to say the 7 a.m. Mass and give the homily. "I'm both the Vicar of Christ and Successor to Peter. I prefer the second role. Peter didn't give out the bread but received it." Some of the cardinals grumbled about her "impiety."

She instigated several pastoral changes. She disliked glamorous receptions, as we saw. She preferred making surprise visits, popping in with little or no notice, comparing them to pop-up summertime thunderstorms like those we grew up with on the Gulf Coast. She claimed she could "see what was really going on before authorities had time to clean up the mess." Sometimes she wore layman's clothing, preferring pantsuits to dresses. On a visit to Kadugli, Sudan, to investigate reports of Black Catholics from South Sudan being enslaved by white Sudanese government officials, police detained her for an hour at the airport for "impersonating the Pope." But the biggest break with the past was the weekly one-hour English-only Vatican Chat, as she called it. In this radio call-in program any one was welcome to ask a question of her or express an opinion. Censors ensured that the questions were legitimate, but they had strict orders not to exclude challenges to her views. The program was an immense success, with as many as 280 million listeners tuned in on any given Saturday. American wives might be listening to Macrina take on her critics or explain some Church policy needing change while their husbands watched a football game in the next room. Or college students would listen in so they could write a report for their sociology class on the Pope's "revolutionary spirituality." Or atheists contemptuous of all religion hoped to see how poorly she held up under the battering of "better minds." What made the program so popular? Whatever else she was, she was a great teacher. And she had a knack for pinning down her opponents, then charitably lifting them back up. Below are some of the conversations, all recorded and placed in the Vatican archives.

Macrina and call-ins, audiotaped:

1. Hello, is this the Pope? Pope Macrina?

Macrina: Yes, it is. And who is this?

1. My name is Melinda.

Macrina: Hi, Melinda.

1. I wanted to ask how you could participate in a Hindu religious ceremony. Some people say you're a Hindu in disguise.

Macrina: Well, I did do that. It was called an "Opening of the Eyes" ceremony, and I was the guest of honor. A new statue was being consecrated at the Krishna Temple in Udupi, India. Here is what happened. Their priest invites Krishna to enter the statue, and he comes down and takes up his post. At that point the priest removes the blindfold from the statue. It's all very moving, and I wanted to show them that Christians are their friends. It's a lot like our Communion service, except that we call down Christ into bread and wine. I think it's important for people to feel that God is near them, so near you can see him in a statue. So, no, I'm not a Hindu, but I love Hindus as my brothers and sisters. Don't you?

1. Well, sort of, I guess. Not really.

Macrina: What a wonderful question you've asked, Melinda. Thank you.

2. Is this the Pope?

Macrina: Yes, it is.

2. I can't believe it. Angie, it's really her! (Spoken to someone in the next room?) I just want to thank you for what you've done for women. Our pastor is a woman, and she is the greatest....

3. I'm a retired Anglican priest living in London. I read that you're dropping the word *Roman* in front of *Catholic*. You don't want to think of yourselves as *Roman* Catholics. You've taken over the name *Catholic* for yourself. That's quite a grab. Have you forgotten that Anglicans also consider themselves Catholic, Anglo Catholic? How do you distinguish yourselves from us?

Macrina: I've thought of this quite a bit actually and thank you for your question. The world usually refers to Anglicans as *Protestant,* which is accurate, and that's enough to distinguish you from us. But you have a point. Your Mass is very close to ours. It would seem the same to an outsider. But there isn't anything especially Roman about us anymore. Of the 18 cardinals I recently appointed, not one is Italian. They come from every continent except Antarctica. *Catholic* means *universal.* And we're that as never before. I don't see how you can qualify *universal.*

3. That seems quite cheeky to me.

Macrina: I grant the point. But let me say how indebted we are to you. You were 80 years ahead of us in opening the priesthood to women. Many of your ministers are divorced, while we can't even make room for a divorced laity. Your carefully prepared sermons put ours to shame. Your hymnal is without an equal. And we have no monopoly on saint-making — the only difference is that we name them! We consider Anglicans our dearest spiritual relatives and hope to reunite with them. Then we wouldn't be having this conversation....

4. I'm a lesbian ex-Catholic. I see the Church as hopelessly homophobic. You consider us disordered, deviant, unnatural. How can you work for such a backward institution?

Macrina: What's your name, and are you married?

4. Not according to you.

Macrina: This isn't — do you mind giving me your name?

4. Let's just say I'm Sylvia.

Macrina: Sylvia, this is not an easy subject. According to Catholic teaching, the reason we're sexually attracted to each other is to bring children into the world. That's true of all primates. And I think you have to grant me this point. So there's something a little odd about people of the same sex being sexually drawn to each other. To biologists it might look like getting your wires crossed. Are you following me?

4. So there is something sick about me, right? Something unnatural. Like maybe I'm possessed by a demonic force or something.

Macrina: Not at all. Because being gay might be entirely natural in cases like yours. Scientists specializing in the memories of little children who claim to remember a previous life tell us they underwent a sex change between lives. In other words, if you were a male in your previous life and sexually enjoyed women, that habit might have carried over into this life. Psychologically there's nothing unnatural about it at all. We are very close to changing our policy on homosexuality, Sylvia. Maybe the key is getting it to accept reincarnation. But even if that doesn't work, the point is that for a lesbian like you it seems completely natural and good to love another woman. And that is enough for me. Will it be enough for my colleagues on the Curia? We'll see. Do you follow me?

4. I do. But reincarnation?

Macrina: Well, neuroscientists tell us the brains of gays and straights look the same. They can't account for it physically. Something's got to be the cause.

4. Well, maybe there's a little hope for the Catholic Church after all.

Macrina: LGBTQ people like you make a difference, Sylvia. Thanks for speaking up.

5. Am I really talking to the pseudo-pope, Macrina?

Macrina: As you say. How can I help?

5. I was thinking about becoming a Catholic until I saw what you were up to. You deny that Jesus died on the cross for our sins. But the whole reason we love Jesus is because he did that. That's what Christianity is all about. I can't see how you could ever be a Christian.

Macrina: What's your name?

5. Gary, from Shreveport, Louisiana.

Macrina: Gary, you'll just have to accept it. I think of myself as a Christian. And I love Jesus, though for reasons different from yours. Which I won't go into here. Try to think of Jesus' death on the cross as a parable, a parable that the Church uses to make a point. It's natural for us to think we have to pay for our sins. That's why we have law courts, right?

5. I don't follow you. What does that have to do with Jesus dying for our sins?

Macrina: Somebody has to pay. And Jesus is that somebody. Think of him as the scapegoat for the sins of the world. And think of God as the one who forgives us because the scapegoat has atoned for our sins. That's the way we think. Somebody has to pay. Does that make sense?

5. But... wait a minute. That's what I believe, not you.

Macrina: You're right. I'm summing up your position. I ask you: Do you really think God thinks in this way? Doesn't it seem a little too human?

5. To me it makes total sense.

Macrina: That's okay with me, dear brother Gary from Shreveport. I can join hands with you any day. There's room for us all.

6. Thank you for taking my call, Your Holiness. I cannot give you my name. I am a retired deputy governor of one of Nigeria's northern states and a Catholic. Last week Fulani jihadists opened fire on another congregation attending Sunday Mass, as I'm sure you know. The priest was one of the victims. He was my eldest son! What would you do to put an end to these massacres—over 3,000 dead already this year? It's been going on for the last 75 years.

Macrina: (Long pause.) I can barely think a rational thought. All I want to do is throw my arms around you and weep. (In a quivering voice after a deep, audible breath.) If I had all power at my disposal, I would send an army into your country and either capture or kill these criminals—all of them. This is no place to turn the other cheek. Many of them are irreformable, but many, especially the teenage boys, are victims themselves. Somewhere deep in their hearts they must already be repenting their crimes. They just don't know it yet. You ask what I can do. The answer is nothing. Any gesture of love I might show them would be interpreted as weakness. They can't be loved out of their hatred. They can only be defeated. But in your country there isn't the will to defeat them. I know, because I have talked to your president, received his assurance that everything possible is being done, yet the atrocities continue. (Long pause.) Here is my advice. Listen to your wife when she tells you she sees him or hears his voice or feels his presence. Your son isn't far away. He is in a good place and will come to comfort you.

6. (Sobbing) Thank you... thank you... my wife...has already told me this. She has seen him. She has seen him. Oh, thank you so much!

7. It's a miracle that I got through to you at last. I've been trying for three months. Thank you!

Macrina: I'm so glad the censors finally let you in. You sound like a fellow American.

7. Yes, I'm Robert from Chico, California. I teach religious studies and some philosophy at the local university.

Macrina: Aha, one of my kind!

7. Yes. Well, let me begin by saying I'm a great fan of yours. I think what you're trying to do for the Church is beyond important. It's the future. But I understand why you tread carefully. You want to stay within the boundaries of the faith, not invent a new religion. Do I have this right?

Macrina: You do.

7. You get a lot of flack from traditionalists who insist that Christ died on the cross for our sins. If I may, might I suggest a way to make sense of this?

Macrina: I'm all ears.

7. As I see it, and as you explained it a few weeks ago, we're all geared to blame bad people for their crimes. We have this thing called a sense of justice. That means people have to suffer for their crimes—jail time, big fines, even a death sentence. But for most of us, our sins are hidden, they go undetected. If we hit someone with our car, even kill them, but get away with it, we live with guilt for the rest of our lives. We wake up in the middle of the night in a cold sweat. That's why Christians look to Christ to atone for all these hidden sins. But that's not justice. Why should an innocent man suffer for my sins? But what if that man was God, as traditional Christians believe? Then God does the suffering. Is that unfair? No, because God made us the way we are. The buck stops with God. He looks down upon all his planets and sees people doing stupid things to each other and grieves. And why? Because he loves us as his

children, his rebelling, abusing, criminal children. His grief is like ours when we see our kids do stupid things, and I speak from experience. He atones for his own flawed creation by suffering with them. And it's natural that he should. So it's not that hard to understand why Christians insist on this way of looking at things, and why they take you to task because you don't. Do you see what I mean?

Macrina: Robert, you believe that God suffers, and so do I. And so do all Christians. So the greens and the reds are not that far apart. I think that's what you are saying.

7. Exactly. Except that you and I know that Christ was not really God. But it's okay if traditionalists do. The point is that for all of us, greens and reds alike, God must suffer. And it's logical that he should. If he didn't, he would be a heartless scientist experimenting with human rats, or a cosmic kid amusing himself with video games using real people.

Macrina: So God is our fellow sufferer, in the same way we suffer for our kids when they make a mistake, or when they make others suffer.

7. That's right. The world is full of mistakes that create suffering, as all of us know.

Macrina: But also joy.

7. Absolutely.

Macrina: You've given me much to ponder, Robert. Lucky are your students to have you as a guide.

8. Thanks for taking my call. I'm an ex-Catholic and want to tell you why.

Macrina: Please do, and what is your name?

8. Priscilla, from Perth, Australia.

Macrina: Go ahead, Priscilla.

8. Seven years ago I married a man, a divorced non-practicing Catholic. He wasn't willing to jump through all the hoops the Church required before you can get married. A personal friend with a ministerial license married us in a small ceremony in my husband's backyard. When I asked my priest what I could do to make myself right in the eyes of the Church, he said I could go to Mass but not receive communion. This made me feel that marrying my husband was a dirty business, a mortal sin. I stopped going to Mass altogether. But then I began to ask myself if Jesus himself would have given me such an answer, and I was sure he wouldn't. Three months later we found a nice Anglican Church that welcomed us with open arms. The priest knew I had married a divorced man but couldn't have cared less. There was never any question about receiving communion. But I miss the Church I was brought up in. What do you say? Am I unworthy to receive communion?

Macrina: Priscilla, when I hear a story like yours, my blood boils. Who is anybody to tell you whether you can receive the Eucharist? That's between you and God. But I can tell you this: I am personally overseeing a commission here at the Vatican that will put an end to these exclusionary canon laws. Not only that: we'll be simplifying the paperwork and the marriage preparation laws for older couples. As for divorce, we are going to recognize it as the business of the couple alone, not the Church's. We will neither bless it nor condemn it. The Church exists for people who are laden with guilt for past mistakes and for people wounded by them. We should be healers, not lawyers. Voices that cry out like yours are hastening change in the Church. Thank you, Priscilla.

9. Is this the Pope? Is this Pope Macrina?

Macrina: Yes. Who am I speaking to?

9. Lars, from Stockholm. My question has to do with your novel view of the Trinity—Father, Mother, and Universe permeated by the Holy Spirit. What happened to the Son?

Macrina: Lars, allow me to use an analogy. Think of the Third Person as a Divine Diamond with as many facets as there are souls in the universe. Jesus for us Christians is the facet that shines the brightest. He is the Father-Mother's most evolved earth-child and our cherished elder brother, all the more lovable because he is so much like us. The Holy Spirit shines within him in a manner we Christians like to think unique.

9. Oh. But why so radical a break with the tradition?

Macrina: Because we can do so much better. Have you ever wondered why there is no mention of Motherliness in the Trinity? The primordial relationship is between Father and Son. What happened to the Mother?

9. The Mother? What Mother?

Macrina: The Mother who got left out.

9. What do you mean? There was no Mother. That isn't Christian.

Macrina: Not yet. But we can make it Christian.

9. How can that be? You can't change God.

Macrina: I agree. God is as God is. All we can do is change the way we talk about God. No one really knows much about God anyway. Do you think the bishops at Nicaea had a private line to heaven?

9. I think they were guided by the Holy Spirit. They couldn't have erred.

Macrina: That's an assumption. They'd have come up with a different formula if women had been respected as equals, don't you think?

9. Well—

Macrina: I can live with the traditional formulation, Lars. Much of our talk about God is a plunge into the unknown anyway. For me, it just makes more sense to think of the Universe as being created by a cosmic husband and wife rather than a cosmic father and son.

9. I follow you, but it's just not the tradition.

Macrina: I agree. So let's make it so. Church teaching has changed down through the ages. There was a time when Catholics claimed there was no salvation outside the Church. The Second Vatican Council put that to rest. We shouldn't feel trapped by bad teaching.

9. So you call the Trinity bad teaching.

Macrina: Ah, sometimes my enthusiasm for reform carries me away! I apologize. It's just that we know better now.

9. I think it's too radical a break.

Macrina: Dear brother, I honor you for your faith. Being Catholic in Sweden cannot be easy. "By this all people will know that you are my disciples, if you have love for one another." So said our master. Can you love me as I love you?

9. I can, but not as a Christian.

Macrina: Thank you, Lars. That's all I ask.

10. I'm an investment counselor with a big company headquartered in Singapore. I'm not a Catholic but a Chinese convert to Christianity. I describe myself as an evangelical. I would like to know what you think about capitalism. You may call me Chu.

Macrina: That's a big subject, Chu, and I have to keep my answer short. Catholic Social Teaching has a lot to say on the subject, and it starts with God. God is not a solitary being but is relational. Whether you think of God as Father, Son, and Holy Spirit, or Father, Mother, and Holy Spirit, God is a social being. Mutual respect and love reign at all times in the very essence of those three coeternal Persons. The same should reign in our lives since we're made in their image. We have to reach out and build relations with our neighbors if we are to live fulfilled lives.

10. But how do I apply these ideals to what I do as an investment counselor?

Macrina: I'm not sure. But I don't see how you can justify dedicating your life to helping the rich get richer if that's in fact what you do. Is there some way you can help the poor and vulnerable get richer? As Catholics, that's what you should try to do. That's what Christ expects us to do. If we don't do it, then conflict and violence follow. Chu, this ideal should be kept close to your heart. Is there a way you can teach your clients to use their fortune for the common good?

10. My clients? (Burst of laughter.)

Macrina: At the very least, can you contribute generously out of the money you make? Catholic Social Services runs field offices all over the impoverished world. They're doing great work.

10. Good idea. How much should I give?

Macrina: Give until it hurts—that's the only rule. It has to hurt a little. For the widow in the Bible it was a penny. For you it would be more.

10. Yes, quite a bit more. I own rental property.

Macrina: Then reduce the rent. Make a fair profit, but not a fortune. You can't justify your greed by comparing yourself to what other landlords are charging. Capitalism is good up to a point, not when it goes unchecked. Be a Catholic capitalist, Chu. Remember Jesus' parable about Judgment Day? And what the King tells the good man who fed the hungry and clothed the naked? "As you did this to one of the least of these brothers of mine, you did it to me." And the man is taken up into eternal life.

10. Thank you. Hmm. Maybe I should look into becoming a Catholic.

Macrina: Not a bad idea. Send me a note if you do.

11. Hello, is this Pope?

Macrina: Yes, it is.

11. Thank you for taking call.

Macrina: You're welcome. Where are you from? I can't place the accent.

11. Moldova, and please forgive accent.

Macrina: I understand you perfectly. And what is your name?

11. Oh, I am Anastasia.

Macrina: Thank you. I think of Moldova as an Orthodox region. Are you Catholic?

11. No, Romanian Orthodox.

Macrina: Romanian Orthodox. What brings you to so distant an outpost as Rome?

11. You are so funny…. I have question about Roman Church claim—I think you say infallible. Do I pronounce the word correct?

Macrina: You do.

11. So you agree you are infallible?

Macrina: (Muffled chuckle.) In 1870 the Church declared the pope infallible when pronouncing on a subject of faith or morality. Its motive was to remove division and doubt among the faithful. It even went so far as declaring that anyone who rejected its claim to infallibility was anathematized. Our people wanted certainty, and the Church gave it to them.

11. I not know that word, excuse me, that long word.

Macrina: Anathematized?

11. Yes, that word.

Macrina: It means, uh, sent to hell. Damned.

11. Ooohh, that is no good! So if I don't believe what pope says, I go to hell?

Macrina: The whole non-Catholic world scoffs at Rome for making such an arrogant claim in the face of reason. This is a doctrine that we will reconsider at a future ecumenical council. And if reason prevails, we'll bury it. We'll bury it alongside the claim that earth was the center of the universe. May God help us. And may you forgive us.

11. Oh, that is good. And I practice English listening to you. And sometimes I even learn something.

Macrina: You are most welcome, and if I ever get to Moldova, please introduce yourself as the woman who asked about infallibility. I'll remember.

11. And learned new word. Thank you, Pope.

12. My name is Alejandro. I've heard rumors about how you pray, and they are contradictory. How *do* you pray?

Macrina: What a wonderful question. I open every day with a prayer of thanks to the Creator for my life, the good and the bad, the pleasant and the painful, successes and failures. Then I center myself and quiet my mind after asking God's spirit to well up within me. I try to stay in that state for ten or fifteen minutes by repeating my prayer word, or rather, phrase. Then I turn to my entreaties. I ask heaven's help for the many intentions I carry into the day—from the well-being of my daughter, to the illumination of my mind as I go about my business, to peace between Muslims and Christians, to the overall health of the Church. If—

12. Do you mind sharing your prayer phrase?

Macrina: Not at all, but it wasn't an easy choice. It's "Come, Master, come, and fill me wholly with thyself." The shortened version is simply "Thyself," a one-word reference to God. But you should choose your own.

12. Thank you. And, if you don't mind, what do you mean by heaven?

Macrina: Heaven. For me it's a catch-all term for all the saints and friends who are there. All those spirits who love me and might want to help me. Sometimes I try to pin down one or another angel or saint by name. But usually I don't try to sort out my helpers. I just trust they are there—thousands, all named by our wise old Church. We call them the "Church Triumphant," and they follow us with compassion. But their power is limited. So don't expect miracles. There are no guarantees.

12. I thought heaven was where they all live.

Macrina: Right you are, so let's get their attention.

13. I am addict to porn and nothing I do helping.

Macrina: What is your name, and where are you from?

13. Fazil. I live in small town not far Ludhiana in Punjab.

Macrina: I'm guessing you are Hindu or Sikh.

13. Hindu.

Macrina: Are you asking this Christian woman how you can break your habit?

13. Yes. I listen to you so I improve my English, and like you say.

Macrina: Your English is good enough for the world to understand. So, you watch porn. Are you married?

13. No. That is problem. Not enough women go around. So what can I do?

Macrina: So you are a victim of selective abortion. Female fetuses are aborted because of dowry considerations?

13. That right. My parents despair finding suitable match.

Macrina: You have my deepest sympathy, Fazil. Obviously I cannot solve your marital problem, but I can offer advice about the porn. Let me tell you in advance it won't be easy.

13. That is okay.

Macrina: First, it's not as easy as making up your mind you're going to stop. That will never work. Ask yourself what is your heart's deepest desire. It sounds to me like it's sex.

13. Yes. I think always sex.

Macrina: You must think of something else. Fill your mind with something else. Eventually your heart will follow. Your religion can be a big help. Read the Gita in a good translation or a biography of a Hindu saint—there are so many. Or any contemporary religious literature. Or even a good Punjabi novel—anything to take your mind off the addiction. Or join a cricket club, or a chess group. If you listen to music or watch movies laden with sexual imagery, change your habits. Explore what you are unfamiliar with. You might like what you discover. Click your phone away from trash and onto something clean. If you hang around with friends who encourage you to watch porn with them, find new friends. What you put into your mind is the key. Feed it a different diet and the heart will eventually follow. Not even therapy can do it for you. You must do it. And you can. You can, Fazil. I'll be praying for you. Does this help?

13. Thank you. Thank so much.

14. Hello, Your Holiness. This is Cardinal Zamora.

Macrina: Cardinal Zamora? What a surprise! I hadn't expected someone so close to home. You could almost sail your message across the yard by paper airplane. What do you have to tell me, or perhaps I should say the world?

14. So much has been written about our rivalry that I thought I'd try to clear it up.

Macrina: Is this the best place? After all—

14. The very best. I hope to make it clear that Christian love guides my feeling toward you. Journalists make their living by inciting passion in their readers. Exaggeration and outright distortion are their common currency. They have damaged our reputations and that of the whole Church.

Macrina: I'm not feeling damaged.

14. Well, then you haven't kept your antennae well-tuned.

Macrina: Oh?

14. Consider the question of what happens when the priest consecrates the bread and wine. I see that you honor the sacrament. That was never in question. What is in question is the degree you honor it.

Macrina: So we disagree only in degree? That's progress.

14. Not exactly. I say the bread and wine are actually the body and blood of Christ, and you say they are only symbols. We agree that the faithful should approach the sacrament with reverence, but you don't go as far as I. And as far as the great majority of Catholics. And as far as the Church says.

Macrina: The majority of Catholics in the pews of our churches are more inclined to agree with me than you—so the polls say. About the cardinals as a whole you're probably right.

14. Well, who knows more?

Macrina: That's an elitist position.

14. Maybe so, but it's the correct position.

Macrina: I see it as an unscientific position.

14. Christ said, "This is my body." He didn't say, "This symbolizes my body."

Macrina: He wanted his disciples to remember him when they broke bread after he was gone. He didn't get technical.

14. Technical? What an odd turn your mind sometimes takes.

Macrina: (She pauses.) I hope you don't think I condemn the tradition out of which you speak. I delight in your faith. Each of our positions has a weakness and a strength. Catholics like you bring greater reverence to the sacrament; they have this wonderful capacity for thinking that the creator of the universe is right before them, really before them, even inside them, body and blood. Their weakness is the scandal they give to non-Catholics who think they are lunatics. They make us look like a superstitious lot. Can the Church afford this reputation in the late twenty-first century? Reverence is a wonderful thing; the world needs much more of it. But we can find it in other places, especially in centering prayer. And in the glory of nature, God's outer garment. That's what I offer.

14. Your own colleagues are against you, Your Holiness. Even those who agree with you say you are moving too fast.

Macrina: Well, it seems you've enflamed our rivalry rather than dimmed it.

14. (Pause.) No, it's not a rivalry between us, but between our views. Please remember that you are the face of the Church. It's not yours to deck out as you like.

Macrina: Deck out? (Spoken with irritation, then more coolly:) Thank you for your frankness, Cardinal Zamora.

Greg: She ended each of her sessions with the Lord's Prayer, unaltered, followed by the Hail Mary, its first half faithful to Luke's gospel, its second non-biblical half changed to read: "Holy Mary and all you saints, shield us from evil now and at the hour of our death, amen." She did not believe in emphasizing sinfulness, as in "pray for us sinners."

Anna, email: Dear Mother, I write you with a sorrowing but happy heart. I have received your birthday and Christmas letters down through the years, read them hurriedly, then thrown them away. Now I regret that, terribly regret that. Now I look forward to seeing you again.

What exactly has happened? For the last two months I've been dating a man, another doctor. He's divorced, about ten years older than me, with two sons. One of them I've never met because he has disowned his dad. I was shocked to see myself in this son. So much misunderstanding. Another reason for my change of heart was something you said to one of the call-ins from your Vatican Chat show, which I was listening to out of curiosity. You might not remember the Nigerian who lost his son, but the compassionate heart I saw in your response to his loss melted me. I had never seen that side of you before. I had assumed all these years that you had a brilliant intellect and a heart of stone. Now I see I was wrong. And there is that mysterious other factor, that saint you've been praying to for a miracle. Who knows? Maybe she had a hand in it. I still don't know whether there is a God, but I don't count it out.

I admire the effort you are making for the women of the world. That you should be my mother is almost beyond belief. Up until now I haven't told anyone about you except my boyfriend, whose name is Blake. Needless to say, he is eager to meet you. For a while he wondered if I was playing a sick joke on him.

We are planning a trip to Italy and hope to meet you in Rome. Or will you be coming home by any chance? I forgot to tell you that I live in Atlanta, where I work for an HMO as an ophthalmologist. It's hard to believe I'm about to turn 39. Still no child but am thinking about it if we marry, which I'm almost sure we will.

I've attached pictures of me and Blake.

With deep love,

Your daughter, Anna

Macrina, Journal: I'm practicing brain-to-screen writing on my new laptop as I travel home on Alitalia. Decided to avoid Castel Gandolfo this summer. Too close to the Vatican. Too close to work. Decided to turn over non-urgent business to Audrey (her assistant at the Vatican). Shame on me for agreeing to travel business class.

But glad I did. Made a new friend, a woman, a secular friend. I'm wearing my wig, a salt-and-pepper bob parted off to the side. I'm unrecognizable, although the flight attendants know I'm aboard. They saw the manifest. Thank God they haven't announced it. I asked them not to.

It starts off by her asking me if I were an American like herself. I can tell she wants to be friendly and will be interested in what I'm doing. The kind of conversation I love. The kind when you get to know a stranger better than friends you've known for years. But I don't want to come clean too early, so I change the subject. I ask her what brought her to Italy, and she says she's an art collector and dealer living in Atlanta. She's probably my age though doesn't look it, with lovely features and a silvery-blonde pixie cut. Not a wrinkle on her blue-eyed tan face. Pure class. Just what you'd expect of an art dealer.

I can't postpone it forever. She asks me what brought me to Italy, and I tell her my job.

"Just like me. Do you spend a lot of time in Italy?"

"I do. In Rome. Actually I live there. I'm traveling home to see my family. My daughter lives in Atlanta, my brother and parents in Mobile."

"How lovely. If I may ask, what sort of work are you in?"

"You might say I work in the area of religion." I can tell this makes her slightly uncomfortable.

"Well, that's pretty far from my expertise, though one of my purchases this time round was an old painting from the Vatican for a Catholic client."

"Really? I'm familiar with some of those paintings."

"Are you? Really? How interesting. It's a painting of the Annunciation. I guess I was wrong in supposing you were a missionary of some sort. I'm afraid I'm completely secular myself." Then her curiosity gets the best of her. "My name is Lois. What exactly do you do, if I may ask?"

"I'm the CEO of a large corporation. My name is Macrina."

"A CEO? How fascinating. A large corporation that has something to do with religion. Did you say Macrina? The same name as the pope. Actually I had hoped to see her weekly address, but she was on vacation. Have you ever seen her in person?"

"I never have. Except in a mirror."

"A mirror?" Then she leans back and gasps. "You're not—? Silly me. For a minute I imagined you were Pope Macrina!" And she laughs an embarrassed laugh.

I remove my wig and display my rather messy white hair. "Your imagination didn't deceive you." She looks at me in amazement, as if I were an angel of the Lord with a disturbing message. I reach over and touch her hand.

She recovers quickly as I reposition my wig on my head, then head to the bathroom to straighten it. Soon we become like sorority sisters talking about old times and our kids. She has no interest in religion, and I don't trouble her with it.

The plane lands in Atlanta, and Lois and I part with a hug in the bustling lobby. I remember the time in Albany when the Haitian gardener never guessed I was the bishop.

Greg: In July 2083 Cassio Balzano, the papal aircar mechanic and programmer, began writing notes to himself on his phone during slack time. Psychologists, criminologists, historians, and sundry opinion-setters have sifted through these scratchings looking for clues to explain what he did. They have spent millions of words describing him to the world in their various languages. Most of my readers will already know a little about him, so I will keep this brief.

Cassio's wife, Bianca, was two months pregnant when she decided to leave him and seek a divorce because he had a violent temper and battered her when she was too tired and sick to prepare him dinner after work. When she divorced him, the judge, a woman, ordered Cassio to refrain from violence of any kind or face a restraining order. At the next court hearing a few months later he testified that Bianca refused to let him see Stefano, their 6-year-old son. Bianca's mother, Veronica, testified that Cassio repeatedly came over and pushed his way into her house, where Bianca and Stefano now lived. The judge slapped the promised restraining order on him. Cassio wrote in his notes that his mother-in-law, whom he passionately hated, "looked like the Pope."

Cassio had other, far better reasons for hating Macrina. When Bianca aborted their baby without consulting Cassio, she claimed that "the Pope authorized it." This of course was ridiculous, but he had read an article somewhere describing Macrina as pro-choice without qualification, so he took Bianca's word at face value. From his point of view, he had lost access to both his children, one to a liar and judge's decree, the other to a murderer.

Then there was the case of his 87-year-old grandmother, "the only person who understood me." She suffered from a painful and degrading affliction known as rectal prolapse, a condition in which the rectum bulges out of the anus. That and a recent pneumonia from which she almost died left her so depressed that she decided to end her life by not drinking water or any other fluids. When Cassio visited her in the hospital, the IVs were disconnected. When he told her that suicide was a grievous sin that leads to hell, she replied that "even the Pope says it's okay." There was nothing he could say that dissuaded her, and she died four days later, leaving him alone in a world that offered only personal pain. He turned bitter and sought retribution.

He knew that Macrina had been under fire from conservative Catholics almost from the beginning. He was a churchgoing Catholic and read rigidly conservative theologians as a hobby that gradually developed into an obsession; he knew that forces in the Church resisted, even condemned what she was doing. But what were they willing to do about it? Nothing. He decided it would take an individual of tremendous courage to set things right. He began to imagine what he might do, even planning it. Sitting idly in his Vatican office beside the car, which mainly ferried the pope and a variety of bigwigs and assistants back and forth between the Vatican and Castel Gandolfo, he visualized how he would get even. Whatever happened to him wouldn't matter. There wasn't much worth living for anyway. He might as well do the world a favor and die a despised hero. Perhaps God would understand and even reward him.

Cassio knew that the Pope attended or said the 7 a.m. Mass at San Marco but couldn't get in without a ticket. One morning as he stood in line Macrina herself, noting his apparent sincerity and repeated attempts to attend, allowed him in without a ticket. From that point he became a regular. In this manner, seated in a pew, he stalked her.

Authorities who studied the notes he made to himself on his computer revealed a deteriorating mental state. Delusions of persecution alternated with delusions of grandeur as the months passed. In the end he saw himself as an instrument of God's will and savior of the Catholic Church.

Greg: During the month she spent with us on her vacation in July 2083, Macrina worked on her encyclical. From overseas came a deeply disturbing note from her secretary that Cardinal Zamora was trying to organize a no-confidence vote on her papacy. A few days later a 22,000-word tract appeared in her email. Zamora summarized what he took to be doctrinal "irregularities" and blasted her for abandoning the "clear and certain teachings" of the Church on abortion, euthanasia, physician-assisted suicide (PAS), and capital punishment. Deeply troubled, she would get up early, stroll a half mile across Spring Hill's campus to the tiny Episcopal chapel where our great great grandparents on our mother's side went to church when they were children, and entered the unlocked, empty chapel to pray. It was for her a place of great beauty and solace with its stained glass windows and altarpiece showing Jesus carrying a lamb on his shoulders—a tiny grotto hidden out of view by a line of ancient azaleas from the large, modern red brick church on the other side of the property. She never spent less than an hour and a half before showing up for breakfast with me and Sophie. Wearing her wig to help hide her identity, she dressed unpretentiously in her work pants on these daily visits. She looked more like a woman with spade in hand intent on digging weeds out of her garden than a saint carrying the burdens of the world, like Jesus, on her shoulders. It was in that humble guise that she gathered strength for the day's tasks.

Free from teaching for the summer, Sophie helped Macrina polish her encyclical, even turn it in a different direction in a place or two. Many years ago I lured Sophie away from a Ph.D. at Georgetown in Christian theology to a career as wife, mother, and high school teacher. I've always felt a little guilty about this and wondered if she regretted her decision, though she never hinted at it. In any case, she got a hefty consolation prize as unofficial copyeditor of a papal encyclical! I am proud of her.

On July 23, Macrina broke her self-imposed silence and emailed Cardinal Zamora in the hope of forging some kind of reconciliation. She didn't ask him to drop his mutiny against her—an action without precedent in the entire history of the Church—but only to reply quickly to her points, as she promised to do to his. Thus began an exchange than ran almost nonstop across the next two days. A fragment from that exchange follows:

Macrina and Cardinal Zamora, email exchange:

Macrina: What I hope to do is bring clarity to our positions. Perhaps we may discover unexpected compatibilities....

Zamora: I look forward to this exchange.... May I refer to you as Pope Thomas?

Macrina: Of course. That's my official name, the name I chose out of deference to the great apostle who dared to doubt.

Zamora: Perhaps you should have chosen a different name....

Macrina: You are aware that biblical inerrancy is a Catholic dogma, yet modern biblical scholars, almost all of them Christian or Jewish, can point to countless errors in the Bible. They range from the first chapter of Genesis, where God is said to divide night from day on the first day of creation, while creating the sun only on the fourth, to St. Paul's claim that Christ would come back to earth in the lifetimes of some of those alive in his day. Do you defend biblical inerrancy? Do you claim that God is the true author of scripture and preserved its human authors from error, as Catholic dogma requires?

Zamora: Yes, in the most important sense: that God was writing for people of that time. If he had written a book containing all we know today about the universe, it would have come across as science fiction and been rejected as preposterous.

Macrina: You have made quite a concession. You are saying that God was more interested in reaching out to ancient people's understanding of the world than to facts about the world. In effect he was propagating error, though with a good intention.

Zamora: God had a far better grasp of what he was doing than you, Your Holiness!

Macrina: The truth begins with scientific evidence and a twenty-first-century view of the universe. We need to reject biblical inerrancy and pay attention to our best biblical scholars. Nothing is lost, everything gained....

Macrina: People are responding well to these revisions. The Church is actually growing in Europe, and Muslims are converting to Christianity in surprising numbers, partly in response to our revisioning of the Trinity.

Zamora: The old growth argument.... Let us suppose for a moment, for the sake of argument, that we can't be sure these dogmas are true. I would argue that it was still necessary to maintain them.

Macrina: Why?

Zamora: Because that's the Tradition.

Macrina: Then let us honor the Tradition. But also make room for progress. There is more than one way to be Catholic. The Church should be quick to advise, recommend, and urge, not condemn. "Hold up a standard, not a disciplinary rod." So wrote Tagore.

Sophie, face to face talk with Greg: All this fuss over doctrine wasn't where Macrina was coming from. She got pulled into it by Zamora and his allies and had to give a lot more time to it than she wanted. For her, Christianity was almost elementary in its simplicity. Love God, love your neighbor, and model your life after Jesus. Not after Paul, not after the theologians of the past, not after the great doctors of the Church. Just Jesus. Jesus the man. Jesus as human as you and me. Any religion that could excite the masses to follow Jesus would be worthy of greatness and would grow. All those nonessential dogmas that Zamora stands for were optional. They have their charm, even great charm. She was so bent on reform that I think she failed to give them their due. I once scolded her: "Who wants to sing 'O little town of Nazareth' at Christmas?" She conceded the point but said she'd actually prefer Nazareth to Bethlehem. She could be stubborn! But she did manage to laugh at herself.

Where did Macrina's spirituality reside? What did she find when she reached down into her depths for the strength to keep going, and going joyously? Even though she claimed to know very little about the divine nature, she met God every morning in her centering prayer. For her, God was mysterious, hidden. Even her prized redefinition of the Trinity was only a wise guess, a better use of words than the old formula. Anyone thinking there was only one way to define God was deceiving themselves. But she did allow herself a few words that worked for her. In the paper I earlier quoted from—the one she wrote at Georgetown for a theology course—she described God as "a joyous, compassionate, loving, powerful, boundless, light-filled Reality at the hub of the universe with an outreach that extended to the epicenter of my soul, a Being that would resonate with a Hindu as well as a Christian." That was the God she met in her daily prayer. In that was her personal theology. That, I believe, was the source of her strength.

She had no illusions about the Church. She knew it wasn't a perfectible institution and that past attempts at perfecting itself led it into great error. Every well-intentioned dogma, every attempt at greater precision, every anathema it spun out to fence off error took it further into error. Macrina wanted the Church to be an institution for seekers, for people on a journey, not just for those who thought they had arrived at a final destination.

Macrina, Journal: Sophie got me to thinking: Maybe religion is better off left alone. My colleagues at the Vatican seem surprisingly unconcerned with scientific accuracy. They don't seem to care whether Mary was really a virgin or not. For most of them the story is what counts, and they like the story. The same with Adam and Eve, Noah and the flood, and the parting of the Red Sea. The same with Jesus' resurrection into a body of flesh after his death, and Thomas reaching through Jesus' clothing into his wound after his great doubt. They like the story and don't want to trouble themselves with the facts. They don't want to wonder too much about the facts and resent me when I try to lead them.

How many are in league with Zamora? Are they counting the months until I resign under pressure? Do they think I'm damaging the Church even though it's growing again, especially in France? Do they regret their votes? Or am I suffering from a little paranoia about Zamora? Is he getting to me in a way he shouldn't? I need to get back to the Vatican but dread it. What would it say about women if the first woman pope got sacked by her colleagues three years into the job? God help me.

The old story is a good one, but there is a better one ahead. We have to be brave enough to tell it.

Greg: The account I now present is known everywhere but needs retelling. A few weeks after returning from her vacation, Macrina paid a visit to the retired Pope Francis II at Castel Gandolfo, where he lives. Francis described her as seeking moral support. Cardinal Zamora's vote-of-no-confidence had faltered, but his forces were designing another strategy for stopping her. Her assistant, Lucille Taggart, accompanied her on the aircar but was not present at their meeting. The day was warm and overcast.

Francis was 90 percent on board the Renewal—the name the press gave it—but he demurred on the liturgical question. She wanted to create new Masses. Why make all Masses reenact the Last Supper? Why not create new rituals? Jesus' life was rich with events that Christians could model themselves after. Why not create a second Mass that reenacted his great Sermon on the Mount, the "Sermon Mass"; or a third that brought to life his three or four greatest parables, the "Parable Mass"; or a fourth celebrating his seven last words before he died, the "Death Mass," or a "Transfiguration Mass" with wonderful light displays? She described the Mass as we know it as wearisome from repetition. She said it bored young people, always in search of novelty. But Francis couldn't be persuaded. He felt that what most Catholics wanted was familiarity. He described her as disappointed in their conversation. It was in this mood that she, Lucille, and a Swiss guard boarded the carbus for the flight back to Rome.

The carbus was guided by a computer in the cockpit that was programmed on the ground. It had been flying back and forth, unpiloted, between the Vatican and Castel Gandolfo for twelve years without a mishap. If the computer on the ground failed for some reason, the carbus was defaulted to land on the old Vatican helipad or the new pad at Gandolfo, whichever was closer. Programming it to land elsewhere required keystrokes.

Cassio Balzano was the chief programmer. He was on duty when Macrina and Lucille boarded the bus for the 10-minute ride back to the Vatican. He helped them into the bus as was the custom.

When the bus was airborne and reached its cruising altitude of 3,400 feet over the green Castelli Romani hills, it happened. "I jerked in my seat," Lucille would later testify. "I looked back at Macrina. 'What was that?' she said. A strange noise, a buzzing or whining sound, came from the cockpit. A few seconds later smoke began creeping through the closed cockpit door. The craft began to lean over on its left side and tipped downward. I remember her saying, 'We're going to crash. My God, we're going to crash.' Andreas, our Swiss guard, released his belt and fell over trying to open the cockpit door. 'Leave it shut,' Macrina cried. She picked up her phone and put in a call to Cassio, but he didn't pick up. Then I think she texted him. I remember Andreas scrambling back to his seat and strapping himself in. He looked back at Macrina and said there was nothing he could do. 'That's okay,' she said, her face tense with alarm. 'Talk to your loved ones. Tell them you love them.' Then I put them out of my mind and began to prepare to die, for I was sure I would."

An Analysis was done on her last phone calls. Mom and Dad and Anna didn't pick up. She left a voice message for Anna: "Anna, my bus is crashing, falling out of the sky. Falling. Listen to me. I love you. I'll be checking in on you. Feel me around. Talk to me. I love you. I'll miss your wedding. So sorry. Got to go." Then she reached me and I did pick up. She described what was happening. "Smoke everywhere, Greg. Going down, going down sideways. Feel dizzy, sick. Green hills below. Trees. This is the end, Greg. The end. With luck, but no.... Greg, the encyclical... almost finished. Send to Francis, both paper and digital.... Greg, couldn't get through, get through to Mom and Dad. Tell them I love them and, and thank them for all they've done. And to you, dear brother, my inseparable brother, all my love." After five seconds she added, "Zamora wins. Oh my God, all my work undone. Zamora wins." Then she quiets and turns inward. I make out the word "Mother." Her final prayer goes to the Mother. "Mother, I come home, come home, coming home." In the last seconds her mind returns to earth, to action. She tries to reach Cardinal Iglesias, but he doesn't pick up. Iglesias called her back just as the bus crashed like a torpedo into a stand of trees.

Catholic News Agency Release:
Pope Thomas (Macrina) Dies in Aircar Crash—Assassin in Custody
In a horrifying crash of the Vatican's private aircar, Pope Thomas (Macrina) was killed while traveling back from Castel Gandolfo to the Vatican. Cassio Balzano, the aircar's programmer, has confessed to planting a plastic explosive device under the bus's computer. He detonated it from his office at Castel Gandolfo.

The device went off at 2:53 p.m. Roman time. The bus crashed approximately four minutes later. The Pope's secretary, Lucille Taggart, survived the crash and is in critical condition at Rome's Agostino Gemelli Polyclinic Hospital. Swiss guard Andreas Blazer also died in the crash.

Expressions of deep grief are pouring in from all over the world. U.S. President Nicholas Denton joined with New York's Cardinal Clara Silvestri in deploring the loss of "a brilliant herald for a better world," and Chinese Premier Li Xeng-ho called her China's "best Catholic friend and a tremendous loss to Chinese-Vatican relations." India's Prime Minister Narendra Bose simply compared her to Gandhi.

Here at the Vatican the College of Cardinals has united to express its grief. Cardinal Zamora, her archfoe and nemesis, told the press: "We had our differences, but her sincerity and love of the Church were never in doubt." Women and school children in Asuncion, Paraguay, marched along the city's main street singing hymns. "She brought me to the Catholic Church," said 17-year-old Cynthia Corwin from Austin, Texas. "I was nothing before her. My heart is breaking." Makeshift streetside altars are popping up all over the Catholic world with her picture surrounded by flowers and candlelight. Devotees are posting photos and portraits of her in her trademark spruce-green robe on internet sites. Even personal robots are mimicking the grief of their masters. Everywhere Masses and rosaries are being said for her as the world mourns. The Womanpriest Society announced that it would begin immediately to seek her canonization as a saint. The whole world is in a state of shock....

The Sun: As the great Hosanna from the Sanctus of Faure's *Requiem* rang out over the crowd standing in St. Peter's vast nave, it was impossible not to imagine Macrina's soul entering heaven to a chorus of angels.... Outside, spread out over the Square, women dabbed at their eyes and lifted their faces skyward, their arms extended, under a chilly overcast sky.... Cardinal Iglesias, Macrina's closest ally, described his friend as the best hope not only for the Church, but for the world. Choking with emotion as he spoke, first in Italian, then In English, he described the love she inspired in people everywhere, from heads of state to children who drew pictures of her on their classroom computers.... Hero, prophet, commander-in-chief, saint, best friend—she was all these things to the people who loved her. Meanwhile, in his jail cell Balzano boasted that he had saved the Church from the "she-devil" and would do it again if given the chance.

Greg: What followed at the next conclave is a story in itself: how the forces behind the American Cardinal Zamora and the Spanish Cardinal Iglesias waged an irresolvable pitched battle; how a sleeper, Mees Van Orden, one of the cardinals Macrina appointed, rose from the melee as the new pope; and how his patient, quiet diplomacy won "cautious support" from her allies while emboldening her enemies who thought they could outflank the meek Dutchman.

He took the name Thomas II, and this time the name stuck.

One of his first decisions dealt with Macrina's remains, and I had much to do with it. Macrina made it clear to me on several occasions, both before and after her elevation to the papacy, that she wanted to be cremated. She would have been the first pope to be so, and the Curia balked at the request. They didn't want an urn residing next to all the papal coffins in St. Peter's basement. As usual, their arguments turned on the question of Tradition.

In a phone conversation with the new Pope (we are friends), I presented Macrina's case: she wanted her ashes preserved at Santa Dorotea, her titular parish church down the street along the Tiber where she said her weekly Mass. When the Curia objected, Pope Thomas came up with a highly original recommendation, and the Curia begrudgingly went along with it. In what became known as the "Tablespoon Compromise," a tablespoon of ashes would be placed in an urn at St. Peter's, another at St. Dorotea's, and the rest distributed across the world in archdiocesan cathedrals. By now the relics are all gone. One tablespoon resides in Mobile's Cathedral of the Immaculate Conception in a small urn the size of a kiwi, surrounded by plexiglass bolted to the floor, near a side altar dedicated to the Virgin.

Jan McGrath, email: Greg, you asked me for a final reflection on

Macrina. As you know, I'm a retired English teacher. I've always felt that her worst enemy was her impetuosity, her unwillingness to settle for lesser achievements. This at times has led to errors in judgment, to miscalculations. You could even call it her tragic flaw. If she had settled for less, she would be alive today. But she was too driven to settle. As always happens with people who shake the world, she made fierce enemies, just as Jesus did. And her many friends mourn excessively her death. They are overcome with fear that such a noble person should come to such a fate, that terrible things like this happen in our world. And they pity her for her loss. Aristotle thought it was good for people to fear and pity in this way. He called it catharsis. He thought that by indulging these feelings they would be tamed, reduced, gradually swept away. I never questioned this until I found myself grieving for Macrina.

I've never stopped grieving. Aristotle didn't know what he was talking about.

Greg: I am thinking back to the video I opened this book with. We were twin babies gradually discovering each other as something more than unstable shifting furniture that we were constantly bumping up against. Wiggling and crawling, climbing on top of each other, we were always together, never out of sight. Side-by-side was the only way of being in the world that we knew. Knowing that I'll never have her by my side again has not been easy. I've come to realize I've still not completely freed myself from thinking of myself as a *we*. Writing this book has only aggravated the feeling. As close as I am to Sophie, there is a void that no one can fill. Living in a world without her has made it harsher. Am I still grieving? That's not quite it. It's just a sadness you never quite outgrow. I never realized how much I loved her until I lost her.

Anna, email to Sophie:
Hi Sophie, thanks for the talk last night. I was sinking fast, feeling crippled, alone. I'm beginning to understand that life is

just too hard without prayer to a God who will make all things right in the end. But for me it's harder than hard to believe such good news. Yet both my mothers believed it and fed off it. And so do you. Why can't I?

Blake is in his office, and I find myself with baby Macrina, who is sleeping. I'm listening to Vaughan Williams' "The Lark Ascending," and I understand why you recommended it. I imagine my soul rising like the lark, like the ascending solo violin—so alone, yet so beautiful. The thought that Greg is getting older while Macrina stays the same, always the same, seems less tragic. The fluttering in my stomach has calmed. I live in a heavily populated world, the world of those who suffer. I do not lack for company.

Where are my two moms? Are they in a good place, like you believe? I need to believe this. I need to believe it for my baby's sake as much as for my own. I cannot bequeath to her my bipolar mood swings. She deserves your optimism.

You say you saw hints of the same disease in Macrina, but she conquered it with prayer and a call to service. That's what I must do. With your guidance I am learning how.

Macrina is waking up. I wish I were better able to enjoy tiny babies, like so many other moms. But I miss my work. I really do. Perhaps I am drawn to service after all. Now if only I can be drawn to faith.

Love to you, dear Sophie,

Anna

Greg: In one of Macrina's trips—to Costa Rica—a peasant reached out to her as her motorcade passed through the streets of San Jose and placed a tiny iron statue in her outstretched hand. The archbishop riding beside her explained that it was La Negrita, the beloved black Madonna and Costa Roca's patron saint. How far Mary had traveled from her home in Nazareth! Experiences like this cemented Macrina's resolve to protect simple folk loving their local Catholic traditions from a bullying introduction to a progressive, science-based revision they are not ready for. She had a horror of what Luther had done to the Church five-and-a-half centuries before. She told me she would shutter her program if it led to schism. A "two-track" Catholicism was born in this way and was a fundamental feature of her vision. Pope Thomas, a worthy and effective ally, shares it. Will he succeed? We will see.

Sophie: Greg has asked me to write the finale for his book. I ask myself, Will the Church move forward into a new but uncertain future, or settle back into the comfortable old ways with its anti-scientific dogmas intact and a declining population among the well-educated? When she was alive, the Church in North America and Europe was adding new members at a remarkable pace. Her revision of the Trinity especially attracted Muslims; hundreds of thousands were converting to Christianity, often turning up at Mass with hijabs intact; baptism of whole families sometimes followed. But with Macrina gone, who knows?

Reading over the manuscript has left me feeling that Greg missed something that needs saying. I'm convinced she didn't seek the papacy for herself. She sought it for women. She told me once that men in general would make better popes because leadership comes more easily to them—not that they would make wiser decisions, but that the rigors of leadership would cost them less emotionally. She took responsibility for all the Church's failures. She slept too little and found it increasingly difficult to pray. She felt that women thrived on service, and that is why they made such good priests. Priests, after all, are expected to serve their congregations, and women, she felt, did it better. But dwelling at the top was another matter. She thought that one woman pope per century would be the norm. She fought valiantly for the right of that one woman, for that exceptional female who could weather the brutal hardship of life at the summit. But she did not wish that hardship on any woman.

Another oddity—perhaps irony is a better word—is that she liked and trusted men more than women. As pastor and bishop she chose them to serve alongside her; she enjoyed them more, felt more comfortable around them. I've always suspected this was due to her relationship to Greg. In their early years they shared life in its totality, in all its innocent intimacy, enjoying the boyish things he liked to do. Her closest friends among the College of Cardinals were not the women she appointed, but a few male colleagues like Cardinal Iglesias and Pope Francis himself.

Macrina was in the habit of transcribing in her paper diary favorite passages from the books she was reading. The last thing she wrote comes from a surprising source: a sermon from St. John Henry Newman, the nineteenth-century English convert to Catholicism: "I sacrifice to Thee this cherished wish, this lust, this weakness, this scheme, this opinion: make me what Thou wouldst have me, I bargain for nothing, I make no terms."

Why did these words impress her so much? Was she pessimistic about getting her reforms through? Or do they hint at her readiness to die? Are they a kind of presentiment of her death a few days later? And why was she reading a conservative theologian like Newman in the first place? She had so many sides.

In this autumn of 2086, we find Macrina's remains spread far across the world. She will certainly be remembered for what she did for women. She will be remembered for what she tried to do for the Church even if it doesn't pan out. Will she be canonized as a saint? Already three miracles have been claimed for her. I can imagine her as busy on the Other Side doing whatever needs to be done as she was on this.

Greg's family has a little plot in the cemetery where the twins played as children, and where their grandparents are buried. On her last visit home when she struggled with her encyclical, she told me she would be happy to occupy a little spot in that plot, a place where ordinary humble people go to be dead, and where their tombs go unvisited.

THE END

ROUNDFIRE
BOOKS

FICTION

Put simply, we publish great stories. Whether it's literary or popular, a gentle tale or a pulsating thriller, the connecting theme in all Roundfire fiction titles is that once you pick them up you won't want to put them down.
If you have enjoyed this book, why not tell other readers by posting a review on your preferred book site.

Recent bestsellers from Roundfire are:

The Bookseller's Sonnets
Andi Rosenthal
The Bookseller's Sonnets intertwines three love stories with a tale of
religious identity and mystery spanning five hundred years and
three countries.
Paperback: 978-1-84694-342-3 ebook: 978-184694-626-4

Birds of the Nile
An Egyptian Adventure
N.E. David
Ex-diplomat Michael Blake wanted a quiet birding trip up the Nile
– he wasn't expecting a revolution.
Paperback: 978-1-78279-158-4 ebook: 978-1-78279-157-7

Blood Profit$
The Lithium Conspiracy
J. Victor Tomaszek, James N. Patrick, Sr.
The blood of the many for the profits of the few… *Blood Profit$* will
take you into the cigar-smoke-filled room where American policy
and laws are really made.
Paperback: 978-1-78279-483-7 ebook: 978-1-78279-277-2

The Burden
A Family Saga
N.E. David
Frank will do anything to keep his mother and father apart. But
he's carrying baggage – and it might just weigh him down …
Paperback: 978-1-78279-936-8 ebook: 978-1-78279-937-5

The Cause
Roderick Vincent
The second American Revolution will be a fire lit from an internal spark.
Paperback: 978-1-78279-763-0 ebook: 978-1-78279-762-3

Don't Drink and Fly
The Story of Bernice O'Hanlon: Part One
Cathie Devitt
Bernice is a witch living in Glasgow. She loses her way in her life and wanders off the beaten track looking for the garden of enlightenment.
Paperback: 978-1-78279-016-7 ebook: 978-1-78279-015-0

Gag
Melissa Unger
One rainy afternoon in a Brooklyn diner, Peter Howland punctures an egg with his fork. Repulsed, Peter pushes the plate away and never eats again.
Paperback: 978-1-78279-564-3 ebook: 978-1-78279-563-6

The Master Yeshua
The Undiscovered Gospel of Joseph
Joyce Luck
Jesus is not who you think he is. The year is 75 CE. Joseph ben Jude is frail and ailing, but he has a prophecy to fulfil …
Paperback: 978-1-78279-974-0 ebook: 978-1-78279-975-7

On the Far Side, There's a Boy
Paula Coston
Martine Haslett, a thirty-something 1980s woman, plays hard on
the fringes of the London drag club scene until one night which
prompts her to sign up to a charity. She writes to a young Sri
Lankan boy, with consequences far and long.
Paperback: 978-1-78279-574-2 ebook: 978-1-78279-573-5

Tuareg
Alberto Vazquez-Figueroa
With over 5 million copies sold worldwide, *Tuareg* is a classic
adventure story from best-selling author Alberto Vazquez-
Figueroa, about honour, revenge and a clash of cultures.
Paperback: 978-1-84694-192-4

Readers of ebooks can buy or view any of these bestsellers by
clicking on the live link in the title. Most titles are published in
paperback and as an ebook. Paperbacks are available in traditional
bookshops. Both print and ebook formats are available online.

Find more titles and sign up to our readers' newsletter at
http://www.johnhuntpublishing.com/fiction

Follow us on Facebook at https://www.facebook.com/JHPfiction
and Twitter at https://twitter.com/JHPFiction